GAIA WILD

PRAISE FOR
JANE RAY'S WILDLIFE RESCUE SERIES

"Diane Haynes has created a world that is as moving and heartfelt as it is funny and hip."
—Brent Piaskoski, executive producer and creator of *The Latest Buzz* (Family Channel)

"Haynes makes good use of the wildlife focus by integrating environmental facts and issues into an entertaining eco-mystery-adventure. The strength of Jane's character helps, too: smart, brave, and independent, she's a good role model."
—Bridget Donald, *Quill & Quire*

"Part modern-day mystery, part environmental tale, Jane Ray's Wildlife Rescue series celebrates teens who've realized—ahead of many adults—that they have the power to change the world."
—*Nanaimo Bulletin*

"*Flight or Fight* is an adventure story with fine Carl Hiaasen-like eco-warrior qualities. [The climax] scene is nothing short of genius on Haynes's behalf."
—Jen Waters, Teen Services librarian, CM *Magazine*

"Jane Ray is a gutsy character who embodies everything I strive to be. Readers will be both entertained and inspired by one young woman's courage to follow her heart."
—Lesley Fox, former humane education director with the Vancouver Humane Society

"I've been looking for this type of novel for over two years, one that integrates science and environmental awareness into a novel. Thank you for finally producing this book."
—Catherine Bentivoglio, teacher, Académie de la Moraine, ON

"This is Nancy Drew with an edge—and a cause. Jane Ray is a true heroine, complete with fears and flaws and an unrelenting drive to follow her heart. The characters are unforgettable. I can't wait to see what Jane and her friends get themselves caught up in next!"
—Lisa Jackson, award-winning Aboriginal filmmaker

JANE RAY'S
WILDLIFE RESCUE SERIES

GAIA WILD

DIANE HAYNES

WALRUS
BOOKS

Walrus Books, an imprint of Whitecap Books

Edited by Sonnet Force
Cover design by Mauve Pagé
Series design and illustration by Five Seventeen
Front cover photos by Mia Robbemont (elephant and calf),
    Devin Manky (Jane), Jonathan Ruchti (butterfly),
    and Vangelis Thomaidis (jungle).
Back cover photo (Siwash Rock) by Gertjan Hofman
Typeset by Setareh Ashrafologhalai
Proofread by Marilyn Bittman

Printed in Canada

Library and Archives Canada Cataloguing in Publication

Haynes, Diane
    Gaia Wild / Diane Haynes.

(Jane Ray's wildlife rescue series)
ISBN 978-1-55285-936-0

    1. Elephants—Juvenile fiction. I. Title. II. Series: Haynes, Diane.
Jane Ray's wildlife rescue series.

PS8615.A85G33 2008   jC813'.6   C2008-900651-8

The publisher acknowledges the financial support of the Canada Council
for the Arts, the British Columbia Arts Council, and the Government of
Canada through the Book Publishing Industry Development Program
(BPIDP). Whitecap Books also acknowledges the financial support of the
Province of British Columbia through the Book Publishing Tax Credit.

 Canada Council
for the Arts
Conseil des Arts
du Canada

 BRITISH COLUMBIA
ARTS COUNCIL

08 09 10 11 12 5 4 3 2 1

The inside pages of this book are made with 100% postconsumer (PCW)
content. For more information, visit www.marketsinitiative.org.

 ANCIENT FOREST
FRIENDLY

In memory of Tina
and in hope for all those who remain

DISCLAIMER

All characters and events in *Gaia Wild* are fictional. However, the experiences the elephant in this story undergoes are based on things that are happening to elephants, wild and captive, all over the world. The wildlife rehabilitation stories are based on the real-life experiences of the author as a volunteer with the Wildlife Rescue Association of British Columbia. Readers should be aware that extensive training as well as specific government permits are required for the keeping and rehabilitating of wild animals, and that the animal rescue and rehabilitation scenarios described in this book are not to be attempted by members of the public. Please see Flory's Files starting on page 308 for information on how you can help elephants and other animals in your community.

CONTENTS

1
THE LAST FIRST DAY

JANE SAID GOODBYE to Amy and Flory and stood, watching and waving, until her two best friends were out of sight. Then she took off at a run.

The early morning sun glanced through the canopy of trees, dappling the path ahead of her and setting Elfin Lake afire. Lilies, rushes, and reeds lined the southwestern shore, which teemed with life and smelled to Jane of marshy water and dirt and summer's decay. Two squirrels raced one another, chattering, up the trunk of a spruce tree, its bark knotted and cracked with age. In the shimmering air above the lakeshore, a trio of barn swallows darted and swooped, their clear, liquid calls gathering others to them in preparation for the long migration ahead.

Darting across a deep ditch to the lower trail, Jane startled a great blue heron out of its hiding spot, the prehistoric-looking bird all beak and neck and dangling legs as it climbed into the sky. For just a moment its wingspan blocked the sun, and in the darkness Jane heard the honking cries of a flock of Canada geese as they passed above her, southward bound. Back in sunlight, she stopped and stood, waving up at them and calling out yet another goodbye.

What a sap I am, Jane thought, wiping her eyes roughly with the back of her hand. She leapt back to the upper trail, the one that led home, and picked up her pace. *Getting all choked up over a bunch of geese. They'll be back next spring*! But it wasn't the geese and she knew it. It was saying goodbye to Amy and Flory after their run this morning that had brought on this odd wistfulness. Amy and Flory, and all the other goodbyes she'd be forced to say this year. Today was the first day of school and she'd see her best friends again in the halls of Cedar's Ridge Senior Secondary in little more than an hour. But this would be their graduating year, and so this was their last first day of school together.

The three girls had been friends since they were small and experienced every milestone and mundane moment together. But beyond next June, the future was dark, a mystery. Jane sped up, tossing her long, dark hair and shaking her hands as if to leave her mood behind her. This was going to be the best year ever! Crazy adventures with Ame and Flor, new friends, dances and parties, and hey, while she was dreaming, why not a date or two and, well yeah, exams, but it *was* school after all, and then grad! And then . . . and then *what*?

Immersing herself once more in the sights and

sounds of the forest, Jane busied her mind identifying the birdcalls she heard. There, off to her left, that sweet, rich whistle ending in a short trill, that was a fox sparrow. She could hear the noisy quacking of mallards across the lake, and that *tsk-a-dee-dee-dee* behind her was a chickadee, one of her favorites. Above, a roost of crows was welcoming the day with hoarse *caahs*, and Jane said hello back as if to old friends. From the middle of the grassy field to the west of the lake, a red-tailed hawk rose up in search of food and screeched its unmistakable *keeeyah!* Jane grinned and raised her hand in salute.

And then from the far eastern shore, that . . . that call . . . okay, was that an *elephant*?

Jane stood stock still on the trail, heart pounding, as the ragged trumpeting rent the air and silenced every other creature in the woods. The sound stopped as abruptly as it had started, and after a long pause during which not even the wind whispered, morning resumed on Elfin Lake.

It had been an alarm call, Jane was sure of it. That elephant's voice had had fear in it. But of what? This was an animal with no predators but man. But what on earth was an elephant doing in sleepy little Cedar's Ridge?

Jane released her breath in a rush, feeling her heartbeat begin to slow and solidity return to her legs. Silently, like a tracker, she made her way to the edge of the woods, maintaining cover behind a broad old fir tree.

Peering around the trunk, she spotted a massive white form making its way off the access road and lumbering toward the lake. In fact, the lot behind Elfin Lake Park was half filled with these massive forms and more were arriving. Suddenly understanding what she was seeing, Jane sagged against the tree trunk, threw back her head, and laughed.

Movie trailers. Rows of them, long white caravans with silver stars emblazoned on the sides. Somebody was making a movie and Elfin Lake was the set. That "elephant call" she'd heard had been a recording! A special effect by the sound department. Jane was surprised she'd been so easily fooled. Well, she was glad she'd been wrong and that all Cedar's Ridge elephants were A-okay! She giggled again. Ame and Flor would love this story. In fact, if she was quick, she could scope out the set, score the day's best gossip, and still make it home in time for breakfast.

Sprinting the length of the south shore trail, Jane emerged panting behind the boathouse and concession stand. The lot was now full and bustling with activity as black-garbed film crew set up sound and camera equipment in preparation for the first scene of the day. Jane inched slowly forward, determined to remain inconspicuous as she scoured the set for celebrities she could mention at school. Intent on her search, she almost tripped over a tent sign pitched at the edge of the lot. She crouched to read it:

Shapeshifter! Jane had read every book in the series and couldn't wait for more. The series was about a group of friends who had the ability to take on animal forms, complete with strength and speed and extra-keen senses, and together they rescued animals and helped save the environment. Jane loved those books, and here they were making a movie! Forgetting all about celebrity-spotting, Jane leapt up and ran smack into two of the tallest people she'd ever seen. "Oh! Oh, I'm so sorry! I . . . I was across the lake and I heard . . . I saw your trailers and I was just wondering . . ."

"No problem," the man said, his eyes dancing. He and the tall woman both had dark hair and dark eyes, and though they were dressed in black fleeces and jeans like the rest of the crew, they looked like movie stars, or models—tall, assured, and gorgeous. "David," he said, extending his hand. Jane shook it, feeling her blush reassert itself. "And this is my wife, Lynn."

The woman smiled and shook Jane's hand in turn. "Did you have some questions about the production?" she asked, glancing at her watch. "We've got a few minutes before we have to be on set."

"How tall are you?" Jane blurted, and then wanted to kick herself. Her blush deepened. "I mean, you're doing *Shapeshifter*! I can't believe it! It's my favorite series!

My two best friends love it, too, but I'm *crazy* about it!" Just plain crazy was more like it. Jane could hear herself gushing like a starstruck fanatic; her mouth seemed to have grown a mind of its own. "Do you know the author? Or if there are any famous people in the movie? Or when it will be in the theaters?"

Lynn laughed. "Yes, yes, and probably next summer. But give us some time—we haven't even started shooting yet!"

"But we're about to!" David interjected excitedly as his watch beeped an alarm. "It's been a pleasure . . . er . . ."

"Jane. Jane Ray."

"Jane." He shook her hand again and was gone.

"Lovely to meet you, Jane," Lynn said as she followed after him. "Drop by the set any time and say hello!"

Thrilled, Jane stared after Lynn as she crossed the lot and entered one of the trailers. Then, glancing at her own watch, she exclaimed at the time and bounded for the trailhead. As she rounded the southeastern point of the lake, she thought she heard voices off to her right. Slowing, she caught the words of two men arguing on an abandoned boat dock below the trail.

"Denny, I swear, you're too hard on her. Somebody's gonna notice somethin'!" The voice was high, pleading, nervous.

"Shut up, Dig. Geez, you're such a bleeding heart sometimes. I thought you'd be used to it by now. Don't tell me you're one of those guys who gets softer with age instead of tougher?" The second man chuckled, his oily voice taunting. "It's all part of the routine and you know it. If she's gonna work for us, she's gonna do what we say. Period. It's all about safety, Dig. Safety. Now, you want your money or what?"

There was a silence, a soft rustling, and then, "Sweet, eh? And there's plenty more where that came from, my man. Now get down there and do your job. I'll handle the big-wigs. Trust me, Dig, once we've broken her in, she'll be eating out of the palm of our hand, and by December, she'll be ours. Our bargain-basement cash cow!" An oily voice laughed.

"Whatever, Denny. Hey . . . it's past call time! We're late. Let's go."

Jane took off, wanting to put as much distance as she could between herself and the conversation she'd just overheard, but the words kept repeating themselves in her head as she ran. She had no idea what "bargain-basement cash cow" meant, but she was disgusted that some poor crew member had to work for such jerks and hoped the woman would find the courage to stand up for herself.

Bounding up the trail toward home, she almost lost her footing when the sound came again—a wild, trumpeting call that reverberated through the sky and turned the forest into jungle. A call of fear. A call of pain. A call for help. Rooted to the earth in the preternatural silence that followed, Jane turned her head slowly in time to see a barge cast off from the eastern shore and drift toward the center of Elfin Lake. Standing on the barge, as beautifully regal as she was utterly out of place, was an elephant. And not just any elephant. Jane stared, her heart racing in recognition. It was Gaia.

2

AN ELEPHANT NEVER FORGETS

"JANE, GET A move on. You're going to be late for school!" Ellen Ray's no-nonsense voice rang out clearly from her home office, where she was answering emails from her East Coast clients before heading downtown.

"Five more minutes!" Jane called back from the living room. She pulled a well-worn photo album out from under the coffee table and began scanning its pages. It was 8:20 and she was still dressed in dirty sweats, having barely remembered to kick off her runners before racing upstairs to search.

At the sound of Jane's voice, Sweet Pea and Minnie climbed down from the kitchen windowsill where they'd been peering, ears cocked, toward the lake. They jumped up on the couch and curled into soft circles on either side of her, purring. "Hey girls," Jane whispered, reaching down to place a hand on each warm body. "You're as curious as I am about those elephant sounds, aren't you? Look at this, maybe you can help me find her."

Breakfast and shower forgotten, she stared intently at the photographs, seeking one she'd looked at many times over the years. Here she was at three, pulling on a pig's tail at the Children's Petting Zoo. Nope, she'd been older. She reached under the table and pulled out another album, turning quickly through its pages. Here she was again, at five, at the Aquarium, soaked by an Orca whale's spray and grinning with glee. Closer. It wasn't long after that. She flipped the album over and began to work backwards, and then she found it.

There.

Three little girls, age six. One chestnut-haired, one red-haired, and one raven-haired, seated atop an elephant, uncertainty mingled with wonder on their small faces. A short dark handsome man walked beside the elephant, his hand resting lightly against her flank, his gaze resting lovingly on her face. "The three best friends meet Gaia at the Raincity Zoo," the photo's caption read.

Gaia.

Jane closed her eyes and saw the dirt track ringing a patch of overgrown grass, felt the summer sun on the back of her neck, and smelled the warm, sweet scents of hay and dung. She rocked with the rolling gait of the giant animal beneath her, marveling at her size, daring, at her friends' urging, to run a tentative hand across the heavy, wrinkled hide, to brush the bristly hairs rising from the sloping back. Daring, as she stepped off the elephant's back and onto the high wooden platform at the end of the ride, to look into the eye that was just about level with hers. And seeing not a strange, unknowable creature but a friend.

Gaia.

She opened her eyes and ran a finger across the elephant's image. In the twelve years since this photo was taken, Jane had gone through school, laughed and learned, traveled and played, fallen in love and survived the breakup, flown a plane and landed herself on national television.

And what had become of this beautiful, intelligent creature in all that time? Had she had friends? Explored new worlds? Played? Loved? Run for miles across open land?

In twelve years, Jane had never thought to wonder about such things, or whether the elephant was well, or content. She had not thought of her at all, except on the rare occasions she rifled through these old albums.

Gaia.

Jane buried her face in her hands, the memory of the elephant's cry resounding in her ears. What had Gaia's life been like all these years? And what had brought her to this, to performing on command on a film set in Cedar's Ridge? Calling in fear? Calling for help?

Jane had heard the expression, "An elephant never forgets." The same could not be said of humans, she thought bitterly. Then a thought struck her: Was it possible Gaia remembered *her*? Suddenly, she wanted very badly to find out. Maybe, just maybe, if the elephant remembered her, she would let her help her.

"*Jane!*"

"Uhhh . . . ?" Sweet Pea and Minnie leapt off the couch and scurried for the stairs, and Jane snapped her head up to find her mom standing in the doorway, hands on her hips, scowling.

"You now have exactly four minutes to be in my car, hair fixed, dressed for school. This is the first and last time I give you a ride. And you will not go out the door looking like *that*, young lady! Honestly, Jane, I don't know what's gotten into you this morning!"

Gaia.

Gaia had gotten into her—or maybe she'd been there all along—and Jane knew that's where the elephant would stay until she found a way to help her.

3
POSTER CHILD

"N IIICE OOUUUTFIT, JAAAAANE!" Amy Airlie MacGillivray sped by at top speed and full volume, hair flying and hordes of startled students parting before her like the Red Sea. Jane and Flory winced as she crashed into a bank of metal lockers at the end of the hall, then rolled their eyes at one another as a gaggle of grade twelve boys battled to be the first to help her up.

"Amy, when did you get Wheelys?" Flory inquired politely once Amy had extracted herself from her admirers and made her way over to the timetable postings. "Aren't they for, well, you know, kids?"

"One, summer garage sale. And two, irrelevant," Amy retorted, rounding on Jane. "Jane, today is the first day of the last year of the rest of your life. Why in the name of all things holy did you let your mother dress you?"

Placing a hand self-consciously on her head, where her unwashed hair was twisted into a wispy updo, Jane looked down, taking in her 1960s psychedelic-print tunic, a secondhand-store bargain she'd lucked into over the summer, bell-bottom jeans (same store) and canvas flats, and shrugged. She thought she'd done pretty well for four minutes.

"And what is that smell?" Amy wrinkled her nose and fanned her hands dramatically. At this, Jane blushed. Worried about skipping her shower after her run, she'd grabbed an old bottle of perfume from her mom's bathroom drawer and sprayed it on liberally. Even she was a bit woozy from the effects.

"Don't be a hypocrite, Amy," Flory interjected in her friend's defense. Jane grinned, feeling vindicated, but too soon. "You create smells almost that bad every day in your laboratory!"

"Did you guys get the timetable email?" Jane questioned them, desperate to change the subject. "According to mine, we don't have a single class together all year long. There must've been a mistake."

"That's why I asked if we could meet here before class," Flory responded, pointing up at the hard-copy schedules posted outside the school office. "These are the originals. These are the ones I'm going to go by."

Amy shook her head. "I already checked. The email was right. It's splitsville." At Jane's and Flory's pained looks, she held up her hands. "Whoa, girls, I'm just callin' it like I see it. After this year, I'm headed for sciences, Flory'll study law, and Jane . . . is set for a life of mystery and adventure!" The pause had been slight, but Jane had caught it. "It only makes sense that we're going to go our own ways more this year. Oh, come on, don't look so miserable. There's still lunch! And the Shack!"

The bell rang, announcing five minutes till the start of classes. "Just be glad you don't have my schedule!" Amy continued, throwing her pack over her shoulder and tipping back on her heels. "That's what the Wheelys are for. I'm back and forth from one end of the school to the other all day long. Gotta go!" And with that, she pushed off and disappeared into the crowd.

"Go, yes, but what about stop?" Flory called after her, laughing. She reached out to give Jane a hug. "See you at lunch," she said, smiling. Jane smiled back, and then Flory was gone, too. Glancing at her schedule one last time, Jane set off down the hall.

In every class all day long, the talk was of summer holidays, of reunions with friends, of grad and dances and parties and dates, and of plans for the future. Many of Jane's classmates had their futures all mapped out, from where they would travel to what they would study to when they'd get married and have kids. Jane tried hard to focus on her class work and ignore the sensation growing inside of her that she had missed some crucial life-planning session everyone else had attended and was destined to spend her life adrift, anonymous, and alone.

English with Mills. History with Khanna—complete with his infamous first-day-of-school detention. PhysEd, her second run of the day. Lunch—a whirlwind of trading stories with Amy and Flory in the cafeteria—and then too soon, Jane was back in class. Biology with Kereman, where almost everyone in the class opted out of dissections in favor of onscreen simulations. Then the last class of the day—Jane's favorite—Creative Writing with Mr. Zachary. The room was buzzing with talk of the film production that had taken over the city of Cedar's Ridge. "They're doing *Shapeshifter*!" Suze Allan reported to those who were finding out about the production for the first time. "I love those books!"

"Supposedly they've got a whole bunch of animals down there on the set," Kim Park added. "And special trainers to get them to do tricks and even people to ride them!"

"Yes, I'd heard that as well," said Mr. Zachary. "In fact, there's been a hint of a hullabaloo in the local paper about the use of the wild animals in this production. Does anyone know anything about that? Jane?"

Flattered that her teacher would ask her a question about animal welfare and embarrassed that she didn't know anything about any "hullabaloo," Jane blushed and stammered out a "N-no, sorry."

"Yeah, hey, animal lady!" Angus Armstrong teased in a friendly way. "Weren't you on TV again this summer, flying a plane or something crazy?"

The class peppered her with questions about her covert trip out of Cedar's Ridge and her flight back from the Rocky Mountains until finally Mr. Zachary had to rein them in. "That must have been some adventure you had, Jane," he said. "I'm hoping you'll write about it for class. Maybe try to get the story published. In fact, I'd like all of you to think in terms of publication this year. I think you're ready. Meanwhile, I'm sure if there's anything to know about the animals being used in the *Shapeshifter* production, Jane will be the first to find out for us. Oh, and before I forget, anyone who's interested in getting a taste of working on a film set, I hear they're looking for student production assistants. Mr. Chin-Goh mentioned he was going to put the posting up on the board outside the library. All right everybody, enough chitchat. Open your notebooks and let's do some stream-of-consciousness pages to warm up."

Published! Me? Is Mr. Zachary kidding? But wait, what did he say about jobs on the Shapeshifter set? That sounds like a great way to get closer to Gaia! As soon as the bell rang, Jane snatched up her books and turned toward the library, when she suddenly remembered she had Khanna's detention at the other end of the school. Three thousand six hundred seconds of listening to twenty-seven pens scrawling out essays, until finally it was four o'clock. Wishing she had Amy's Wheelys, Jane raced the full length of the hall to the library.

The bulletin board was blank. The library was dark. Someone had beat her here and stolen the job posting to boot. But just as she was turning to go, the library door opened and out popped Mr. Chin-Goh, books, briefcase, and keys threatening to outmaneuver the diminutive man as he attempted to lock up. Jane grabbed the stack of books from his arms and waited as he dropped his briefcase and fumbled with his keys. "Oh, thank you so much, Jane. You are very kind! But my goodness, why so glum?"

"Oh, sorry, Mr. Chin-Goh," she replied. "I didn't realize it showed on my face." She smiled at the friendly librarian who'd helped her many times over the years. "I heard there was a job posting for the production company that's in town, but it looks like somebody else got here first."

Mr. Chin-Goh's eyes went wide and his mouth formed a small, silent O. "False!" he pronounced. Then he bent low and reached into his briefcase. "What is true is that I forgot entirely to post the notice on the board. Here it is," he said, handing Jane a sheet of bright yellow paper. "It must be meant for you!"

Hugging the astonished librarian and laughing over her luck, Jane called a heartfelt "Thank you!" over her shoulder as she raced out of the school, heading directly for the Shack.

4
SHACK TO THE FUTURE

"FLORY MORALES, WHAT is that rotten, reeking . . . Oh, Jane, it's *you*! Er, what I mean is, I didn't hear you come in! Here you are! And looking great, I might add. Nice hair. Pull up a chair. I was just about to power down these Bunsen burners and head to the house for some chai. You want?" Amy turned back to her lab table and busied herself filling a series of test tubes with a viscous, opaque black substance that smelled suspiciously like burnt rubber.

Once the MacGillivray family's gardening shed, the Shack became a playhouse the year Amy's dad discovered three little girls ensconced in its peaty depths one summer afternoon. Now furnished with a table and chairs and fully wired with computer and phone, it was Amy's laboratory, the girls' after-school retreat, their research headquarters, and their secret hideaway. It was where they'd begun to unravel the mystery of SeaKing Shipping and the oil spill, and last summer when they'd needed to get out of town fast, the passage that ran underground from the MacGillivray home to the Shack had helped them throw pursuers off their trail.

Jane joined Flory at the old wooden table and raised her eyebrows. Flory was struggling not to laugh. "Amy, how you can smell anything over that experiment of yours is a miracle." Flory crossed herself as she spoke. "Jane, Amy had just started to describe her experiment for me when you walked in. Amy, why don't you tell us both what fascinating concoction you're brewing!"

Amy glared at Flory, suspecting the petite Philippina girl was making fun of her, but Flory's face was all innocence. "Hmph. Well, to start with, it's a *de*coction."

"Of what? Used car tires?" Jane interrupted, wrinkling her nose.

"As a matter of fact, Miss Smarty Pants, yes, of used car tires," Amy shot back. Then her expression softened as she began to warm to her subject. "I've been wracking my brain for a money-making idea, see, something where the raw materials are cheap, or better yet free, so I can make a product practically everybody needs and sell a million of them cheap and become insanely wealthy. My mom and dad are going to force me to get a job this year and put all the money away for university. This way, I get a little somethin' going on the side, earn myself some mad money, and no one's the wiser! No, please, hold your applause!" Amy bowed.

"And you're inventing . . . ?" Jane prompted.

"Feelys!" Amy squealed.

"Sounds suggestive," Flory muttered to Jane, crossing herself again.

Amy rushed on, oblivious. "I noticed a lot of incompetent parallel parking in the school lot today, I must say. So what Feelys do is attach to a car's hubcaps by some sort of suction, I haven't quite worked that part out yet, and stick out about six inches, and as you're parallel parking and getting close to the curb, you'll be able to *feel-y* the curb and thus avoid hitting it! *Ka-ching*! Five bucks a pop, everybody'll want them, and Mad Scientist MacGillivray will be rich! *Rich*! *Mwah-ha-ha-ha-ha*!"

"Amy . . . ," Jane started.

"Now Jane, I know you killed your car in Crowsnest Pass last summer," Amy rattled on, "otherwise I would have had you beta-test the prototypes. Voluntarily, I mean. I couldn't afford to pay you at this stage in the design process. I'm sure you understand."

"AMY!" Jane and Flory shouted together.

"What? Sheesh, you don't have to yell!" Amy huffed.

"They already exist," Jane said.

"Huh?"

"Feelys," Jane continued, hating to burst her friend's bubble. "They've already been invented. They're called curb feelers."

For a moment, Amy stared straight at Jane, her expression frozen in a look that seemed to register physical pain. Then slowly, she reached down, turned off the

Bunsen burners, placed the rack of test tubes in the sink, and stored the chemical additives in the mini fridge. Without a word, she stepped down into the center of the room, lifted the trap door in the floor, and disappeared into the ground, pulling the trap closed behind her.

Unfazed, Jane and Flory busied themselves with homework assignments until Amy's return. The floorboards creaked and the trap door flipped open revealing a mass of red curls and a tray laden with glasses of spicy-smelling chai and a plate of oatmeal raisin cookies. "Snack time!" Amy called brightly, Feelys apparently forgotten. "Sorry I was gone so long. Ben called."

The girls dug into the snacks, dunking their cookies in the hot drinks and eating till there was nothing left but crumbs. "So how *is* the Fantastic Frenchman?" Jane asked through her last mouthful of food. Benoît Tremblay had gotten off a bus in Cedar's Ridge last year after setting out from Ontario on an open-ended journey and had promptly fallen head over heels for Amy. Short, dark, and stocky, the Francophone had a wicked sense of humor and a raucous *joie de vivre* that made him more than a match for the energetic little redhead. Used to having a different boy by her side every week, Amy had been surprised to find her interest held by this picture-painting, rugby-playing, romance-making enigma. But as Jane watched her friend brush imaginary crumbs from her hands over and over again, she sensed something wasn't right.

"Mm, fantastic, I guess," Amy answered, standing as she stacked mugs on the tray and avoiding Jane's eyes.

"You guess?" Jane echoed.

"Yeah, well, you know, same old, same old," Amy said. Jane and Flory looked at each other, perplexed. And then suddenly Jane figured it out.

"You met some new guy at school today, didn't you?" she said, trying unsuccessfully to keep envy and accusation out of her voice. Amy looked guilty.

"So you did! I can't believe it!" Jane knew her voice was rising but she couldn't seem to pull back. "You've got this amazing guy who absolutely adores you and you want to chuck him? For what, to flirt?"

"Jane," Flory said quietly.

"Look, I know, I'm insane, right?" Amy wailed. "Ben's incredible. It's just . . . I'm not ready . . . I'm not . . . I'm not Flory!" She turned to the smaller girl. "You've known since you were fourteen that Mark was the guy for you. You guys'll go to university, get married, get matching power jobs, have kids, the works. You will! And it'll be perfect and amazing. For *you*."

"Married?" Jane choked out, astounded. Flory reddened but kept silent and Jane realized that Amy had gotten it exactly right.

"But I'm just not sure I'm one of those respectable types that mates for life, you know?" Amy continued. "I want a new mate every season! I want adventure!" Amy breathed. "I want a few more years to be free, a wild child, you know? Or at least as wild as anybody can be with parents like mine." She grinned, glancing at Jane to see if her friend had understood. Jane looked away.

Amy lowered her eyes, her voice strained. "I almost feel like I met the perfect guy for me, only ten years too soon. I just wish I hadn't waited till now to break up with him, but I just couldn't give him up! I'm a horrible, selfish person, I know." She sat down again miserably and lay her head on the table.

Flory reached over and placed a small hand on her friend's shoulder. "Mark and I were lucky to be so sure so soon," she said. "Everybody's different, Amy. If you're not sure—about him, the timing, anything—it's better to break it off. Better for him, too." Amy's curls bounced as she nodded into the table. "And Jane, you won't be alone for much longer," Flory finished.

The comment sounded like a non sequitur, but Jane realized Flory had cut to the heart of the matter, as she so often did. That's what was bothering her most about Amy's decision to break up with Ben: the fact that Amy had so many options when she, Jane, had none.

"She wouldn't be alone at all if my idiot brother would grow some brain cells on that organic farm of his and ask her out!" Amy blurted, coming suddenly to life again. Jane flushed a deep red. "And don't even try to deny it this time, Lady Ray. You're mad for the boy."

Jane sighed and then began to laugh. Both her friends had caught her out this afternoon. Well, after all, what were friends for? It was true: she was crazy about Michael Malcolm MacGillivray. She'd known him as long as she'd known Amy, which was all her life, and up until just a couple of years ago, thought of him as nothing more than her friend's older brother. Then something had changed. The gap in their ages had seemed to close; she'd begun to notice the way the sandy waves of his hair curled to frame his face; how his blue eyes sparkled when he teased her; how he'd begun to notice *her*. But she'd been dating Jake Harbinsale at the time, and until just a couple of months ago, he'd been dating Katrina D'Angelo, one of Jane's fellow volunteers at the Urban Wildlife Rescue Center. So that had been that.

But this past summer, he'd chosen to abandon his engineering program at university and commit himself to becoming an organic farmer, a decision Jane had championed but that had cost him both his relationship with Katrina and the support of his family. Jane had hardly dared wonder if these events might be the catalyst that would bring them together. But now he was living on a farm on Cortes Island, banished from the MacGillivray home and miles and an ocean away from Cedar's Ridge.

"So you admit it!" Amy crowed, her own problems temporarily forgotten. "*Jane MacGillivray*! Listen to that . . . has a nice ring to it, doesn't it?" Then she squealed: "We'd be sisters!" Flory sat silently beaming.

Jane could feel herself grinning stupidly and looked down to hide her embarrassment. A sheet of bright yellow paper poking out of her bag caught her eye—the job posting!—and in a flash she'd changed the subject and was telling Amy and Flory about her adventures on Elfin Lake that morning.

"So you're saying that elephant we rode at Raincity Zoo when we were little is still alive?" Flory asked.

Jane nodded. "And I'm scared something's wrong," she said. "Those calls I heard this morning weren't social calls. They were calls of terror." Jane shuddered, remembering.

Flory was already at the computer conducting a search on the production company. "Here's the Production Assistant job posting," she called from the computer desk. "It sounds like they want more than one. Oh, and listen to this: 'SayWhat? Productions brings the internationally renowned *Shapeshifter* series to life at last on the silver screen!'" she read from the official website. "'Shot on location in picturesque Cedar's Ridge, British Columbia, Canada, *Shapeshifter* makes use of all the technology Hollywood North has to offer—but producers David and Lynn Sayers say the real stars are the animals!'"

"Say again?" Jane said, suddenly alert.

"SayWhat?" Amy corrected.

"No, I mean, what was that last bit, Flory? About the producers?" Jane listened as Flory reread the sentence.

David, she heard in her mind. *And this is my wife, Lynn.* "I met them on set this morning!" she gasped. "David and Lynn! I met the producers!"

"Jane, don't tease—are you saying we have a shot at nepotism here?" Amy asked eagerly.

"Oh, Jane, this could be the answer to all our prayers!" Flory said reverently, joining them at the table. "I'd get a break from working at my family's law firm *and* we'd all be together!"

"I'd be making money and rubbing shoulders with movie stars!" said Amy.

"And I'd be close to Gaia," Jane whispered.

"So what are we waiting for?" Amy hollered, tightening the laces on her Wheelys. "Let's go get those jobs! Race ya!"

5
NOAH'S SECRET

Heads turned on set as Noah Stevenson
walked by.

Five-foot-ten, maybe eleven, the girls in the crew
mused as makeup brushes paused in midair and coffees
went cold. Not so tall—but tall enough. Dark, almost
black hair buzzed close to his head, hair that would curl
in tendrils around fingers if allowed to grow long. A
solid physique that looked as though it had been disci-
plined by martial arts, and a strong jaw to match. The
square-cut features softened by a full, sensuous mouth
that smiled now as though animated by some Mona
Lisa secret, and starlit blue eyes with lashes the makeup
crew would have paid a fortune for.

But it was the walk. The casual confidence stopped
well short of a swagger, but there was a presence in
every step, in every movement, that commanded attention. And Noah Stevenson was getting attention.

From beside trailers and inside crew tents and
across the lot, eyes took in the black fisherman's turtle-

neck sweater and jeans, the camera in the left hand, the smile, the sheer vital presence. *Stills photographer for the production company? Nah, too good looking to hide behind the camera. Actor for sure. Some up-and-coming star, no doubt. Have to check the cast list, put a name to that face. Wonder when he gets his dinner break?*

Noah continued to make his way across the lot through the tents and trailers, nodding acknowledgment to a few smiles and stares but ignoring most. *Let them wonder,* he thought as he listened to the conversations swirl around him and kept his eyes open for clues that would lead him to his destination. *Their snap judgments are my best disguise, and the less everybody knows for now, the better.*

Noah Stevenson was a cub reporter with the *Cedar's Ridge City Herald* and the local cable news station. Just entering third-year humanities at university and determined to get into journalism school in a couple of years, he'd juggled multiple jobs in the news industry all the way through school, and thanks to breaking the summer's top story—about corruption within Cedar's Ridge City Council—while still an intern at the paper, he'd been promoted to full reporter.

He was here to follow up on a story the paper had run last week, about the film production and the economic boom it would mean for Cedar's Ridge. The crew was in town till at least December according to the shooting schedule filed with City Hall, and that meant lots of extra people spending lots of money. After the story ran, a vocal contingent of animal rights activists had written to express their displeasure over the film's use of live animals in the production, and his editor had sent him to interview the producers and at the same time keep his eyes open for signs of trouble. There were regulations governing the use of animals on a television or film set, but there were no laws against it, so Noah didn't expect to encounter any problems. Still, he had his own reason for wanting to make sure everything was on the up and up where animals were concerned. A tall, beautiful, very passionate reason.

Noah could still remember the first time he'd seen Jane Ray. She'd been dressed in muddy gray sweats and was soaked from head to toe in sea water and oil, her expressive face a kaleidoscope of emotions as she stormed out of the Urban Wildlife Rescue Center that October day. The oil spill had been his first assignment with the local TV station and he'd arrived at the Center with his camera operator and without any idea of how to tackle the story. Then he'd spotted Jane, clearly a firsthand witness to what had taken place and so obviously moved by what she'd seen. Praying she'd be able to articulate the myriad passions that played across her face, he'd held out his microphone and asked her if she'd rescued an oiled bird. Her answer—clear, eloquent, furious— became the cornerstone of his news segment, and the story had gone national with the six o'clock news.

He'd used that success to keep up media pressure on the oil company while they were under investigation, and he'd learned through the grapevine that Jane was conducting a campaign of her own to try to bring the culprit to justice. When he received an urgent message from a trusted PR source about a takedown at the Plaza of Nations last winter, he was there at the front of the media scrum in time to catch the oil company's top executive whisper a damning confession. That coup had won him an award and got him his internship with the *Herald*. He was only mildly surprised to discover later that Jane Ray had orchestrated the whole event. Where Jane was concerned, anything seemed possible.

This past summer, he'd had his hands full keeping up with the firestorm of controversy that had plagued the little wildlife center as the threat of West Nile Virus hung over Cedar's Ridge, and he'd been among the reporters present on the dock the day Jane had landed a float plane carrying a life-saving vaccine.

While everyone's attention was focused there, a few greedy city councillors had used the diversion to rob taxpayers, and managed to poison a great number of animals in the process. Their *modus operandi* was revealed in an anonymous package delivered to the *Herald's* offices one midsummer evening. Working late that night, Noah found the package and was the first to learn the truth. He checked the facts and broke the story the next day. The scandal rocked the city and cost four councillors their positions on council as well as their jobs. No one had ever claimed authorship of the package, but Noah had his theories. They began and ended with Jane Ray.

At the sound of shouts off to his left, Noah snapped out of his reverie and leapt from between two tents to find himself face to face with an elephant's behind. He stopped short, melting into the late-afternoon shadows once again as two animal wranglers struggled to push and prod the reluctant pachyderm into a trailer. Their hollering and shoving, along with their sweat-soaked faces and grim looks puzzled Noah. Sure, that's how *he'd* look if *he* tried to move an elephant, but weren't these guys professionals? The elephant never made a sound, but Noah sensed her distress. *Cut them some slack, old girl*, Noah thought. *Your handlers don't appear to be half as smart as you are.*

Once the two men had finally closed the trailer doors, Noah emerged from the shadows and held out his hand to the shorter, more rotund of the pair. "Evening, boys," he said congenially. He noticed the tall, thin, wiry one was glancing nervously at the camera he carried. "Any idea where I might find the producers of this little flick?"

"You see that willow tree?" The short greasy one shoved a muscled arm between Noah and the tall skinny sidekick, pointing into the distance. "Well, you gotta cross a little bridge when you get to the creek, and then you hang a left at the willow tree, and bingo!"

"SayWhat?" Noah prompted.

"Well, you gotta cross this bridge . . . ," the sidekick repeated.

"Say what!" Short and Greasy wheezed, doubling over with laughter. His guffaws emerged from a point not much higher than ground level and he slapped at knees lost to view beneath his ample belly. "*Say what*! Good one, dude!"

"Hey, thanks, eh?" Noah said as he turned to go. "Catch you later!" As he strode away, his sharp ears caught Shorty's last words:

"See that loser, Dig? I seen a million guys like him come and go—out-of-work actors. Worm their way onto film sets any way they can. Man, I feel sorry for him."

Noah smiled as he headed toward the little wooden bridge that spanned Chickadee Creek. Sometimes he couldn't believe he got paid to have this much fun.

The willows' leaves had turned from bright green to a deep, mottled yellow and were beginning to carpet the ground. Noah paused, breathing in the crisp, earthy air that had meant "back to school" for as long as he could remember. The sun lit the backs of the ancient cedars on the western shore with a deep orange glow and the rest of the sky was a starless swath of indigo. It would be dark soon. It would be fall soon.

In the fading light, he spotted a sign hanging above the entrance to the large, square white tent ahead: SayWhat? Productions HQ. He'd arrived at his destination. Pausing outside the tent flap, where a scattering of canvas director's chairs sat empty, he reached for his notebook, intending to scan the questions he'd written down earlier. But then he heard voices coming from inside the tent and realized someone else had usurped his appointment. He sat himself in one of the chairs and flipped open his pad.

A voice drifted out of the tent on the cool evening air, clear as birdsong. *Her* voice. Jane Ray.

Noah felt himself break into a sweat. What was she doing here? He wanted to see her, wanted to meet her, but here? Now? He wasn't prepared for this. He shifted in the chair, his body trying and failing to find a nonchalant pose. He dropped his notebook in the dirt and as he bent to pick it up, his camera fell from his lap and clunked against a rock. He could hear the voices inside coming closer and closer to the flap of the tent. In a moment, the flap would lift and she'd see him. And then . . . and then what? It wasn't as though she'd recognize him. It wasn't as if, after all this time, she even knew he existed. He was just a camera, a microphone, a byline in a newspaper.

Well, so, maybe he could stop her and introduce himself, tell her how impressed he was with all she'd done for animals, let her know he was working on a story about the animals in the film production. Yes, that's what he'd do. He cleared his throat and wiped his palms on his pant legs, practicing his opening line.

And when the tent flap swayed, as though someone inside had brushed up against it, he grabbed his notebook and his camera and he ran. Like a grade-school geek. Like an idiot. Like he was in love.

6
THE MAHOUT

NIGHT FELL OVER the Raincity Zoo. One by one, the lights in the animal enclosures were extinguished and the outbuildings threw solid black shadows to the ground as floodlights came on in the compound. One by one, the staff changed their clothes, got in their cars, and drove away. One by one, the diurnal animals lay themselves to rest, a few with their own kind, many alone. And one by one, the nocturnal animals began to prowl the limits of their pens.

The zoo housed over seven hundred animals and a hundred different species within its confines. Many had been captured in faraway countries, whole families or colonies sold piecemeal to zoos across the continent. A few had been rescued from pet owners who'd been surprised to discover that their African spurred tortoise could grow to be over a hundred and fifty pounds or that a python didn't play well with their children. The rest had been born here and had known nothing else.

The reptiles and the exotic birds lived in glass or

wire mesh caging; the African beasts such as the rhinoceros, giraffe, and zebra had outdoor enclosures, as did the lion, tigers, jaguar, and cougars. Local wildlife such as the grizzly and black bears, wolf, and elk roamed in yet other outdoor pens. These discrete areas were linked together by paved pathways and a miniature railway track, all designed to provide zoo visitors with maximum viewing pleasure.

Raincity Zoo had been open three hundred and sixty-five days a year for over forty years and in that time had evolved from a slapdash dusty roadside attraction to a major operation spread over one hundred and twenty acres and taking in over a million visitors each year. Four owners had come and gone, each adding several crowd-pleasing "attractions" to the zoo's eclectic menagerie. Now, the zoo—and all the creatures within it—belonged to a European businessman by the name of Timo Lausanne.

A rumbling shook the second-storey offices like a small earthquake. Timo Lausanne rose from his desk. *She's here.* Extinguishing the desk lamp, he moved in darkness to the window that overlooked the courtyard and watched the truck and trailer roll into view. It was well after seven o'clock—what had taken them so long? He should be home with Anna and the kids, not poring over the books trying to figure out how to pay yet another veterinary specialist's bill. She'd been out of his hands and out of his hair, he'd been sure of it, the head-bobbing and the foot rot under control long enough to get her through her probationary period with his prospective buyers. Four months—that was all he needed. She just had to put on a good act till December and then she was somebody else's problem.

But tonight, clearly, she was his.

Gaia.

"Foot problems," that Arcola fellow had said on the phone that afternoon. "Holding up the production," he'd said. Timo had tried to sound surprised but of course he'd seen it all before. He'd been watching her condition worsen since buying the zoo four years before. Even then, she'd stood as though pigeon-toed, displacing her weight—all nine thousand pounds of it—to the outsides of her front feet in an attempt to relieve the pain caused by the chronically infected foot pads and nails on the insides. Foot rot was common in circus and zoo elephants, he knew. It came of standing idle for long periods of time on hard surfaces instead of roaming and migrating over miles of soft jungle floor. What he hadn't anticipated was that after he sold Gaia's last pen-mate to an American wild animal park, Gaia refused to lie down. For almost four years, she had spent twenty-four hours of every day on her feet, and the unrelenting pressure was taking its toll.

What on earth did other zoos do with their elephants, he wondered? Paid their vet bills and looked away, no doubt. But the truth was, Timo knew, Gaia didn't need more medicine. She needed to roam wild.

Timo scrubbed his face hard with his hands and shook his head to clear it. Such thoughts were an unaffordable luxury for a zoo owner. Besides, he was a businessman, not an animal handler. Really, how could he know what she needed? It was his job to make sure she was sheltered and fed and free of disease, and he fulfilled his duty in those regards. But she had become a liability. She was old now, and lethargic, didn't draw the crowds the way she used to. Expensive to feed, expensive to maintain. It was time to sell her while he could still get a decent price.

He watched from the window as Sen Chanta and the on-call vet appeared in the courtyard and made their way to the back of the trailer. It took the traditional mahout trainer less than five minutes to coax Gaia backward down the ramp and into the concrete enclosure that had been hosed out in anticipation of her arrival. Timo's expression softened as he watched the two move side by side, the mahout's right hand pressed gently against the huge creature's left front flank, the vet trailing behind. Timo knew that if it weren't for Sen Chanta, these vet visits would be a whole lot more frequent. Sen tended to the elephant almost as if she were his child, talking to her, feeding her by hand, giving her baths, treating her feet, just sitting with her for hours at a time. The sight of the pair of them—the gentle, lumbering elephant with the small, dark, nimble man—filled him with a feeling he could not name, but which always made him think of his own children.

Timo still hadn't told Sen the news of Gaia's sale. He didn't know how to do it. Sen had come with Gaia when he bought the zoo, a package deal. As far as he knew, the man was single, childless. That elephant was his life. Well, the deal remained to be sealed. He'd talk to Sen about it when the time came. Still at the window, Timo stared down, seeing nothing now except a glow of light from the enclosure.

Sen Chanta stood by Gaia's side within the concrete enclosure, a hand on her flank and his face turned up to the orb of her eye, telling her why she was here and what the vet was about to do. Beyond the commands they had practiced together over the years, he didn't suppose she understood his words, but he believed she could sense things from his tone—that she was safe, that he would stay with her, that the stranger was here to take some of the pain away. As the vet moved about the enclosure gathering the hose, the large metal foot basins, his medicines, Sen pressed himself against the massive, solid warmth of Gaia's left side, feeling the crêpey flap of her ear fold round him like a caress, and laughing softly as he always did when she began to explore his head and shoulders with her trunk. He was struck now, as he was every time he was near her, by the power of her presence. Her mind was nowhere else at this moment, not on hunger or thoughts of her strange day or even on her pain. She was entirely with him. He let his own worries go and gave her the same gift in return.

On his way across the courtyard, Sen had caught sight of his boss in the window of the zoo's offices. With his tall, athletic build and blonde, blue-eyed good looks, Timo Lausanne cut an imposing figure. To Sen, though, he seemed benign, even passive, although frankly that was an improvement over his last boss at this zoo. It was strange to Sen that Lausanne knew so little about animals. He seemed to like them well enough, and welcomed advice about improvements to diets and housing and so on. But to him, the zoo was a business and the animals were his commodities. Sen had never had cause to be concerned with his boss's philosophy until last week, when Lausanne had announced that he'd rented Gaia out to a film production company from September through December. And just Gaia. Not Sen. Sen had been distraught—Gaia was in pain, needed to rest, needed him near her—but his arguments had been silenced by Lausanne's bottom line. She was costing the zoo a lot of money; she needed to start making some, too.

Sen had done all he could to prepare, dictating care instructions onto cassette tapes for the temporary handlers and telling Gaia what to expect—although he did not know himself—before the truck and trailer arrived last week to take her away. Then he'd left the compound, sent home on "sick pay," until the call had come today letting him know Gaia was returning to the zoo overnight for treatment. He felt ashamed to know that her pain was the cause of his good fortune, but he couldn't help his joy at being near her again.

He crossed now to the bucket he'd filled before her arrival and began to roll its contents toward her across the concrete floor. A watermelon, two grapefruits, three oranges, a banana, and a bunch of grapes he would feed her by hand. Out of the corner of his eye he caught a flash of silver and glanced over to see the vet preparing a long-needled syringe. Pain medication. A wave of guilt and sadness washed over him and he turned his head back only to find himself caught in Gaia's wondering gaze.

In that gaze were the memories and secrets of all their years together, Gaia and Sen. But beyond that, of all the elephants that came before her. Couched in soft folds of flesh and rimmed by long, sweeping lashes, those eyes held the wisdom of the ancient ones, transmitted from generation to generation—where the watering holes are; how to choose the best mate; where the grasses are tall and sweet and where the river mud is cool and deep; when the rainy time will come. And also, who the two-legged ones are with their hooks and chains and fire machines; how long the fences run; where the hidden holes are; where their young have been taken; and why their forest is vanishing, tree by tree.

All of that history and wisdom, all their memories and secrets. All of the past and all of the future, too. Don't get mired in this moment, she seemed to be saying to him. There is another one just past it, and then another. Anything is possible!

There was a sharp crack and Sen blinked and then laughed as Gaia popped the watermelon beneath her foot as easily as he might crush an egg. Strong enough to lift six hundred pounds and sensitive enough to pluck a single berry off a bush, Gaia's trunk easily found the choice, juicy meat of the melon and delivered it, chunk by dripping chunk, to her mouth. Next, she sought out the oranges, lifted and peeled them with her trunk and mouth, and then dropped the peels to the ground as she savored the sweet fruit.

As she ate, the vet positioned the basins near her front feet. Using tactile commands they'd practiced thousands of times, Sen asked her to lift each foot and place it in a basin. While the vet treated her feet, Sen fed her grapes, holding one at a time in the palm of his hand and waiting until her seeking trunk had found it before offering another. He ran out of grapes before the vet finished, and before he could stop her, Gaia reached her trunk into one of the buckets, siphoned up its contents and sprayed them in an exuberant shower over her back. Laughing, he helped the vet refill the first bucket while Gaia proceeded to do the same with the second. Both buckets refilled, Sen turned the hose on her, letting the stream of water play across her back. In thanks, she reached down with her trunk, supporting its great weight as she gently explored his head and shoulders in an affectionate caress.

The vet signaled that he was ready to administer the pain medication. Leaning into Gaia to let her know she could step back out of the basins, Sen caught the sweet, earthy sent of her skin, heightened now by her bath. He closed his eyes and drew a deep breath, overcome suddenly by thoughts of home. Home. She remembered it far better than he did now, after all these years, and often he pressed himself to her side as though she might somehow transmit those memories to him.

They came to him now: scents, sights, and sounds— long buried in his heart—of the place where everything and everyone he loved had been born. The place that sang with life in every hour, that shimmered and cracked with heat and then flooded again each year like a promise. Lush greens and blues and startling crimson, the very palette of life. The place that to him was the world itself, round and fulsome and fecund, every other place an exile. The long migrations on land and through the sky overhead, all creatures returning, always returning home. Except for them. He and Gaia could never go back. In truth, the place she held in her memory, the place he dreamed of, was no longer there.

Sen rested against Gaia's side, feeling a slight tremor go through her as the veterinarian's needle found its mark. Tomorrow she would return to the film set. But tonight she would rest, and he would stay by her side. And as long as he was with her, he was home.

The phone rang, startling Timo out of his reverie. He left the window and crossed to his desk. Who could be calling at this hour? His wife, no doubt. He switched on his desk lamp and glanced at the call display: no, a strange number. Annoyed, he took the call, and afterward was glad he had. A Fraser Valley mom booking a birthday party at the zoo for twelve little girls and their parents. Excellent. That would cover tonight's vet bill.

Timo relaxed as he hung up the phone, but only slightly. There would be another bill. And another. And this deal with Animal Actors Inc. wasn't in the bag yet, not by any means. He needed a Plan B. Without allowing himself to consider what he was doing, he grabbed his cell phone from its holster, punched in a number he now knew by heart, and listened to a message he'd heard many times before.

"Marcozi, it's Lausanne. Tuesday night, late. As it turns out, I may have an elephant for your client after all. I'll know for certain by the end of December. Asian female, around thirty-five years old, no tusks of course and not a fast mover, but eight-foot-six, nine thousand pounds, still an impressive prize for the right individual. Let me know if you think you might be able to place her. Oh, and call my cell. Thanks." Timo flipped his phone shut and simultaneously shut out the image of Gaia and Sen Chanta walking side by side through the courtyard earlier. This was business.

He tore a check from the book, switched off his desk lamp, and locked his office behind him. He would go downstairs and pay the vet, bid good night to Sen, and then go home. Home. To Anna and the kids. To eat. To sleep. To forget.

7

SCAUP . . . IN THE NAME OF LOVE

JANE LOFTED THE tray of thawing salmon above her head, kicked the refrigerator door closed, and backed up hard into Katrina D'Angelo. Dropping tray and fish to the floor with a clatter, she spun around and in a swift glance took in the swinging blonde ponytail, flawless makeup, pink and white track suit, and scowling face. "Oh, Katrina! I didn't . . . I'm so sorry!" Thoughts of Mike MacGillivray and memories of the summer flooded in as fast as the blood rushed to her face. She was taken aback to find Katrina still here instead of attending college or working full-time somewhere. Sure that it all showed in her face now, she stuttered out, "I'm really, really sorry."

"Yeah, so you said," Katrina replied, turning away. "Anybody seen the bucket of insectivorous? We've got a couple of Steller's jays that are going to start making some serious noise if they don't get their daily dose of ground insects." Katrina worked as she talked, banging dishes on the counter, slamming cupboards closed, and upsetting a tray of dirty dishes into the sink with a crash. Two young work experience students hurried out of the kitchen, out of the line of fire. "Anybody else ever notice ground bugs smell like Christmas fruitcake?" Katrina continued. "Oh, and speaking of cake, anybody else notice Beefcake Boy in the exam room with Evie right now? Hello, *hottie*! Oh, but Jane, you've probably already scoped him out, haven't you?" Dishes rattled as Katrina stacked diets into a teetering pile on her tray.

"What in the name of heaven is that infernal racket?" a strident voice called from the far side of the outer door. "This is an animal hospital, not a discotheque!" Jane hurried to pull open the door and Avis Morton stepped into the kitchen, dressed head to toe in fawn-colored wool tweeds and carrying a stack of excrement-soaked towels.

Tall, silver-haired, and always impeccably groomed, Avis preferred the wildlife center's kitchen to run with a certain militaristic precision when she was on shift. She made a habit of reprimanding new volunteers whenever they failed to operate according to the laws of common sense. In the beginning, the regular tongue-lashings had almost convinced Jane to quit. But when she'd found herself in trouble with a vengeful oil company and then later with violent protestors, Avis had proven to be a powerful ally. The older woman had become both mentor and friend, and her dedication to animals was an ongoing inspiration to Jane.

"It's my fault," Jane said now, avoiding Katrina's gaze. "I, uh, tripped and dropped a bunch of stuff. Sorry."

"Oh, well, if it was an accident . . . ," Avis conceded. Then she promptly dropped her stack of soiled towels to the floor. "*Fiddlesticks*!" Jane jumped. Fiddlesticks was Avis's F-word.

"What's wrong?" Jane asked, bending to scoop up the towels.

"It's this darned arthritis again!" Avis exclaimed, holding knobbled hands out before her. "Everything aches these days and my hands won't do anything I tell them to!" She sighed. "I hate to admit it, but I think I may need some help getting the outside animals fed and cleaned this morning. With any luck, I'll be fit as a fiddle again next Thursday."

"No problem, Avis," Katrina interjected perkily. "Jane, why don't you join Avis outside? As far as the care room goes, I'm on it, so there wouldn't be much for you to do anyway."

Jane held her tongue. She resented the implication that she wasn't needed in the care room, but she was happy to work with Avis, and frankly it would be a relief to escape this tension between Katrina and herself. She dropped the stack of towels in the laundry room, checked the display board for the list of animals currently in care, and set to work preparing their diets.

It was the tail end of busy season at the Urban Wildlife Rescue Center. Nestled in the woods on the south shore of Aerie Lake, the little wild animal hospital admitted the bulk of its patients in the spring and summer months, when animals were mating and producing offspring. More than two thousand injured, orphaned, or pollution-damaged animals came through the Cedar's Ridge facility's doors between April and September, and the small wooden building resounded from dawn till dusk with the cries of hungry babies.

Working inside, Katrina would feed the last few fledgling robins, jays, starlings, and sparrows of the year. Outside, Jane and Avis would take care of the animals—fourteen Canada geese, seventeen mallard ducks, nine gulls, six songbirds, and a lesser scaup—that were almost ready to be released to the wild.

Jane found she enjoyed working side by side with Avis, preparing diets, laying out fresh towels, draining and refilling bathing pools, hazing gulls that had become too comfortable in the presence of humans. Avis had each task down to a routine, and by watching carefully, Jane learned the most efficient way to move through the pens and aviaries that dotted the UWRC's sprawling grounds. She also noticed, though, that Avis moved more slowly than usual, bending and lifting and navigating the dirt paths with obvious difficulty.

"Coffee!" Avis huffed after they'd chased a particularly insolent gull around its pen. "I need a rest!"

After scrubbing down, they headed for the small heritage home that stood next to the care center.

Upstairs, it housed the UWRC's administration offices and downstairs there were lockers and a lunchroom for the volunteers. Passing the exam room window, Jane's gaze was drawn by the glare of a bright light. She remembered Katrina's comment about Beefcake Boy and wondered if he was a visiting rehabilitator here to assist Evie, the UWRC's head of animal care; that made sense since Daniel Jackson, Evie's usual second in command, was away interviewing for veterinary jobs. She reminded herself to check on the way back.

In the lunchroom, Jane set out the chocolate chip pecan cookies she'd brought while Avis made the coffee. This weekly ritual with her elderly friend had become one of her favorite things about volunteering at the wildlife center, and she missed it in the summers when they were too busy to take a break. It felt like a kind of homecoming to reach September and be able to sit together for a while. Jane was already looking forward to more of Avis's stories about her time in the Navy, of the animals she'd encountered over the years, of adventures with her husband George.

Avis filled two mugs with the dark, steaming liquid and then they sat, sipping companionably and munching on cookies. "Mmm, tasty," Avis complimented her, reaching for seconds.

"Thanks!" Jane answered, pleased her baking had passed muster.

As she dusted crumbs from her hands, Avis said

casually, "I don't know how much longer I've got here."

Jane glanced at her watch, uncomprehending. "We can spare another few minutes, I'm sure. Everybody's fed, and the list on the odd-job board didn't look that long." She reached for another cookie.

"No, Jane," Avis responded quietly. "I mean, I don't know how much longer I'll be able to keep volunteering here. I'm tired, and everything's so much harder these days."

Jane stared at Avis. *Quit volunteering? What's she talking about? She's been coming here for over fifteen years. What would she do instead? And why, just because she's tired? Is something else going on?* Jane's mind raced with questions, but she couldn't think of a single thing to say.

"Anyway," Avis said, her voice bright, "I'm fine for now. I'm sure my retirement from the UWRC is a long way off!" She stood uncertainly and then moved slowly to the sink to wash out their mugs. Jane zipped up her pack and stood wordlessly by the door.

"Oh, don't wait for me, Jane," Avis called over her shoulder. "Evie left some envelopes for me to stuff in the upstairs office. You go on and give Katrina a hand. I'll see you next week."

Jane mumbled an awkward goodbye and fled. As she hurried up the path to the care center, she berated herself for her callous response to Avis. It wasn't the first time she'd failed to speak up when it really mattered.

The stronger her feelings, it seemed, the bigger the knot in her throat. Well, so, she'd say something to her next week. She'd offer to help her care for the outside animals every week from now on. Make the coffee while Avis sat and rested. Make things easier for her. That's what she'd do.

Feeling a little better, she yanked open the care center door, failing to notice the DO NOT ENTER sign taped to the outside. Immediately, Anthony Lau, the UWRC's receptionist, leapt to his feet on the far side of the desk, shot a hand out to Jane, palm forward, and cried, "SCAUP! in the name of love . . . before you break my heart!" Anthony's stylish black shag swung over his eyes as he bopped one knee and hip in time to his singing. "Scaup! in the name of love . . . before you break my heart! Think it o-o-ver. Haven't I been goo-ood to you? Think it o-o-ver. Haven't I been twee-eet to you?"

By this time, Jane was doubled over laughing and didn't see the exam room door swing open. She looked up to find the UWRC senior staffer, eyebrows raised, taking in both performer and audience. Evie Jordan did not look amused.

"Uh, the interview is still in progress, guys," Evie said, clearly trying hard to keep her exasperation out of her voice, "and I'm pretty sure my last answer was underscored by the Supremes. Would you mind taking this show on the road?"

Anthony nodded sheepishly and sat back down at the desk. "Sorry, Eves. What can I say? I got the music in me." Suppressing a giggle, Jane took a step toward the care room when a figure behind Evie caught her eye. Deliberately. Stopped in her tracks, Jane took in dark, closely shaved hair, muscular build, green open-necked sweater and well-worn jeans. And eyes. Magnetic blue eyes that held hers. For much longer than was comfortable. His gaze stirred a faint but familiar sensation in her. And then the exam room door swung shut and the memory was lost.

"Who . . . urgh?" Jane's voice gave out on her for the second time that morning.

"I don't know, girlfriend," Anthony answered, sizing up her reaction, "but by the look on your face, I'd say you'd better find out!"

8
DEVIL'S ADVOCATE

"IF YOU DON'T want to be caught on camera, work elsewhere!" Evie was marching down the hall, face grim, with Blue Eyes hot on her heels. Jane, who had begun stacking towels in the care room, paused in mid-fold, unsure what was happening. "Our intrepid reporter has decided he wants more animals and 'volunteer action' in the background of our interview, and against my better judgment I acquiesced." Evie rolled her eyes and Blue Eyes smiled at Jane. Jane blushed and dropped her gaze to the floor. "So if you want to be on tonight's news, stick around. If you don't, there are dishes to wash in the kitchen, kennels to clean on the pad outside, and perches to scrub in the laundry room. So go!"

The two young students scurried from the care room. Katrina flashed a brilliant smile at the reporter and angled herself on her stool so that the camera could catch her hand-feeding the fledgling jays. Jane froze, shyness battling with her desire to learn more about this reporter and to hear what Evie had to say. In the end, curiosity won out, and she resumed sorting, folding, and stacking. She kept her back to the room, but tuned every one of her senses to the reporter and his questions, Evie and her answers.

The spotlight came on, the video camera began to whir, and the reporter spoke: "Ms. Jordan, as head of animal care at the Urban Wildlife Rescue Center, can you tell me, has the UWRC taken an official position with respect to the use of wild animals in the production currently being filmed on Elfin Lake?"

So that's what he was here about—*Shapeshifter*! Jane was glad she'd stuck around. Maybe Evie would say something about Gaia!

"It's not the role of this organization to speak out for or against the activities of any other organization," Evie answered carefully. "Our job is to rescue and rehabilitate urban wildlife. What I will say personally, though, is that no matter how well the wild animals on that set are being cared for, you're still dealing with an element of exploitation." Jane straightened, surprised, then hurriedly resumed folding. "Those animals have been rented out for the purpose of creating entertainment. The money from the rentals will go directly into the pockets of the animal handlers or the keepers of the zoo where the animals came from. When the film gets shown in theaters, the money from ticket sales will go back to the filmmakers. Of all the money that changes hands, little or none of it will go to improve the lives of those animals, or to conserve those of their kind that are left in the wild. Everyone benefits except the animals."

Jane kneaded a small cloth with shaking hands. She'd never thought of it that way. And then it struck her: she would be part of the very problem Evie was talking about! She'd just accepted an after-school job on set, and the money she'd earn would be tied to the exploitation of animals in the production, including Gaia! She felt sick. She'd have to speak with Evie as soon as this interview was over.

Katrina sidled up beside her and began removing towels from shelves, re-folding them, and then replacing them in their stacks. Jane realized the reporter's camera must be focused on them.

"But Ms. Jordan, this 'exploitation' you're speaking of is actually legal commerce, is it not?" the reporter asked. "The Raincity Zoo, Animal Actors Inc., and SayWhat? Productions aren't actually doing anything wrong, are they?"

"Yes, it's all legal," Evie answered, "because according to the law in this country, owned animals are property, just like your camera there, or my car. And subject to just about the same whims. Don't like the color any more? Want a newer model? Trade it in! Doesn't perform like it used to? Get rid of it and buy a new one!" Evie's voice had taken on an intensity Jane had never heard before. "There are film industry standards governing the use of animals on set, which is a good thing, since the laws protecting wildlife generally have fewer teeth than a lion in a roadside circus. So these animals will probably be quite well cared for, as far as captive wild animals go. But it's my view that these animals shouldn't be in captivity in the first place! And the fact that the elephant in this production is a member of an endangered species doesn't seem to have been factored in at all."

"But isn't that why she's in a zoo?" the reporter pressed.

"She's in a zoo to sell tickets!" Evie shot back.

"But surely, if she's endangered, she's safer in a zoo than in the wild?" the reporter persisted.

Jane felt the tension mounting between the reporter and the wild animal rehabilitator, and fought the desire to escape by leaving the room. She didn't have answers to the reporter's questions herself, but after a year of volunteering under Evie's guidance, she trusted the senior staffer's experience and perspective on animal-related issues. She wanted . . . no, she *needed* to hear what Evie would say. She sought Katrina in her peripheral vision and found her, still close by, cutting newspaper to line the birds' cages. She knew that Katrina was trying to stay in the picture, and Jane realized the reporter's camera must be panning over to the laundry shelves with some regularity.

"The sad thing is, you're partly right," Evie replied, surprising Jane. Between poachers hunting for ivory, habitat loss, and conflicts with farmers when the elephants turn up seeking space and food, living in the wild has become a crapshoot for elephants. But what people forget is that safety isn't the only factor in an animal's welfare. Being wild is having the freedom to exhibit natural behaviors and preferences, like how and where to spend their day, whether to be alone or with others of their kind, when and where and what to eat, choosing when to mate and whom to mate with. All of those freedoms are denied in captivity. Zoo animals are, for the most part, bored, cramped, lonely, deprived of all control over their lives, and far from their natural homes. For a wild animal, a zoo is a prison."

"But isn't it true, Ms. Jordan, that most zoos focus on conservation now?" the reporter asked. "Breeding endangered species for re-introduction to the wild?"

"Do you know how many zoos there are in the world?" Evie quizzed back. She didn't wait for an answer. "*Ten thousand*! And do you know how many of those are registered for breeding and conservation?" Again, she answered her own question. "Twelve hundred. To top it off, only two percent of the world's threatened or endangered species are even registered in the breeding programs! Zoos aren't breeding their animals to save endangered species, Mr. Stevenson. They're breeding to produce babies. And that's because cute little baby animals draw crowds, and crowds buy tickets. Just don't ask what happens to those cute little babies when—or if—they grow up."

"So you're saying zoos are not significant players in conservation efforts worldwide?" the reporter persevered.

It suddenly seemed to Jane that the reporter wasn't listening to Evie, or worse, that he'd arrived with an agenda and was trying to get her to say things that would support his point of view. She began to wonder if this interview was some kind of setup.

"Zoos couldn't survive without animals imported from the wild," Evie said flatly, "and the worldwide trade in rare animals probably couldn't survive without zoos! Countries in Africa, Asia, and South America have absolutely no incentive to protect endangered animals when they can make money by selling them!"

Evie's voice changed, sounding more like the patient teacher that Jane was used to. "The only way we're going to save endangered animals is by preserving their habitats in the wild and eliminating the reasons they're captured or killed by people in the first place. The idea that animals are this endless supply of free product to be captured and sold for our benefit is the only thing that should be extinct!"

The reporter matched Evie's more measured tones: "And what about the argument that zoos teach people— especially children—to care for the natural world?"

Jane stopped what she was doing and listened carefully. Her parents had taken her to the Aquarium and to various petting zoos when she was little, and they'd all visited the Raincity Zoo on their way to Cultus Lake almost every time they went. She had also grown up with animals as part of the family. Since becoming a volunteer with the UWRC, she'd come to the conclusion that all of those things had helped inspire her love for animals and her desire to help them and protect them. She was pretty sure the reporter was finally on track.

"All zoos teach people is that it's okay to keep animals in captivity," Evie answered simply. "To buy and sell and trade them like stocks and bonds. To rent them out for profit. To confine them, to sacrifice their freedom, their family bonds, their most basic well-being for *our* amusement. That when they stop drawing crowds or performing on command, it's acceptable to then dispose of them, like garbage." Evie kept her voice low, but it vibrated with the intensity of the passion behind her words.

"Animals are sentient beings, Mr. Stevenson," Evie continued. "In that way, at the very least, they are exactly like you and me. This elephant, who is no doubt being required to walk and kneel and trumpet on command, has the ability to communicate her emotional state with an astonishing variety of vocalizations and physical displays. She has the capacity to form relationships with others of her kind in which she is loyal and caring, and for which she will grieve when they come to an end. She can be gentle, despite her enormous strength, and she can be dignified, despite the oppression of her captivity.

But she and all of her kind are not long for this world unless something drastic is done. And zoos cannot expect to inspire us to take those drastic measures when they themselves treat these animals as disposable."

Jane thought again of how she'd forgotten about Gaia all these years and her eyes filled with tears. Before anyone could catch *that* on camera, she hurried from the care room and took refuge in the kitchen. She listened as Evie and the reporter exchanged a few final words and then the back door swung open and shut. It was over.

She followed Evie to the exam room, taking the senior staffer by surprise: "Evie, I'm working there! I took a job on the *Shapeshifter* production. I'm part of the exploitation!" she confessed in a rush. "But I just started yesterday. I can still quit. Should I quit? I don't want to make things worse for Gaia, I want to help her!"

Evie placed both hands on Jane's shoulders. "Whoa, girl. Take it easy. Tell me again, but slower this time. What's going on?"

Slowly, Jane related to Evie all that had happened since early Tuesday morning: hearing the elephant's alarm call on the Elfin Lake trails, visiting the *Shapeshifter* set, recognizing Gaia and deciding she wanted to help her, learning about the production assistant jobs and applying for them with Amy and Flory. "But after listening to your interview, I feel terrible, Evie! Being on set will be like saying I think keeping wild animals in zoos and renting them out to film companies is okay!"

"Will it?" Evie asked. "*Is* that what you think? Because another way to look at it is that being on set with your knowledge of animal welfare might just keep everybody a little more on their toes. Right? I, for one, would feel a lot better about this whole film thing knowing Jane Ray was present on the set."

Jane glowed, her eyes wide with the surprise of Evie's compliment.

"Listen, like I said to that reporter, I'm sure everything's on the up and up with these guys," Evie went on. "But if you're right, and that elephant needs help of some kind, you're in a much better position to figure that out if you're right there." She grinned. "Just don't do anything crazy, like getting into an elephant suit or trying to airlift her out of there by yourself!" Jane laughed. "Hey, Jane . . . it's after noon—don't you have to get to school?"

Jane gasped, hugged Evie in a quick goodbye, grabbed her bag, and tore out the front door, giving Anthony a high-five as she ran by. Where had the morning gone? She'd be lucky if she got fifteen minutes with Ame and Flor before lunch hour was over. Unlocking her bike from the wooden bench in the garden, she was just about to push off when a hand gripped her arm, pinning her in place.

9

RED LETTER DAY

"**I** DIDN'T MEAN TO startle you . . . I just wanted to talk with you before you left!" The hand on Jane's arm burned like an iron, but the grip was gentle, almost hesitant. She looked up into blue eyes that were gazing back at her as if the lake and trees and buildings around them had fallen away and she was all that was left. "Hi," he said. And then he smiled.

"Hi," Jane replied softly.

"I'm Noah," he said.

"I'm Jane," she responded.

"I know." He smiled again. She blushed.

He looked down and cleared his throat, and Jane realized, astonished, that he was shy, too. "I, uh, I just need to get some contact information and your signature in case you appear in any of the shots that get aired tonight." He handed her a standard release form and a pen.

She filled it out and signed the bottom. As he took it from her, his hand brushed hers and again she felt that alarming burning sensation.

"Well, uh, thanks!" he said, suddenly not meeting her eyes. "I . . . I guess that's all, then." She realized he was about to leave, and she realized at the same time that she didn't want him to. She grasped for something fun and flirty to say, the kind of thing Katrina would say.

"Sounds like you're a real zoo freak!" was what came out. She glanced wildly about the garden for a pillow she could stuff into her mouth, but found none. "I mean, back there, your questions, you think zoos are a good idea." Fun and flirty? She was oh-for-two.

He looked at her intently as if gauging what she was really asking him. Then he said, "You won't hear my questions in the news segment tonight, only the answers of my interview subjects—Ms. Jordan, the film's producers, and the owner of the zoo. Here's my card. If you think the segment misrepresents the issues, let me know. Please. I'd like to hear from you, Jane." And then he was striding up the path to the parking lot, to his car, and gone.

Jane gripped the card, kicking herself for what she'd said, sure she'd offended him. But what *did* he think about zoos? More importantly, why did she care? She pocketed the card, jumped on her bike, and rocketed onto the trail. Amy and Flory were never going to believe the morning she'd just had. But there was proof— Noah Stevenson's business card in her jeans pocket, its contents already committed to memory. Suddenly she grinned, realizing she'd just given a guy her phone number for the first time ever. Okay, so it was on a news release form, but whatever! Amy would be proud.

Pedaling hard, she thought about the answer Noah had given to her question. Watch the segment, he'd said, and judge for yourself. *I'd like to hear from you.* Well, it might surprise the heck out of her mom, but she would definitely be watching the six o'clock news tonight.

Skidding into the lot at Cedar's Ridge Senior Secondary, Jane locked up her bike and tore downstairs to the cafeteria. There they were in their usual corner. Jane had to elbow her way through a crowd of boys to get to her friends.

"You guys won't believe this . . . !" she started.

"Oh, hi, Jane!" Flory jumped up and gave her a hug. "Make sure you tell me later, okay? I have to run. Mark and I are cramming for our history quiz. Bye!" She disappeared into the crowd.

"Wait . . ."

"Janeykins!" Amy exclaimed, bouncing to her feet. "I saved you some of my mom's famous three-bean-and-tofu casserole! Yum!" She handed Jane a full container.

"Some?" Jane asked. "This looks like 'all.'"

"Like I said, 'Yum!'" Amy threw the rest of her lunch things into her bag. "Hey, I can't stick around, kiddo. Can your news wait? I busted a nut in my left Wheely and I need to go to Mall-Mart during my spare to get it fixed. See you later on set!"

Jane sighed and sat down at the empty table to scarf

her sandwich before the bell rang. Suddenly Amy was by her side again, huffing with the exertion of walking instead of Wheelying. "Almost forgot," she wheezed. "This came for you in this morning's mail." She dropped an envelope on the table and was gone again.

Jane put her sandwich down and picked up the envelope. Business size, plain white. Thin, just a single sheet inside. On the front, in neat block letters, a draftsman's hand, it read:

JANE RAY c/o AMY MacGILLIVRAY

Her heart racing, she turned the envelope over to find a name she recognized, the name she'd hoped for, printed in the same hand:

M. MacGILLIVRAY

It was a letter from Mike.

10
REUNION

Gaia had been called for a night sequence and it was up to Jane to see that she was ready.

Across Elfin Lake, the western sky was still light, a smoky blue ribboned with orange. Here on set, the animal quarters were warm and dry and dimly lit by low-hanging bulbs and the last vestiges of daylight that managed to slip in through the open doorway and the slats of the roof and walls. Jane breathed in the smells of fresh hay and clean animal bodies and the tang of grassy dung and let out a sigh of contentment. There was no place on earth she'd rather be.

For the past two afternoons, Jane, Amy, and Flory had reported to the *Shapeshifter* set after school where the fantastical story was coming to life before their eyes. Jane's encounter with David and Lynn Sayers had proved fortuitous—the producers hired the three of them on the spot Tuesday afternoon. Amy was assigned to Technical Assistance, which so far mainly involved transporting heavy equipment on dollies from one area of the set to another. Already, she knew almost everyone on the crew by name. One look at Flory's curriculum vitae and the producers slotted her into Administration, where she had immediately implemented a system for tracking the whereabouts of all crew members and equipment at any given time. Her employers were thrilled. Jane was appointed Animal Care Assistant, reporting to Animal Actors Inc., the animal wrangler company hired by the production. The three of them were in heaven.

Jane had done a double-take when David introduced her to the Animal Actors Inc. wranglers late Tuesday. Mr. Arcola, the short, round swarthy fellow with the greasy black comb-over and Mr. Hutchinson, his tall, nervous, reed-thin partner weren't familiar to her at all. But as soon as they spoke, she realized she knew their voices. They were the two men she'd heard arguing on the boat dock that morning—something about a cash cow and breaking someone in so she'd eat out of the palm of their hands. Jane was suddenly uncertain about taking the job if it meant working for people who could speak that way about an employee. But the moment they led her into the barn, all her concerns were forgotten.

Her eyes adjusted to the dim light in the corridors, and then suddenly, standing just a few feet away from her, with nothing but a wooden gate between them, there was Gaia. Jane gazed up, open-mouthed, into the dark globe of her eye and felt a well of joy and recognition spring up within her. "*It's you!*" she breathed.

As if in response, Gaia turned her head and, reaching across the gate with her trunk, began gently to explore Jane's head and face with her sensitive nose. "Stand still, there," said Mr. Arcola from behind her. "She's just checking you out." But Jane didn't need any prompting. Fear and wonder rooted her to the spot as she listened to the snuffling sounds Gaia made with her long nose, taking in Jane's scent. She closed her eyes as the tip of Gaia's trunk—precise, delicate, insistent—measured every contour of her face. Satisfied at last, the elephant lifted her trunk and let out a deep, huffing sigh, and then reached back over the gate and into the pocket of Jane's hoodie, searching for food. Jane had packed along an apple as a snack for herself but delightedly offered it to Gaia on her palm. Gaia plucked it up and delivered it to her mouth, then reached her trunk back across the gate and touched Jane's shoulder as if in thanks. Jane couldn't tell for sure whether the elephant had recognized her after all these years, but it didn't matter. She'd accepted her as a friend.

Back at production headquarters, Lynn had handed her a folder containing a cassette tape and a set of notes written in a small, looping hand. "These came with Gaia from her caretaker at the zoo," the producer explained. "The Animal Actors Inc. folks said they didn't need them, but you may find it helpful to review them before you start work tomorrow."

Tuesday night, alone in her room, Jane had devoured

the notes and played and replayed the tape. It was all about Gaia—what foods she liked, what kinds of toys and activities she enjoyed, when she preferred to sleep, how much she needed to move to keep her feet healthy, what commands she understood—and was dictated by the voice of a man who sounded to Jane as though he had come here from a far distant place. Maybe the same place Gaia had come from. And it was evident in his words and in his soft tones that the man cared very much about Gaia.

Wednesday afternoon, as Mr. Arcola and Mr. Hutchinson had led her through her tasks, she noticed right away that they didn't feed Gaia what the zoo care-taker recommended, nor did they provide her with the toys and other stimulating activities he suggested. Unless Gaia was called for a scene, they kept her alone inside the barn in a barren pen, with buckets of water and molasses-soaked grain as her feed.

Shyly, Jane had asked them about the caretaker's instructions. Mr. Hutchinson had said, "What instruc-tions?" but Mr. Arcola had jumped in, laughing, and answered, "Structions, smuctions, eh, Dig? You see this supposed caretaker anywhere around? No. See, Jane, we're the experts here, and we do things our way. Everybody has their own little tricks of the trade, know what I'm sayin'? There's a girl! Now, listen up, all the horses are on set right now, so be a good little Produc-tion Assistant and go muck out their stalls, alrighty?"

With an uneasy feeling in the pit of her stomach, Jane had done as she was told. But at the end of her shift, she'd stopped by Craft Services and asked one of the line cooks if she could have some leftover fruit for Gaia the elephant. Grinning, he handed her a bulging bag and told her to come back at the same time each day. She smiled in thanks, realizing she'd made another friend, and then she headed home, tired and happy.

At 4:30 this afternoon, she'd run into Amy and Flory in the producers' tent and had finally been able to tell them about her morning at the wildlife center and her strange conversation with the reporter named Noah. "Looks like I'm stuck here after six tonight. Would one of you be able to record the news for me? I really want to see how he uses Evie's interview. Thank you!" Then she'd rushed off before either of them could ask about the letter from Mike.

Now, here she was by Gaia's side, holding a hose aloft so that the spray fell in a soft arc across the elephant's back. Gaia reached into her water bucket, siphoned up the contents and splashed them down the fronts of her legs. Laughing, Jane said, "Thanks for the help, Gaia. Bathing you is definitely a two-person job!"

"How about drying her?" Jane startled as Mr. Arcola approached the pen from behind her. "You need to get that water off pronto so we can saddle her up. Ilsa's riding her tonight." Hastening to grab a handful of soft chamois cloths, Jane rubbed the elephant's flanks as high up as she could reach, all the while wondering how on earth she was going to dry Gaia's back. Recalling her Tuesday-night study session, Jane attempted an authoritative voice and commanded, "Down, Gaia, come down!" But Gaia didn't budge.

"All right, all right, that's enough, kid," Mr. Arcola snickered and shooed her away from the elephant with a wave of his hand. "Why don't you call it a day? We'll catch you tomorrow, eh?"

Jane said good night and hurried from the barn. She was halfway across the lot when she realized she'd left her pack behind. She ran back and scooted in through the rear door. Making her way along the corridors toward Gaia's enclosure, she was stopped short by a low electrical buzzing and a sharp crack that sounded like a gunshot. Jane dropped to the ground, her senses on high alert, and then shuddered as Gaia's trumpet call resounded through the barn. Before she could move, she heard Denny Arcola's voice shouting over Gaia's, and she made out the words, "When I say . . . behave . . . Ilsa . . . do it *now*!" What on earth was going on?

In the next moment, the barn doors swung wide, letting in the last of the day's light in a great, sweeping shaft. Jane pressed herself against one of the horse's stalls, clinging to a sliver of shadow and breathing hard as slow, heavy footfalls made their way from the far right corner of the barn toward the open door. Gaia's trunk came into view first, and then her eye and ear.

Jane held her breath, awed as always by the sight of her. Then she bit back a cry of pain as a strong hand clamped down on her shoulder.

"Thought I heard Denny tell you it was quittin' time!" Digger Hutchison pressed his face close to hers, his breath sour with old coffee and cigarette smoke.

Jane wrested her shoulder from his grasp and answered as calmly as she could: "You heard right, Mr. Hutchison. I just forgot my pack and came back for it, that's all." She held her backpack in front of her, although she wasn't sure if she meant it as proof of her story or as a shield.

"That's all, eh?" Digger raised his eyebrows. "Looks to me like you were snoopin'! Damn kid. I told him we didn't need no kid helpin' us. Get outta here! You got your precious pack? So scram!"

Jane took off toward the back of the barn. But on some instinct she couldn't explain, she turned around again just before she opened the door. Digger was gone, and there, silhouetted in the barn's front entrance, was Gaia. Denny Arcola walked at her side, and astride her back sat a woman gowned in silk. She was seated on a fine carpet woven in threads the colors of jewels. Her flaxen hair was piled high on her head and her dress was the same shade of violet the sky would be in another half hour. Petite as she was, on Gaia she towered above all the world. She bore herself like royalty, and Jane could easily believe her to be a queen. What she couldn't believe was the way Mr. Arcola was treating her, and she realized now that Gaia's alarm calls had been caused by the elephant's own concern for the pretty little performer.

Before Jane could decide what to do next, the three figures moved through the entranceway toward the setting sun and disappeared.

11
THERE'S NO PLACE LIKE HOME

Donna Lise Harbinsale popped a meatloaf in the oven, wiped her hands on her apron, and ducked into the bathroom to give her hair one last little spray. Tossing her apron into the laundry basket, she spritzed some *L'Air du Temps* on her wrists and checked her watch again: 5:47 p.m. Less than fifteen minutes and Rand would be home.

Home. She looked around, her glance taking in the mismatched linoleum floors, beige walls, low ceilings, and high windows in the few small rooms she and Rand now shared. It was still hard to believe that just a few months ago they'd been living in a mansion on the east shore of Elfin Lake, hosting dinner parties by the pool and deciding how much to bonus the grounds-keeper and the maid. Back then, Rand had been General Manager of the Cedar's Ridge Golf & Country Club and held a seat on City Council, and his incomes combined with his side investments had allowed the Harbinsale family to live a very luxurious lifestyle. But last summer, when he and three other Council cronies used their positions to line their own pockets, he'd been forced to resign his seat, and the fallout had cost him his job at the Club as well.

While Rand ranted and railed, they'd lost the house and then the cars. But Donna Lise barely registered those losses. Her two younger boys, Jake and Bobby, had run away earlier in the year, and her eldest, Randall Jr., was so embarrassed by them that he stopped coming to visit; houses and cars hardly mattered after that.

Still desperate to maintain a presence in the community, Rand had rented them a basement suite in their old neighborhood. Traditional as ever, he wouldn't allow Donna Lise to get a job, but found one himself in the only place that would take him—as a greeter at Mall-Mart. Every morning, he showered and then dressed in one of the three-thousand-dollar power suits left over from his General Manager days and waited for the bus, and then the SkyTrain, and then another bus. He arrived home each night wrinkled and damp, pummeled by the hordes of bargain-hunters and smelling of sweat and despair.

Donna Lise would have preferred to move away and start over again. But the belief that her boys would eventually come home kept her rooted here. She'd received word toward the end of the summer that Jake and Bobby were alive and well, and it was that thin strand of hope that kept her tied to Cedar's Ridge.

There was a crunch of footfalls on gravel—Rand. Donna Lise patted her hair with a nervous hand and hurried to the kitchen to check on the potatoes. She listened to the key turn in the lock and the door swing open and she held her breath: would today be the day he remembered to duck?

THUD. "*Owwwww*! Dammit! What kind of idiot makes ceilings this low? Geez, Donna Lise, can't something be done about this? Donna Lise? *Hello*? Now what? Has my wife gone and left me, too? *DONNA LISE*?"

"I'm right here, Rand," she called from the kitchen. "Dinner'll just be a minute. Have a seat and relax, honey. You've had a hard day."

She could hear him in the other room muttering about how she had no concept of what a hard day was as he took off his jacket and shoes and switched on the television. The opening theme of the six o'clock news blared through the suite and she relaxed a little, knowing his attention would be elsewhere for a while. She set Rand's PitBull energy drink and her tea on a tray along with the two plates of meatloaf and mashed potatoes, the gravy boat and the cutlery, and headed into the living room.

"How are you, honey?" she asked when a commercial came on. She assembled two TV tables and laid out their meals in front of their brown velour recliners. It was only as she was finally sitting down herself that she noticed his pants were torn at the knee and he had a gauze patch fastened above his right eye. "Oh, Rand, what happened?"

"Oh, I'll tell you what happened, Donna Lise," he said, attacking his meatloaf. "My day was just fine and dandy—missed my bus, showed up late, discovered it was the day of my one-month performance review, can you believe it, and they do it over lunch, so I miss lunch, get back out on the floor and I'm thinking, haven't the kids gone back to school? Because if they have, most of them are skipping out to 'hang' with their gangs at the mall. And then just when I think the coast is clear and it's just me and the retirees for the rest of the afternoon, *BLAM*!" Donna Lise dropped her fork and it clattered to the floor. Rand ignored her.

"*BLAM*!" he repeated. "This red-haired she-devil from hell comes out of nowhere, doing *easy* forty clicks, I'm talking *in the store*, on some kind of skateboard-shoe-hybrid damn contraption and takes me out! *Takes me clean* OUT!" He shook his head as he worked a mouthful of mashed potatoes and gravy. "Never says a word, never even stops. Going so fast security didn't even get her on camera! Godalmighty, Donna Lise, kids these days. Sometimes I think Jake and Bobby did us a favor by taking off, you know? Just the two of us, eh, honey? Just like old times." The commercials ended and Rand leaned back in his recliner and turned up the volume. Donna Lise stared straight ahead, pushing her food around her plate.

"Cedar's Ridge, are you ready for your close-up?" the newscaster blared as a montage of images of the city played across the screen. "The first book of the phenomenally popular *Shapeshifter* series is being made into a movie, and filming is happening right here in Cedar's Ridge! Best of all, it stars everybody's favorite pachyderm and the darling of the Raincity Zoo, Gaia the elephant!"

"You hear about this, hon?" Rand asked through sips of his PitBull energy drink. "I was reading about it in the paper. Elephant's going to be in Cedar's Ridge till Christmas. That's got my wheels turning, you know what I mean? The merchandising opportunities, the cross-branding, the spin-offs. Seriously, Donna Lise, I think there might be a way to make some money on the back of this whole elephant thing. People go nuts for crap like that!" He took a hearty swig of PitBull to underscore his enthusiasm.

"Now, Rand, haven't you done enough scheming for one year?" Donna Lise replied as she gathered up the dinner things. "You've finally got a steady job and we're just getting back on our feet. Let's not go looking for trouble." She hurried into the kitchen too quickly to make out his muttered reply, but she knew she'd angered him. Why couldn't she learn to keep her mouth shut?

Over the clatter of dishes in the sink, she heard the news announcer talk about the controversy that was already brewing over the use of wild animals in the production. She could hear the zoo's owner and the film's producers talking about how well their animals were being cared for. When she returned to the living room with two bowls of strawberry ice cream, the TV screen was filled with images of the little wildlife rescue center down by Aerie Lake and someone named Evelyn Jordan was speaking about the lives of wild animals kept in captivity. As she leaned over to place Rand's bowl on his TV table, she caught sight of her husband's face—jaw grinding, eyes narrowed, the skin flushed a deep red.

Quickly she glanced to the screen, seeking whatever it was that had caused his reaction but fearing that it may well have been her own discouraging comments earlier. In the background, behind this Evelyn Jordan person, was a familiar figure hard at work in the wildlife center. Her back was to the camera but Donna Lise recognized her immediately. It was her son Jake's ex-girlfriend, Jane Ray.

Before she could put the pieces together, Rand rose up, knocking his TV table and the bowl of strawberry ice cream to the floor, and dashed his can of PitBull into the shattered crystal and melting pink froth. As she watched the drink spread across the linoleum and saw her husband turn toward her, her only thought was that the floor must not be level, that everything was running toward the door. And then she heard a small voice that must have been her own crying, "No, Rand, no! *No, not again.*"

12

BABY ELEPHANT TALK

SEN CHANTA PAUSED outside his boss's office door turning the letter over in his hands. He shouldn't even be here but he couldn't sit at home any longer, wondering what was going on and waiting for Gaia to be brought back to the zoo. He'd written Timo Lausanne requesting permission to visit Gaia on the *Shapeshifter* set in Cedar's Ridge. He would take the bus in from the valley, pack his own lunch, spend the day with her, meet her handlers, make sure his instructions had been clear. That's what the letter said. That was all. He hadn't written anything about the connection that existed between himself and the elephant or how he sensed across the distance that she needed him right now. He didn't know how to write of such things, at least not to a man for whom such things were nonsense.

He bent to slide the letter under the door when Lausanne's voice rose on the other side, loud and clear. Hesitating, he realized after a moment that his boss was talking on the phone with someone and reached down again with the letter. Then he heard the words "Gaia" and "baby elephant," and he stood stock still, his senses trained on the voice on the other side of the door. Not a devious man by nature, Sen did not intend to eavesdrop, but as the phone conversation continued, he found he could not pull himself away.

"I thought you said you could get a baby elephant from San Diego," Lausanne was saying. "Wild capture is against the law, Marcozi, and even *you* . . . Make it look like a rescue? How? . . . I don't know, it sounds risky. Besides, I've only got till December and then I'm without my star attraction. I need a local baby, some-where on the continent, we fill out the papers, wire the money, we're *done*." Lausanne slammed a hand down on his desk for emphasis. Sen jumped, suddenly re-membering where he was, and turned to leave, when he heard her name again.

"Gaia? So far so good, from what I hear. I had my girl draw up the transfer papers today, actually—the studio wranglers should have them in hand next week. If she behaves, I've got myself a sale in December. If not, your client has got himself a nine-tonner." Lausanne groaned and muttered, "Either way, I've got myself one hell of a conversation ahead with her caretaker here." His voice rose again: "But either way, Marcozi, I need a baby elephant, you know? Cute? Draws crowds? Gives rides? Steals hats? Makes me money?" He sighed dramatically, listening for a moment. "No, you know what, Marcozi?

Don't even tell me. I don't want to know. Whatever you have to do to procure a baby elephant, just do it, okay? And keep my end of it clean. Yeah, perfect, exactly. You're a lifesaver. Okay, cheers."

Sen stood paralyzed, the letter crushed in his grip. Baby elephant. Wild capture. Memories he thought he'd left behind forever replayed themselves now in his mind. He'd known it was still happening all these years later, but he hadn't realized that the demand was coming from here, a continent that presented itself to the rest of the world as so civilized, so enlightened. He shut his eyes in an effort to shut out the images in his head and felt tears course down his cheeks.

And Gaia? The reason he'd endured it all, the reason he was here . . . for sale? To be handed over in December? To whom? Not to anyone who knew her, who knew her history, not to anyone who would care for her as he had. Of that he was certain.

Not to anyone. *Not to anyone.* The phrase ran through his head, obliterating his painful memories and turning itself into a decision. Gaia would not be sold, *not to anyone.*

The floorboards creaked. Lausanne had risen from his desk, was coming toward the door. The letter in Sen's hand felt like a lead weight, its polite request for permission to see Gaia seeming ridiculously naive to him now. He made up his mind: he would not ask permission—not of anyone. Crumpling the letter in his fist, he turned and fled.

13
FLORY OPENS A FILE

"'Group *Proboscidea*,'" FLORY read from the computer screen as she made notes on a yellow legal pad. "'Large mammals having tusks and a long, flexible, tubular snout, as the elephant.' That's pro-bo-SID-ee-uh," she repeated, glancing behind her to make sure Jane and Amy were absorbing the correct pronunciation.

"Proboscis," Amy intoned with mock formality from behind her lab table as she fussed with a CD-sized opening in the wall. "A, like, totally tubular organ for sucking, food-gathering, sensing and, if you're my father when he has a cold, which he does right now, spewing. That's pro-BOSS-cuss." She picked up the receiver of the old red phone and dialed ten digits. "Big Mama? Hey, it's Little Red. I'm ready for our test run. We'll take three of the small and browns, please. No, make that six. We're ravenous over here. Roger, and over!"

It was Friday afternoon, and the girls had been sent home early from set. "Equipment malfunction," David

Sayers had explained wearily. "We're shut down till it can be repaired, and meanwhile all my union people are still on the clock. But not you three. Go enjoy your weekend. We'll see you Monday."

Thrilled to have the unexpected free time, Jane, Amy, and Flory had bounded to the lake trails and headed straight for the MacGillivray house. "I need a hit of Shack time," Amy had said. "Three days away and I'm in withdrawal!"

Now, as Amy hung up the red phone, Flory said, "May I ask with whom you were just speaking?"

"Yeah," Jane jumped in, "and what exactly the 'small and browns' are that we're supposedly going to eat?"

"My latest invention," Amy said, her back to them as she lowered a flap over the hole in the wall. "The Pneumatic Afternoon Snack Sender—PASS™. Built according to the principles of suction, peristalsis, and expulsion employed by an elephant's trunk. It's going to revolutionize snacking! No more leaving your desk in the middle of homework to go down to the kitchen for cookies. Just place your order and keep right on working!"

"Ame," Jane broke in cautiously, "isn't the whole point of snacking to take a break from working?"

"Hush!" Amy ordered. "Irrelevant! Now watch: Big Mama . . . er, my mom will pop six chocolate brownies into the hole in her kitchen wall, *which* I noticed she was not too thrilled about, I must say, despite the pride I know she feels at having a scientist daughter. Now keep your eyes on this opening, girls. Twenty, thirty seconds tops, and we'll be snacking on the best homemade brownies on the Ridge!"

"What about drinks?" Jane asked.

"Shush!" Amy cried. "Details! I'm working on it!"

There was a distant clunk, as if someone very far away had dropped a soup can into a garbage pail. The girls waited, counting off the seconds in their head. At thirty, Amy bent down and peered into the dark shaft beyond the hole. Jane thought about warning her to keep her face at a safe distance from the exit point, but after several more seconds concluded it might not be necessary. At fifty, Jane glanced at Flory, who was grinning at the ceiling, and stifled a laugh. At sixty, Amy flopped down at her lab table and buried her head in her hands with a groan.

"As I was saying," Flory continued as though there had been no interruption, "elephants belong to group *Proboscidea* and their closest relative is the hyrax, a small, tailless mammal that looks like a guinea pig! They are also related to sea cows, such as manatees and dugongs, and to aardvarks." Amy looked up at the sound of Flory pulling a fresh file folder from the computer desk. Catching Jane's eye, she managed a wink and a small smile.

Flory's favorite after-school activity was research, the way other people's was pick-up basketball or hanging out at the mall. She opened a new black file folder on every subject that caught her interest and had filled enough cabinets with them to warrant her own home office. Despite her facility with modern technology, she had a penchant for paper and usually had several files going at any given time. Her research skills had proven invaluable during the girls' animal rescue adventures, filling in gaps and turning up clues her friends had never imagined. They liked to tease her, but in fact they counted on her, and she always came through.

"'In prehistoric times,'" Flory continued, "'over three hundred and fifty species of elephant roamed every continent except Australia and Antarctica. The three lone survivors are the African elephants—*Loxodonta africana* and *Loxodonta cyclotis*—and the Asian elephant, or *Elephas maximus*. All three are listed as endangered species, with the Asian elephant at highest risk. Their remaining population is just one tenth that of African elephants.'"

"Gaia's an Asian elephant," Jane said quietly.

"Well, so that's good, isn't it?" Amy broke in. "That she's safe in a zoo, I mean?"

"Amy, it says here there are only forty-four thousand Asian elephants left in the whole world," Flory responded, "and a third of those are in captivity! They're hunted for their ivory and for their meat. They're captured and trained to haul logs out of forests. They've even been forced to fight in wars! Growing human populations have destroyed most of their territory, and struggling farmers are killing them over what little is left. If we humans don't find a way to live in balance with them, they're doomed! It won't matter how many elephants are left in zoos then!"

"But don't we breed them in captivity and send the offspring back to the wild?" Amy pressed.

"Raincity sent Gaia to a zoo in the States a few years ago," Jane broke in, "to breed with one of their bulls. She never got pregnant. All that travel and stress and confusion for nothing."

Flory nodded, tapping the computer screen. "It says here that captive breeding programs have limited success, and even when there are offspring, they can't be released to the wild. They don't have the same instincts and skills or the genetic makeup to survive. The sad fact is, most zoos breed just to create a cute new exhibit, or a product to sell to another zoo."

"But Flory," Amy said in her best "be reasonable" voice, "at least if there are Asian elephants in zoos, people in future generations will be able to see them, unlike the three hundred and forty-seven other species that have completely disappeared."

"When was the last time you visited Gaia at the zoo?" Flory asked sharply. The question was directed at Amy but it was Jane who felt it hit home as she was overcome once more by remorse for having forgotten about Gaia for so very long. She reddened and looked down at her hands. "My family went in the summer because my little sisters wanted to go," Flory went on. "Let me tell you, Amy, *that* was not an elephant we saw. Standing alone all day in a yard half the size of a soccer field. Wild Asian elephants travel up to thirty miles in a day, forage and feed for up to sixteen hours a day, and migrate three to six *thousand* miles in a year in search of food and water! That was not an elephant we saw, lifting one foot and then the other out of pain. Weaving her head from side to side, over and over again, out of boredom and frustration and loneliness. For years, Amy. Not days or months. For *years*! But now that's what my sisters think an elephant is!"

Amy frowned, taking in Flory's words. "You'd think after all this time Gaia might have adjusted," she said.

"In this handbook for mahouts," Flory replied, clicking on another link, "it says, 'Elephants can never be completely domesticated. They always have a desire to return to the wild, unlike some other domesticated species, such as dogs and cats.'"

"The Hooters handbook is online now?" Amy asked innocently.

"I said 'mahouts,' not 'hooters,'" Flory repeated, ignoring Amy's laughter. "A mahout is an elephant driver, kind of like a trainer or guide. There are three types: *Balwaan*, who control elephants with strength and cruelty; *Yuktimaan*, who use ingenuity to outsmart them; and *Reghawaan*, who communicate with their elephants through love. Given elephants' aversion to violence and their great intelligence, love seems the only option that makes any sense."

Flory flipped quickly through the sheets of paper she'd slotted into the black folder, then rose from the desk to face Jane and Amy.

"Elephants have the largest and most complex brain of any land mammal," Flory told them, "and you know the saying that an elephant never forgets?" Jane nodded; she'd thought of it herself on recognizing Gaia. "Well, the area of their brains that's responsible for memory is so large it bulges out at the sides! They can use their brains to make tools and solve problems the way primates do, and to remember where to forage and find water, even years later."

Flory dropped her file onto the desk behind her. She was speaking from memory herself now. "But what's really amazing about them is their social life." Amy snorted, clearly picturing an elephant toga party and drinking games, and was silenced by a look from Flory. "They live in families and clans and raise their babies together as a community. The males go off on their own or with other males as they get older, but the females stay with their herd throughout their entire lives, even after they have babies of their own. In the wild, a female elephant is never alone."

"The way they are in zoos," Amy said the words Jane was thinking.

Flory nodded. "The herd is led by the matriarch, the oldest and most experienced female. She becomes the herd's living memory, the one who knows every inch of their home range, who remembers the migration routes, the best feeding spots and secret water holes, and knows how to avoid threats. She'll even turn and face hunters alone if it means saving the rest of her herd. And she's often the one the hunters want, because her head makes the biggest trophy."

Jane felt the shock of Flory's words like a punch in the gut, but Flory carried on, relentless. "Elephants care for one another, they touch and caress one another, they stop when one of the herd is injured, they even talk to one another! Elephants have really complex physical and vocal communication systems—researchers have recorded over seventy-five different vocalizations, from grunts, rumbles, and snorts much like yours, Amy, to barks and even purrs! And even more amazing . . . they can communicate using infrasound, sounds so low humans can't hear them! They can sense a mating signal or a warning from more than two miles away!" By this time, Amy was taking notes herself and Jane guessed she was laying plans for her next invention.

"They care for their ill and elderly," Flory continued, "and they grieve their dead, staying with a body for days and even laying leaves and branches over it as if in some kind of burial ceremony. Often they'll do the same for themselves if they die alone in captivity. If they come across the bones of a former herd member during their travels, they stop and spend time in that place, and the living animals will examine the bones of the dead one, as though acknowledging their own mortality.

"*These* are the animals people shut up in a pen alone, like Gaia, or hunt for their tusks leaving the bodies to rot, or butcher for meat. *These* are the animals we've almost wiped off the face of the Earth."

14

THE GAIA HYPOTHESIS

INTO THE SILENCE that followed, Jane said quietly, "Gaia is the goddess of the Earth."

Amy glanced up at her friend, worry creasing her forehead. "Jane, I know you really care about this elephant, but don't you think calling her a goddess is putting her on a bit of a pedestal somehow? I mean . . ."

"Her name!" Flory interrupted, understanding. "Gaia—Greek for 'Earth' and 'grandmother.' Grandmother of the Earth!"

Jane nodded, marveling at her friend's arcane knowledge. "I did a little research myself, although I didn't find what I expected. I was looking for information about Gaia the elephant, but when I Googled her name, up popped this Greek goddess. *And* it seems she has a scientific hypothesis named after her."

"Ooo . . . a hypothesis!" Amy squealed. "I love hypotheses! Do tell!"

"Well," Jane said slowly, "if I understood it correctly, a scientist named Dr. James Lovelock working in the

1960s proposed that all living matter on planet Earth functions as a single organism, and that, left to its own devices, life as a whole just naturally creates an environment on Earth that will allow life to continue."

"I've heard of that!" Amy waved her hands in excitement. "That's Earth system science—the idea that the planet is a single living system!"

"Except that human ignorance and greed have pushed that system way out of balance!" Flory chimed in.

"Right!" Jane responded. "Dr. Lovelock was criticized by other scientists because he went so far as to characterize the planet as a being, to give that being the name 'Gaia,' and to talk about Gaia as though she were ill. But you know how seeing that first photo of Earth from space helped so many people learn to love the planet? I think maybe he thought giving her a name would help people learn to heal her, too."

"When a system's out of balance," Amy said thoughtfully, "it starts to break down. Eventually, if it doesn't regain equilibrium, it shuts down completely. If that system is an organism, we say that it dies."

"Little Gaia and Big Gaia," Flory said, suddenly seeing a connection between the elephant and the Earth. "Both facing the same predicament—greed, ignorance, habitat loss, violence. Maybe even complete destruction. It's like Little Gaia is the canary!"

"Uh, Flor?" Amy waved a hand to attract her friend's attention. "Who is your science teacher this year?

Because I need to have a little chat with him. Elephants and canaries are not even in the same family classification, never mind genus . . ."

"The canary in the coal mine!" Jane cried. "Flory, you're right!"

"Okay, do we even go to the same *school*?" Amy cried in exasperation.

"Miners used to take birds down the mine shafts with them," Jane explained in a rush. "Canaries were so sensitive that if the air quality suddenly deteriorated, they'd die, and the miners would know to get out right away. Those birds saved a lot of lives. People now use the expression 'canary in the coal mine' to mean a signal that things are out of balance in nature."

"In other words," Amy paraphrased to make sure she understood, "alter your course or die."

An ominous rumbling erupted in the vicinity of the computer desk and quickly increased in intensity. Amy jumped up, legs splayed and arms held out from her sides like a traffic cop. "EARTHQUAKE!" she shouted. "Stop, drop, and roll!" She tumbled to the floor and rolled to a stop beneath her lab table.

"Amy, that's for fire!" Jane shouted over the rumbling. She gripped the old wooden gardening table, not sure herself what was happening.

"Fire? There's a fire, too?" Amy screamed from under the lab table. "FIRE! *FIIIRE!!!*"

Suddenly the rumbling stopped and was replaced

by a series of loud grunts and snorts. Flory started to giggle and then bent double in her chair, laughing hysterically. "I . . . hee hee . . . website . . . ah haha haha . . . vocalizations . . . hee hee . . . elephants!"

Jane did a quick translation, and when she realized Flory had tuned into a website that played recordings of elephant vocalizations, she started to laugh, too. Flory cranked the volume on the speakers and the Shack filled with the voices of a herd of elephants. The recordings ran through a series of rumbles, bellows, barks, and screams, even a trumpet call that Jane recognized immediately as the kind of call Gaia had made the night before.

By this time, realizing that the ground was not shaking and the Shack was not burning, Amy was laughing hysterically while rolling from side to side beneath the lab table. Each new elephant call prompted fresh gales of laughter, and tears streamed down her face.

A sudden frantic banging on the door of the Shack caused all three girls to scream and then erupt into laughter again. "What's going on in there?" a deep voice demanded. "Is everybody okay?"

"Ooooo!" Amy squealed, scrambling to her feet. "Speaking of Guy-a . . ." She ran to the door, flung it wide, and threw herself into the arms of a tall, lanky boy Jane recognized from school. From behind him emerged Mark Co, Flory's boyfriend, who quickly crossed the floor to her and wrapped his arms around the petite girl, reassuring himself that she was all right. The sounds emanating from the computer had subsided to a series of rolling purrs.

"Everybody, this is Sanjay Mehta, basketball captain extraordinaire!" Amy said, sliding an arm around his waist. Jane and Flory said hi.

"From outside, it sounded like one of your experiments had gone quite wrong, Amy," Mark said, grinning.

Flory ruffled his hair playfully. "It was one of mine, actually!" she giggled.

"No kidding!" Mark looked at her admiringly.

"You girls up for a walk around the lake before it gets dark?" Sanjay asked in his deep, gravelly voice.

As Amy and Flory donned their coats and gathered up their things, Jane said, "You know, I think I'll stay behind. I've got a letter to write." Amy shot her a meaningful glance, but neither she nor Flory said a word. *And a newscast to watch*, Jane thought, looking down at the DVD Flory had made for her.

As the door closed behind the two couples, Jane sighed and sat back down at the old table. Rummaging in her bag for paper and a pen, she heard a sudden whooshing sound behind her. Reacting on instinct, she leapt up and spun just in time to catch six of the best homemade brownies on the Ridge as they came shooting out of the wall.

15
WILD

SEPTEMBER SPED BY in a whirlwind of classes, school projects, lunch hours with friends, afternoons on set, and, for Jane, long sessions of letter writing and weekly shifts at the wildlife center. Every morning as she and Amy and Flory ran through the lakeside trails, Jane noticed changes: the turning of leaves, the browning of the creekside rushes, the quietening of the woods as more and more birds migrated south, the arrival of winter visitors like the dark-eyed juncos. The earthy smell of decay grew stronger and the morning air was cool now against her skin. Fall had arrived.

Every week at the wildlife center, there were fewer animals in care and more to be released back to the wild at the end of a shift. Jane never grew tired of lifting a bird aloft in her hands and setting it free into the sky over Aerie Lake. That momentary hesitation as it took its bearings, the flutter of feathers against her fingertips, the weightless sensation she felt before her mind knew that her hands were empty. Every rehabilitation case was different, but in this one way they were all the same: at the moment of release, every wild animal embraced freedom with every fiber and feather: *Yes.*

It was the first Thursday morning in October. Jane and Avis were preparing diets in the kitchen when they heard a commotion in the reception area. Raising her eyebrows, Avis said, "Go get the scoop, Missy. I'll finish up here."

Jane met up with Katrina in the hallway. The older girl looked like the cat that swallowed the canary. *Another good canary expression,* Jane thought, but she didn't have time to investigate because as they arrived at reception, they were engulfed in waves of a smell like rotting cheese. Standing in the doorway to keep out of the way, they observed as an SPCA officer answered Evie's questions and Anthony carefully noted the answers—where the animal had been found, what the circumstances of capture were, what condition it was in. Jane could see Daniel in the exam room hurriedly laying blankets on the floor and preparing a sedative along with syringes of anti-inflammatory and antibiotic medications. What she *couldn't* see was an animal.

Then the SPCA officer hoisted a large kennel over the counter and the smell hit Jane afresh. She peered through the grill as Evie carried the kennel into the exam room—*coyote*!

"Stand back, girls," Evie cautioned. "I'm afraid this is a rehabber-only situation. But if you've got a few minutes to spare from your rounds, you can watch through the observation window if you like." With that, the exam room door swung shut. Jane, Katrina, and Anthony looked at one another for a moment, then rushed to the observation window, each jostling for the best view.

Evie draped a blanket over the kennel, covering the side vents and blocking the coyote's view of the outer room. Then, wearing shoulder-high gloves and using blankets as blinds, she opened the kennel door, using a blind to keep herself and Daniel out of the animal's sight. Daniel reached in and injected a sedative into the coyote's left hip muscle, jumping back as the animal lunged at him from the kennel's depths. "I think I got most of it into him," Jane heard him say.

Minutes later, sure that the animal was unconscious, Evie and Daniel reached in together, grasping the pad that lay under the coyote's body and lifting him onto the blankets on the floor. Jane let out a small groan; the coyote's body bore a number of abrasions and lacerations and his fur was matted with blood. "Hit by a car," Anthony murmured. There was fur missing in patches on one side of his body and several cuts looked as though they'd need stitches.

Jane lost track of time as she watched the two professional rehabilitators work, gently determining that there were no broken bones and then cleaning and debriding the wounds before stitching up the longer lacerations. Daniel injected the coyote with a steroid to reduce any swelling around the brain that might result from the impact of being hit, and lastly he applied a topical antibiotic ointment to all of the wounds.

The three onlookers backed up as Evie approached the exam room door. Poking her head out, she said, "Jane, Katrina, could you prep Isolation Room 2 for him, please? Newspaper, pads, and blankets on the floor, lots of cushioning, and no food, just water for now. Got it? Good, okay, let me know when you're ready for him."

Jane and Katrina went to work, following Evie's directions. Again, they stood back as Evie and Daniel carried the unconscious animal into ISO 2, holding a blanket taut between them as a stretcher. Overcome by the animal's powerful scent, Jane unconsciously brought a hand to her nose. Noticing the gesture, Evie said, "You'll never forget it, will you?" Jane shook her head.

Jane returned to the kitchen only to find that Avis had managed the feeding and cleaning of all the outside animals on her own and was ready for a break. "You should have waited for me!" Jane said, dismayed. She was doing as much as she could to help her elderly friend each week, but sometimes it was hard to keep up with her.

"That's quite all right, Missy," Avis patted her on the hand. "I'm making hay while the sun shines." Jane grinned as Avis waved her hands, did a couple of deep knee bends, and performed a little dance across the linoleum. "I'm feeling good today and I'm going to take advantage of it! Spend it all in one place—here!" She cackled and grabbed Jane by the hand, twirling her around the tiny room. "How's about some coffee, Miss Jane? Bring any of those cookies of yours this week?" Arm in arm, the two of them headed out through the garden to the lunchroom, talking of the coyote in the care center and of the many coyotes Avis had encountered through the years. "Impossible to catch," Avis told her, "even when they're sick and need help. It's no matter to them . . . they'd rather be free."

After coffee, Avis helped out in administration while Jane returned to the care center to finish the inside rounds with Katrina. The older girl was in an ebullient mood today, a one-hundred-and-eighty-degree switch from her demeanor of the past several weeks, and Jane's curiosity was piqued.

"That was *craziness*, hey, that coyote?" Katrina said to her as Jane started to clean the rock pigeons' cages.

"Pretty amazing," Jane agreed, gently wrapping the pigeons and placing them in a kennel while she cleaned. "So, you're, um, extra bubbly today, Katrina," she said, keeping her eyes on her work. "Get some good news or something?"

"No, you know what, Jane?" Katrina replied as she filled a small pool for a gull. "I didn't get out of this nothing town all summer long and as it turns out I was seriously overdue for a vacation. You know? Anyway, so this past weekend I packed a couple of bags, hopped on a ferry, headed up the coast, hung out with an old friend. Sun, salt spray, fresh air, and a lot of lying around." She giggled then. "A *lot*. It was perfect."

"Just what you needed, hey?" Jane said, recalling her own family's road trip through the Rocky Mountains.

"Oh, you have no idea," Katrina agreed, winking. Jane got the sense that there was something the girl wasn't saying that she was just supposed to understand. But Katrina was right; Jane really did have no idea.

She lifted one of the pigeons back into a clean cage and bent to retrieve a second one when ISO 2 erupted in a massive clatter. Heart pounding, Jane quickly closed the cage and ran to the two-way mirror that looked into ISO 2. The coyote had come to, obviously much sooner than Evie and Daniel had expected, and was leaping up, over and over again, five, six feet into the air, throwing its body against the high window in the opposite wall— the one that led to the outside.

Jane heard Katrina gasp beside her and the sound propelled her into action. "Evie!" she cried. "Daniel! Come quick!"

She ran down the hallway to the exam room and banged on the door. "Easy, girlfriend!" Anthony stood, alarmed. "What's the buzz?"

"The coyote!" Jane cried as Evie and Daniel hurried to the door. "It's trying to escape!"

There was a crash in ISO 2. Jane, Evie, Daniel, and Anthony ran down the hallway to join Katrina at the two-way mirror. Jane looked in just in time to see the tail end of the coyote as it leapt through the shattered glass of the window and lost itself in the surrounding woods.

After a few moments of silence, Daniel said quietly, "You ever want to know what it means to be a wild animal? That—right there. No car crash, no sedative, no locked room more powerful than the call to be free."

Impossible to catch, Avis's words echoed in Jane's head, *even when they're sick and need help. It's no matter to them . . . they'd rather be free.*

You'll never forget it, Evie had said. No, she never would.

16

SOLO PERFORMANCE

T HE FOLLOWING WEEK, Evie led Jane around the care center establishing a strategy for handling all of the feeding and cleaning, inside and out, by herself. "Smallest birds first," she explained, "and insides before outsides. Make sure they all have fresh food and water, and if you have to leave some of the cleaning for the afternoon shift, so be it. Just do your best."

The two work experience students were away on a school assignment. Katrina had suddenly rushed outside and been sick in the garden, and Evie had sent her home. Then Avis's husband George had called to say that Avis would not be coming in today, or for the next several weeks; she'd fallen and broken her hip.

Anthony had taken the call. "Hubby says she was taking out the trash," he related to Jane, "and I didn't want to be sexist and ask him why *he* wasn't doing that but really, at her age?" He held up his hands in mock surrender. "Anyhoo, she had the dog with her and the leash got tangled around her legs and suddenly she was all like, 'help, I've fallen and I can't get up' and George had to call an ambulance and now she's in the hospital waiting to have surgery!"

Jane felt a wave of emotion well up in her—fear for her friend? for herself at being left alone?—and fought it back. There were the animals to care for. She worked like a machine and by noon, every animal in care had been fed and cleaned. Evie, who was administering meds without Daniel's help that morning, hugged her in gratitude. "You rock the UWRC, Jane!" Evie laughed. "Sorry you had to miss your coffee break, though."

"That's okay," Jane replied. "It wouldn't have been any fun without Avis anyway." She paused. "Hey, Evie, what would you think if we all sent her some flowers?"

"Brilliant!" Evie exclaimed. "We'll set up a little collection in this jar, and when we've got enough, Anthony, maybe you could order something online?"

Jane had just cashed her paycheck from SayWhat? Productions, and now she put half the money into the jar. Avis had always been generous with her, but this was the first time she'd been in a position to return the favor. "We've got enough," she said, smiling shyly.

Anthony whistled. "Nothing but the best for our Avis!" He gave her the thumbs-up and then set about surfing florists' sites with one hand as he waved her goodbye with the other.

Pedaling through the lake trails, leaves crunching beneath her tires and cold rain stinging her face, Jane found herself wondering again how long Avis would be away, when Katrina would be over her flu, and whether she'd be the only volunteer on duty again next week. A year ago, it would have been unthinkable. Today, it had been hard work, but she'd managed. Sure, she'd left the laundry in a heap and the dishes in a stack by the sink, but every animal, inside and out, had clean dry shelter and enough to eat. A growing sense of pride overcame her fears about having to repeat her solo performance again in weeks to come, and the feeling kept her warm all the way to school.

17
DISQUIET ON THE SET

A S OCTOBER PROGRESSED on the *Shapeshifter* set, Jane's anxiety grew. Each afternoon at 3:15, she, Amy, and Flory punched in and reported to their various posts, Flory to the Producers' tent, Amy to the Crew Chief, and Jane to the barn. More often than not, Mr. Arcola and Mr. Hutchinson were on set with a group of horses or one of the exotic animals, and Jane had the barn—and Gaia—to herself. She loved these afternoons: roaming through the barn corridors, feeding, grooming, and talking with each of the animals; organizing the tack room and polishing the tack and harnesses; cleaning out the stalls and making them comfortable for the animals that were away working.

But as time passed, she noticed that each afternoon when she arrived, things were a little more disheveled than they had been the day before. Small things—equipment left lying around, tack hung up still dirty, stall doors not properly latched. Things she could dismiss at first, knowing the animal wranglers were busy. But then Jane started to notice a change in the animals.

"It's as if they're scared of something," Jane said to Amy and Flory during their break one late October afternoon. "Spooked!"

The three girls had met at Hilltop Grocery & Café, just a short walk from the set. "I call it 'retox,'" Amy had explained when she suggested going there. "Between Mama MacGillivray's beans and greens and the gourmet fare from Craft Services, I don't really feel I'm getting all the chemicals and additives I need as a normal, growing teenager. It's all about balance, you know?"

Placing a soda and a package of Twinkies on the counter now and winking at Flory, she said, "What if it's you, Jane? What if the animals are dreading your arrival every day?" Flory whacked her on the arm. "*Oww*! Okay, joking!"

"Believe me, I thought of that," Jane replied grimly, selecting a kiwi fruit for Gaia and a peppermint patty and a hot chocolate for herself. "But they're agitated when I arrive and calmer by the time I leave, not the other way around. If I thought it was me, I'd quit my job!"

"Of course it's not you, Jane," Flory retorted, sticking her tongue out at Amy. "I'm sure you have a very positive influence on them." She chose a package of red licorice whips and a lemon tea and lined up at the cashier's desk behind her friends.

"Thanks, Flor," Jane replied. "I just wish I knew what it was. And the weirdest part? Gaia's gotten *calmer*! She was agitated, too, a few weeks ago, but not now. There she is, alone most days in her stall, in pain with her foot infections, surrounded by restless animals, and yet seemingly fine!"

"Maybe it's because she knows she's queen of the jungle," Amy suggested, trying to redeem herself. "Maybe the rest of them are scared of her!"

Flory considered this for a moment, then said, "Elephants are herbivores. The other animals would sense that she's not a predator and wouldn't attack them unless severely provoked. In this situation I don't think . . ."

"Jungle Queen!" Jane breathed, standing stock still and staring out the door of the little grocery.

"Actually, Jane, I have to admit I think Flory did a good job of discrediting my theory," Amy responded. "Oh, hey, Ilsa! How's it going?" A lithe, petite woman dressed in a fitted, gold-colored jacket, black capri tights, and gold ballet flats glided into the store followed by several male crew members. The woman was older than she'd first appeared, Jane realized. Still in demand in the industry thanks to her unique talent, no doubt. And still undeniably glamorous.

"Why, Amy! Hello!" Ilsa smiled and paused by the counter. The men jostled to a stop behind her. Jane took in her crimson lips, bright blue eyes lined in jet black, and flaxen hair swept back in a tight chignon and stammered an inaudible hello. "Escaping from work as well, I see! Good for you. Alright, boys, let's go see what we can find!" With that, she swept down the aisle, entourage in tow.

Jane, Amy, and Flory paid for their snacks and left the store, emerging into the waning light of the late afternoon. Jane rounded on Amy: "You know her? I can't believe you know her! You never told us you know her!"

"Know Ilsa? Well, sure!" Amy answered, not understanding the intensity of Jane's reaction. "I know everybody!"

"Why, Jane?" Flory asked, guessing there was a reason for Jane's question.

"She's the one!" Jane said, working to keep her voice from carrying. "Remember I told you I overheard my bosses talking about making one of their employees behave 'or else?' She's the one they were talking about!" Flory winced as Jane relayed what she'd heard in the barn the night she'd returned for her pack, the strange buzzing and cracking sounds, Mr. Arcola's shouting at Ilsa. "It's the reason for all Gaia's alarm calls! They're mistreating Ilsa!"

Amy shook her head doubtfully. "I can't see it, Jane. That girl can hold her own. She's spent years with circuses and on sets, and she's got most of the crew guys wrapped around her little finger. Besides, she doesn't look very mistreated to me!" Jane and Flory followed her gaze and saw Ilsa inside the store at the center of a circle of crewmen, holding a cigarette to her lips as the men all scrambled for their lighters.

"Well, she's certainly mistreating *herself* if she's a smoker!" Flory said primly.

"Oh, for ... ," Amy sputtered, then gasped as she caught sight of her watch. "Yikes! I was supposed to be helping to build a scaffold, like, five minutes ago!" She chugged her soda and let out a belch that echoed off the lakeside houses. "Smell ya later!" Popping the wheels into the heels of her shoes, she sped away.

Wrinkling her nose, Flory checked her own watch. "Gosh, Jane, we *are* late. Makes me wish I had a pair of those Wheelys."

"I guess our morning training is finally going to pay off!" Jane fastened the lid on her travel mug and took off at a run.

Flory caught up to her quickly and tagged her on the shoulder. "Race you!" Laughing, they ran along the lakeshore drive to the set.

Back in the barn, Jane found Gaia in her stall, having just returned from shooting a scene in the woods. Her feet were caked in muck from the lake bottom and she had obviously used her trunk to give the rest of her body a mud shower. Jane groaned in mock dismay. "Look at you, Gaia girl! I just gave you a bath a couple of hours ago and already you need another one!" Gaia erupted in a series of whistles and chortles. She knew the word "bath." Facing Jane, she reached out with her trunk and wrapped it gently, almost protectively, over the girl's left shoulder and around her waist. Jane stiffened slightly, unsure of what might happen next. She felt that Gaia might lift her off the ground at any moment. But then the trunk loosened and Jane felt herself still firmly planted on the barn floor. "Whoa . . . ," she breathed. "You hugged me!" She laughed quietly, astounded.

Fetching the hose from the corridor outside Gaia's stall, Jane turned the water on full force and began to wash away the mud. She filled a small tub and let Gaia help her with the job. Soon they were both soaked, Jane laughing and Gaia snuffling and snorting in delight. "I always need a change of clothes around you, girl," she said, walking the hose around to Gaia's ample behind. Suddenly she felt something touch her own behind. She yelped and leapt forward, then laughed as she realized Gaia had discovered the kiwi fruit in her jacket pocket. "Go ahead, take it!" she said, giving the top of the elephant's head a playful spray. "I bought it for you!"

Circling to Gaia's other side, Jane realized there were leaves and bits of debris clinging to the elephant's back where she couldn't reach high enough with the hose. Pausing for a moment to consider the problem, she heard a sound—so soft and surreal she thought she was imagining it. A singsong voice calling, "Come down, Gaia, come down now, girl!" She twisted around and peered into the dim light beyond the stall. Nothing. She *had* imagined it.

She turned back to Gaia. The elephant was on her knees.

Jane gasped. "Gaia! . . . How? . . . Did you read my mind?" She shook her head, struggling to believe her own eyes. Slowly, she raised the hose and washed the last of the dirt off Gaia's back, making sure to direct the hose into the deep wrinkles in her skin.

When Gaia was clean, Jane coiled the hose and replaced it on the rack in the corridor. She returned to the stall, half expecting to see Gaia in some new position, but she was still on her knees, sphinx-like. Waiting.

Oh-oh. Jane suddenly thought that maybe Gaia had understood she needed to kneel so that Jane could wash her back, but now she needed instructions to get back up. Or maybe she couldn't get back up. Maybe she was stuck! Jane froze, trying to decide whether she should fetch the wranglers or wait another few minutes to see what Gaia would do.

After a time, when Gaia didn't rise on her own, Jane glanced around and then uttered a tentative, "Up, Gaia! Up!" Gaia blinked at her, but other than that, didn't move. *Even Sweet Pea and Minnie wouldn't listen to that wimpy command,* she thought in disgust.

And then, quiet as a thought in her own mind, the singsong voice came again: "Go up, Gaia girl, okay now, go up!" As Jane watched, Gaia placed one front foot and then the other flat on the dirt floor of the barn and raised the front of her body. Then she got her back feet up under her hips and lifted her massive tonnage off the ground until she was standing once again. Droplets of water glistened on her bristly, wrinkled hide.

Jane gazed up at her wonderingly. "How, girl?" she asked. In answer, Gaia simply sighed. Determined to solve the mystery, Jane hurried out of the stall and made a quick search of the barn corridors, seeking the source of the voice. She found nothing out of the ordinary—except that the animals, all of which had been restless upon her arrival that afternoon, were now calmly eating or resting or sleeping. The mystery had only deepened.

Deciding that it was about time to enlist her two sidekicks in this conundrum, she quickly wrapped up her evening rounds, said good night to Gaia, and then buzzed Flory and Amy on her walkie-talkie: "Can you two spare an hour to meet me at the Shack? You won't believe what just happened!"

"I'm there," Amy affirmed. "I'll grab some leftovers from Craft Services."

"And I'll open a fresh file," Flory chimed in. "This sounds juicy!"

"See you there in ten minutes," Jane said. "Over and out!"

18

THE SPARE ROOM

DONNA LISE HARBINSALE paused with one hand on the doorknob, wondering what she was really doing. She held a bucket filled with rags and cleaning supplies in her other hand. In theory, she was cleaning. But her husband had asked her not to clean this room. Had told her, in fact, to stay out of this room. It was his room, he'd announced when they'd moved into the basement suite. His office.

She'd respected that, respected his wishes, stayed out. But lately he was spending more and more time in that room, heading in there as soon as he got home from work, taking his dinners in there, remaining in there long after she'd gone to bed. And lately she'd begun to wonder what a Mall-Mart greeter needed with an office anyway. Maybe he'd taken on some contract work for extra money? Maybe... she hardly dared hope, but maybe he was conducting some sort of search for Jake and Bobby? She told herself she was wrong to wonder, that husbands and wives just needed to trust one another. But here she was in the middle of a Friday afternoon with her hand on the doorknob.

She took a deep breath and turned the knob. As the door swung open, she let her breath out in a gasp. The far wall of the room was papered from floor to ceiling and corner to corner with paintings. Watercolors. Bad ones. Splotchy, two- and three-color abstract blots that looked as though a child had done them. With his eyes closed.

Donna Lise stood staring, struggling with the idea that her husband had been holed up in here making art. Rand *hated* art, called it self-indulgent and meaning-less. His descriptions of artists were more scathing yet. What in heaven's name had made him decide to want to be one himself?

Money—that's what motivated Rand Harbinsale. Not art, not self-expression, not . . . Wait a minute. Money . . . did he think . . . was he planning to . . . ? Donna Lise crossed to the desk that sat pushed up against the right wall. A notepad with some phone numbers she didn't recognize. Desk calendar with Xs marked across two dates in October that had already passed. Sticky note with the name Asia Pacific International Warehouse and an East Vancouver address scrawled in Rand's block lettering. She felt as though she was looking at clues in some dime-store detective novel.

Then she spotted the stack of invoices. Each was headed with the name and logo of one Asia Exotic

Emporium Ltd. Flipping through the stack, she scanned codes she didn't understand:

e-misc toy	500 units @ .98	$490
e-dung ppr	100 units @ 2.00	$200
e-eloo can	250 units @ 1.50	$375

Mercy ... these first three added up to over a thousand dollars! That was more than their rent each month and they could barely afford to pay that. What was Rand thinking? What was he buying? Where was he getting the money to pay for all this? And what did he plan to do with 850 units of anything?

Turning slightly, Donna Lise caught sight of the closet on the far side of the room. The hinged pull-doors were closed, but one sat slightly ajar as though something inside the closet was pushing on it. Hesitating only a moment, she crossed the room and pulled open the doors. Boxes. Floor to ceiling. All marked Asia Exotic Emporium Ltd.

They'd been opened already—by Rand, presumably—so she didn't have to break any seals to see what was inside. She reached into the first and pulled out a handful of ... elephants. Elephant bracelets, elephant necklaces, elephant charms, medallions, pendants, earrings, key chains, can openers, and pens. Trinkets. Pure junk. Pushing her way farther into the closet, she found a lighter box and pulled back the flaps. Inside were sets of stationery, thick, roughly textured paper and envelopes in shades of pale pastels. Turning one over, she read:

> This paper is made from 100% pure Asian elephant dung. The proceeds from this sale will help care for the elephants of Thailand's Nâng Sang Elephant Sanctuary. Thank you!

Elephant rescue? That was even less Rand's style than his new artistic pursuits. Donna Lise was more confused than ever. Groping in a box on the upper shelf, her hand closed around a cylinder of cool metal. It was heavy. She had to stand on her toes to lift it out of the box, then she almost dropped it when she saw what it was. The cheery yellow and red striped label read:

> Eloolo Corned Elephant Meat. With 5 Grain Cereals. Feeds the Whole Family.

Donna Lise felt sick. Her mind reeled: trinkets and stationery and canned meat, all to do with elephants. What did it add up to? Wanting to push the image of the elephant meat out of her mind, she closed the closet and returned to the desk to grab her cleaning supplies and leave. Reaching for the bucket, her hand brushed the mouse on Rand's desk and the computer screen, formerly black, suddenly lit up. The browser was open to the website of the Nâng Sang Sanctuary—the same one named on the back of the stationery. On screen were images of paintings much like the ones in Rand's office, only better. Simpler, sweeter somehow. Most were abstract, unidentifiable images, but one looked exactly like a purple iris. It was entitled, *Iris.*

As Donna Lise scrolled down the page she came to a photograph of an elephant. It seemed to be in a jungle setting, and a young woman stood by its side, smiling. The elephant was holding a paintbrush in its trunk and dabbing paint onto a large sheet of paper that was tacked to a wall in front of it. The elephant was painting! Reading as fast as she could, Donna Lise gathered that these elephants had been abused while working to haul logs out of the teak forests, then rescued and brought to this sanctuary. There, they were taught to paint, and the sanctuary sold their paintings to help pay for the elephants' care. The paintings shown on the website were priced from three hundred and fifty to seven hundred dollars.

Donna Lise looked from the prices on the screen to the fake elephant paintings in her husband's office, to the closet doors, and then back to the screen. Suddenly she recalled something he'd said to her weeks ago: *That elephant's going to be in Cedar's Ridge till Christmas. That's got my wheels turning, you know what I mean? Seriously, I think there might be a way to make some money on the back of this whole elephant thing!*

Money. There it was. Rand had set up a get-rich-again-quick scheme right under her nose, and she'd been oblivious to the whole thing. Here he was, all set to take advantage of the elephant frenzy that had gripped Cedar's Ridge ever since Gaia's arrival on the movie set.

Feeling defeated, she placed everything back exactly where it had been when she entered the room. Closing the door behind her, she leaned against the cool wall, exhausted. Once again, he'd gone against her wishes and spent their money on some crazy secret plan, and there was nothing she could do about it.

Or was there?

19

THE BODY IN THE BARN

SEN CHANTA WAS singing. It was a song his mother had taught him as a boy, about the jungle at night and the animals and their babies, about the moon and the stars and sleep, and the promise of a new day tomorrow. Sen sang so quietly he could hear the animals breathing all around him, and he listened as he sang, so that he could be sure they followed his voice. The song was for them.

It was dark in the barn except for a feeble shaft of moonlight that trickled in through a window. There was frost on the glass. With November's arrival the weather had turned cold, and on set the exotic animals especially felt fall's damp chill. Sen had made his usual rounds that night, filling empty feed and water troughs, pitching out soiled hay and laying fresh, blanketing the horses' backs and setting the space heaters aglow. Before daybreak, he would waken and shut off the heaters, fold and store the blankets, cover his tracks, and disappear into town for the day. He had been following this routine for a month now, walking the streets of Cedar's Ridge by day, and living in the *Shapeshifter* barn at night.

He had come to be with Gaia, to figure out a way to thwart her sale, even to steal her away if necessary. But when he arrived, he had discovered the other animals needed him as well. They were restless, agitated by something, and he knew how to calm them. With words and sounds, with a gentle touch here and there, by keeping their stalls warm and dry, by singing his songs. He found crop marks on the horses' flanks, and burn marks on the tiger's nose and on the bear's paws. So this was life on a movie set, was it? He found puncture wounds in Gaia's neck and in her knees and feet. And so he brought out his tools, his antiseptic and his gauze, his ointments and salves, and he treated them.

Early on, before he figured out the schedule on set, he had arrived to find a young girl making rounds and caring for his Gaia. At first he wondered if she was the cause of the animals' distress. But soon it became apparent to him that she calmed them as he did, naturally, instinctively. He could see her communicating with them, not only talking to them but listening, understanding, responding to what they needed and wanted. He saw a great affection between her and Gaia. That didn't surprise him—everyone loved Gaia. But it was clear Gaia loved her in return.

After that, he came a little early each evening so that he could watch this young woman care for the animals.

So many times, he almost gave himself away, wanting to spare her the struggle to understand something or to persuade an animal to do something. There were so many things he could tell her, secrets he had kept for so long, information about animals that so few people wanted but that this girl might want, might appreciate. Risking everything, he'd shown her how Gaia responded to gentle verbal commands, hoping the girl might make them her own. He heard her try, but without any confidence. He longed to explain how she simply had to trust that Gaia would understand in order for the commands to work. He had never before met anyone he felt he could pass this information to, but in this girl he saw the person he'd been looking for. Still, it would jeopardize both Gaia and himself if anyone knew he was here, so he remained in the shadows.

Now, with Gaia's trunk draped across his shoulder and around his waist like an embrace, he finished his song, kissed Gaia's five-foot-long nose, and made a bed for himself in the hay in the corner of her stall. Gaia would sleep standing, but even asleep, each would know the other was there. Sen closed his eyes and listened to the rustlings and snufflings and whispers that drifted through the barn, until finally when there was just his own breathing, and Gaia's, he fell asleep.

"Flory, when I said 'cat suit,' I didn't mean..." Jane hesitated, not wanting to hurt her friend's feelings. She glanced down at her own running tights and black turtleneck sweater. Flory reached up and touched the ears that sprouted from the tight black spandex hood covering her head. She was sheathed head to toe in a spandex unitard. The ears were non-detachable, part of the package.

"I found it on sale at Mall-Mart," she explained sheepishly. "They were getting rid of all their Halloween stuff."

"Nice tail!" Amy exclaimed as she appeared through the trap door in the Shack floor. Then she let out a wolf whistle. "Geez, Flor, you ever think about showing yourself off a little more often? I'd kill for that bod!" She emerged dressed in a set of her brother's old sweats, complete with stains and holes. Her mass of red curls threatened to break free of the balaclava she'd pulled over her head and face. "What's up with you, Jane? Cat got your tongue?" She threw back her head, guffawing at her own joke.

"I've got a funny feeling about this," Jane answered, pacing nervously.

"Yeah, it's called *fear*!" Amy responded, instantly serious. "We're about to cross the lake in a rowboat in November in the middle of the night and break into a building on the set where we work, where the producers trust us with their confidential files and their expensive equipment and their animals every single day. We screw this up, we've got a lot more to lose than our after-school jobs!"

"Well, when you put it like that . . . ," Jane said miserably.

"Jane, your instincts haven't led us wrong yet," Flory broke in quietly. "If you think something is going on with the animals then something is going on and we need to find out what it is." Jane shot her friend a grateful look. "Amy, maybe you would prefer to stay here and wait for the phone to ring?" Flory pointed to the cell phone clipped to her belt. "I can call you if we need anything . . ."

"Whoa, whoa, whoa . . . *easy*, Pussycat!" Amy exclaimed. "You're not going anywhere without the wee MacGillivray lass! Besides, I'm the one with the handheld Global Positioning System—*which* I made myself, by the way—and the snacks." She held up what looked like a lead weight shot through with a rusty bolt and a bag of peanut-butter marshmallow squares.

"Great," Flory muttered. "We'll be lost *and* fat."

"What was that, Cat?" Amy countered sharply.

"I said, 'Great!' You must be ex*haust*ed after all *that* . . . baking!" Flory finished lamely.

"*Hmph*," Amy huffed. "Well, yes I am, as a matter of fact . . ."

"Enough!" Jane exclaimed. Amy and Flory jumped. "I can't take this tension any more! Either we go now together or I go alone. What's it going to be?" She stared at her friends, the deep silence of the November night pressing in against the walls of the Shack.

Amy stepped forward: "I'm in," she said quietly. The two of them turned to Flory. The girl stared back, her dark eyes like two points of light in her small, dark form. She was silent for so long that Jane began to wonder if she'd changed her mind. And then her mouth moved and a tiny sound emerged.

"*Meow!*"

The three of them collapsed on the floor of the Shack, laughing hysterically. Tension dispelled for the moment, they collected themselves and quietly emerged from the Shack. With Amy in the lead, they moved out into the darkness and made their way down to the MacGillivrays' dock and the waiting boat.

Sen dreamed of home, and of the ocean. He could smell the salt tang in the air and hear the waves lapping gently against the rocks along the shore. Then he was awake, eyes open, body immobile, listening. Nothing. No, wait . . . there. And again. The gentle slapping of oars against water. He hadn't been dreaming it. There was someone out on the lake and they were getting closer. He heard the bottom of a boat grind against gravel and sand, the splash of feet—more than one pair!—muffled whispers, the sound of the boat being dragged out of the water. He held his breath, straining to catch every sound.

Lovers! As soon as the thought crossed his mind, he relaxed and breathed again. "Go back to sleep, Gaia girl," he whispered. She had awakened when he had; she always did. "It's just some crazy kids enjoying a midnight tryst!" He smiled to himself. Young love. Any time, any place, any temperature. Well, good for them, he thought wistfully. Lucky them.

He was drifting off to sleep again when another sound brought him back to full alert. Footsteps, right outside the barn. The back door creaked open and then closed again. Footfalls on the dirt floor, more muffled whispers. They were right inside the barn . . . and coming this way! Sen listened for a telltale restlessness among the animals, but they slept on. Even Gaia was still, though he knew she must hear and smell the trespassers. He couldn't understand it. Why wasn't she huffing and stamping her feet? The footfalls drew closer. Surprised and confused by the animals' non-reactions, Sen had just enough time to bury himself in hay where he lay before he heard the intruders come to a standstill just outside Gaia's stall!

"Now what?" Flory whispered.

"It seriously smells in here," Amy said, also whispering.

"I love this smell!" Jane responded. "It's a clean, happy animal smell. Your lab, on the other hand . . ."

"*Now what*?" Flory whispered again.

There was a pause. "Well . . . ," Jane said, "I guess we just observe. See if anything happens that upsets the animals. I don't know what we're looking for, but I have a gut feeling that we'll know it when we see it."

"I hate to say it, girls," Amy said, "but they all seem pretty okay right now."

"I know," Jane replied, biting nervously on her lower lip. "They really do. Maybe I got it wrong."

Just then, a vehicle crunched into the gravel lot behind the barn. Jane froze, her breath lodging in her throat, and she felt her friends stiffen beside her. All around them, the animals rose into wakefulness, getting to their feet, stamping their hooves, pacing the walls of their stalls. *There it is*, Jane thought. *This is what I come to work to every afternoon.*

That was all she had time to think before the back door of the barn opened. Two people spoke in low voices. She couldn't make out the words, but she knew those tones: it was Denny Arcola and Digger Hutchinson. "My bosses!" she hissed to Amy and Flory. "If they find us in here we're hooped! Get down!" There was an empty stall next to Gaia's. Jane had cleaned it out just that afternoon. "Quick, in here!" The three threw themselves into the hay and Jane latched the stall door behind them.

"There . . . you hear that?" Digger Hutchinson was whispering urgently. "Just like I told you—ghosts! Animal whisperers!"

"Yeah, Dig," came Denny Arcola's patronizing tones. "That's why we're here at freakin' 2:00 a.m. Your damn ghosts. You got me here, okay? So let's see somethin'. Show me your ghosts, Scaredy Man. Otherwise I swear you can take that permanent vacation I been promising and I'll find myself another assistant!"

The two men moved through the barn corridors searching for Digger Hutchinson's ghosts. Though Jane couldn't see them from where she lay, she knew exactly where they were in the barn by the sounds the animals made as they passed them by. Everywhere they went, they left a trail of agitated animals behind them. Suddenly Gaia let out a loud huff and began to stamp her front feet. The men were on their way to the elephant's quarters. Jane glanced through the slats of the stall and had to clamp a hand over her mouth to keep herself from screaming. A small, dark head was rising out of the hay. The head whispered something to Gaia. The elephant stopped her stamping and stood trembling slightly, her trunk reaching toward the spot in the hay where the head had once again disappeared.

Jane jumped as a hand touched her shoulder. "What's wrong, Jane?" Flory whispered. But there was no time to explain. The men had arrived in their corridor.

"There!" Digger exclaimed, terror in his voice. "You hear that? It's down here, jus' like I said!"

"Down here, eh?" Denny taunted sarcastically. "Cuz, Dig, the rest of the place is clean, man. Not a ghost in sight." There was a pause, and then, *"Boo!"* Digger let out a yelp and crashed into the door of the girls' stall, knocking it open. Denny was laughing hysterically.

Jane glanced around frantically. Caught behind the open door, she backed into the far end of the stall. That lump of hay in the opposite corner must be Amy. But what on earth was Flory doing? In the middle of the stall, too exposed to hide, she had instead risen up on her hands and knees, completely in view of anyone who happened to be looking. In the wan moonlight, Jane had to admit she looked rather remarkably like a . . .

"Aaaaaiiiieeee!!!!" Digger screamed. Leaping into the air, he landed back out in the corridor, slamming the stall door closed behind him. Breathing hard, he grabbed Denny: "When the hell did the panther arrive? I thought we weren't getting her till December!"

"What panther?" Denny had given up all pretense of whispering by now and was yelling back at Digger. "Calm the hell down, would you, Digger? Talk some sense, you stupid knucklehead. We don't have a panther. We aren't getting a panther till next month."

"Okay, then you tell me what's in there!" Digger choked out, nearly hysterical.

Jane knew she had seconds before they were discovered. Meanwhile, the real troublemaker was going undetected! She groped frantically in the hay, searching for anything she might use as a weapon. Feeling a soft touch at her back, she turned to find Flory holding out Amy's global positioning device and miming throwing it over the wall of the stall. Without thinking, she grabbed it and tossed it high and hard. She watched as, in slow motion, it spun over the wall, then over Gaia's wall, and bore down on the exact spot in the hay where the disembodied head was hidden. It hit the head with an audible thwack, signaling time to resume its normal speed.

There was a cry of pain from the hay in Gaia's stall. Gaia stamped her feet and blasted the barn with a mighty trumpet. Flory started to scream. Digger Hutchinson shrieked, "Panther on the loose!" and ran screeching from the barn. The dark head emerged from the hay in Gaia's stall, followed by a body. Together, head and body leapt over the stall wall, knocking Denny Arcola to the ground, and tore off down the corridor. Howling in fury, Denny leapt up and ran in pursuit of his attacker. Amy popped out of the hay moaning like a phantom, ran into the corridor, and bolted off after Denny. Turning and seeing nothing behind him but a few tendrils of red hair suspended in midair, Denny screamed and tore out of the barn after Digger. Jane leapt up, pulling Flory after her, and caught up to Amy at the front entrance. Every animal in the barn was crying out in fear.

"Go!" Jane cried. "Get the boat into the water. I'll meet you out there in a minute!"

"But what if . . . ?" Flory was hyperventilating.

"Just go!" Jane repeated. "Two minutes. *Just go!*"

As Amy and Flory dragged the boat back across the beach and into the water, they heard the panicked sounds in the barn slowly subside. True to her word, within minutes, Jane was by their side.

"What did you do in there, Jane?" Flory asked wonderingly as they sculled away from shore.

But Jane was silent. She had no idea how she did what she did with animals. She had some instinct for which there seemed to be no words.

"So I guess your worries are over, Jane!" Amy huffed between strokes of the oars. "We sent your intruder packing. Gave your bosses something to think about, too!" Her wicked grin glowed neon in the moonlight.

But as they made their way back across the lake, Jane spotted a small dark figure running away through the woods on the far shore, running as if for his life. The sight knotted a ball of fear in her gut. She had a terrible feeling that whatever had happened tonight had not made things better for the animals, but worse.

20

JUST THE FAX, MA'AM

IT WAS THE first of December. The woods surrounding Elfin Lake were cold and quiet, as though every creature, and even the trees themselves, held still to conserve enough energy to last through the coming winter. The same stillness hung over the UWRC, where the care center was nearly bare and the outdoor aviaries stood mostly empty, waiting for next spring's arrivals. Despite Avis's and Katrina's absence, Jane found herself increasingly able to manage the full caseload on her own. School was another story, however, as teachers piled on homework in anticipation of winter exams. Still, there was an excitement in the air as Christmas holidays approached, with the promise of two whole weeks off.

Mike MacGillivray continued to write, and Jane returned two letters for every one of his. She described the changes autumn had brought to Cedar's Ridge, guessing he was missing home, told him of Avis's fall and surgery, reported gossip from school, and relayed stories of the animals that came into the UWRC—their injuries, their progress, their release back to the wild. Beneath these things were all the things she *didn't* write—how much she missed him and wished he'd write more often, how she wondered when she'd see him next, how she hoped there was a chance that maybe . . . someday . . . She wondered if, beneath his stories of harvesting and preserving, of communal life on the farm, of the wild beauty of Cortes Island, there were things he was holding back, too.

On set, Denny Arcola and Digger Hutchinson had reported a break-in to the film's producers. Amy said that the story circulating among crew members didn't contain any mention of ghosts, only of an intruder that had been caught sleeping in the elephant's quarters. The producers had responded by increasing security around the barn, so that Jane was now required to report to a guard before she could start work. The changes left her uneasy, but none so much as the changes in the animals.

Jane's fears had proven true: the animals' distress was greater than ever. At first she blamed it on the pandemonium that had erupted the night of their break-in. But it worsened steadily as the days progressed. It took all her concentration to maintain her own sense of calm as she worked. Some days, she was able to impart that sense of calm to the animals. But most days, she took on their anxiety instead and left work overcome with a sense of dread.

She kept thinking about the man she'd seen hiding in Gaia's stall, the one who'd been able to calm Gaia down that night, the one who'd run from the scene as though his life depended on it. Was he connected to the voice she'd heard earlier? The one that helped Gaia to her knees for her bath and then back to her feet? Certainly, she'd never heard the voice again, nor had she been able to produce the same response in Gaia herself, no matter how many times she tried the commands.

Gaia. Of all the animals, Gaia was worst—agitated, restless, starting at small noises, responding less and less to Jane's touch. It was as though something had been helping her cope before, and now that thing was gone. *Thing*, Jane thought, *or person*? The person with the singsong voice? The person who had been sleeping by Gaia's side? Had he been her comfort? And had Jane's clumsy detective work simply taken that comfort away?

Jane sat now at the old wooden table in the Shack running these thoughts through her head for the thousandth time as she watched Flory nail an advent calendar to the wall by the door. December first. Flory scanned the sparkling woodland scene for the tiny door marked "1" and popped it open, folding it back to reveal the picture hidden beneath the flap. "There," she pronounced. "If we alternate between the three of us, that's eight doors each by the twenty-fourth, and we can all open number twenty-five together." Jane smiled. They'd been sharing an advent calendar in the Shack for as long as she could remember, but every year, Flory insisted on reviewing her instructions. They were as much a part of the tradition as the calendar itself. She watched as Flory tacked a sprig of mistletoe above the door and then moved to hang ornaments over Amy's lab table. Amy batted her away. That, too, was tradition.

"C'mon, Flory," Jane said. "I'll help you put up the outdoor lights."

"Forget it," Amy broke in. "Wait till tomorrow. It's way too dark out now. Besides, where's the cheer? The spirit? The gaiety? The laughter? Flory, you called this Shack Summit, girl. I was expecting singing, carols, harmony even! No, wait, stop, you two can't hang lights like this! You both look as though you're headed to a funeral. What's the deal?"

Amy and Flory listened as Jane haltingly laid out her theory about the animals on set. "I think when we assumed that the man in the hay was the problem," she said, "we got it backwards. I'm beginning to think now that he was the solution, the glue that was keeping them together. Without him, they're nearly impossible to calm. And now he's long gone, and I have no idea who he was. Not that it matters, because with all the new security, he couldn't get back into the barn without an army tank!"

"Okay, but what's actually wrong?" Amy pressed. "We still don't know what the problem is. And now any chance of us getting into that barn again is out the window, too!"

"I know," Jane responded miserably. "I've been afraid to say anything to my bosses in case they think I'm the problem and decide I can't do my job. But maybe it's time to go talk to them. Because maybe it *is* me! Maybe I'm just not cut out for this job!".

"Ridiculous!" Amy sputtered peremptorily. "I saw you with those critters. They love you. No, the problem ain't you, Jane girl. But maybe you *should* talk to your bosses. Maybe they've noticed something, too, you know? Maybe they could help."

"Ahem." It was Flory. Jane and Amy raised their eyebrows in invitation. "I called this meeting tonight because I have some news that . . . concerns those bosses of yours, Jane."

"*My* bosses?" Jane asked, surprised. "What do you mean?"

"Well," Flory hesitated, "I'm not sure that it's *bad* news exactly, but I'm not sure that it's good, either."

"What is it?" Amy asked, impatient.

"I can't help but feel it's somehow connected to our breaking into the barn," Flory responded, "but I'm not sure how."

"What's the news, Flory?" Amy pushed, her voice hard.

"Oh, gosh," Flory twisted her hands together. "I'm wondering now if I'd be breaking David and Lynn's confidence by telling you this."

"THEN *DON'T!*" Amy shouted, slamming her hands down on her lab table. "Jane, what do you say we grab a snack back at the house? I'm sure Flory'll be happy to sit here and chew on her morals!"

"Gaia's for sale," Flory said softly into the silence that followed Amy's outburst. "The zoo doesn't want her anymore. Too old, I guess. The prospective buyers are Animal Actors Inc."

Jane felt her heart miss a beat. *Gaia for sale? What did this mean? Animals were bought and sold between various entertainment venues all the time. And at pet stores, over the Internet, at auctions. So why did this feel so wrong? Was it because it was Gaia? Was it because she knew her? Loved her? Or was it always wrong and she'd just never thought about it before?*

"How do you know all this, Flory?" Jane asked urgently.

"The zoo sent a fax today," Flory explained. "I was in the production office when it came. I saw Gaia's name and I . . . I read it. The whole thing. She's on probation with Animal Actors. This is her last month. If everything goes well, they buy her at the end of December."

"Hoo, boy!" Amy whistled, scratching her head until her hair stood on end. "The plot thickens!"

A sharp rap from the underside of the trap door in the Shack floor caused them all to jump. "Girls?" came Mrs. MacGillivray's muffled voice from the tunnel below. "You have a visitor." Jane, Amy, and Flory looked around at one another questioningly and shrugged. Slowly, the trap door opened, hinges squeaking. There was a click of heels on wood, and then from the stairs below appeared Mrs. Donna Lise Harbinsale.

21
TWO ELEPHANT TALES

WORKING HARD TO hide their surprise, the girls seated Mrs. Harbinsale at the old gardening table and laid out the tea and shortbread Mrs. MacGillivray passed up. "If you need anything else, Donna Lise, Amy knows how to reach me at the house," Mrs. MacGillivray said, and then retreated discreetly down the steps.

"You're very kind," Mrs. Harbinsale murmured after her.

The trap door closed. Flory poured the tea and Amy passed the cups and saucers. Out of the corner of her eye, Jane took in Mrs. Harbinsale's neat blond coif and expensive charcoal suit. The idea that she'd dressed up to visit them was almost as strange as the fact that she was here at all.

Her hands shook in her lap. Jane's first memory of Mrs. Harbinsale was of those shaking hands, diamond rings slipping in place. Then Jane noticed that her own hands were shaking, too.

"I'm here about Jake and Bobby," Mrs. Harbsinsale said without preamble. "My boys. They're still . . . missing," she struggled to control her voice, "and it's almost Christmas and I just want them home. Home, or just safe—just to know they're safe." She looked directly at Jane then, her expression a mixture of fear and hope. "I was wondering, Jane, has Jake contacted you again?"

Jane closed her eyes and shook her head. It hurt to have nothing to offer this woman who was so obviously distraught. "Nothing since the summer, Mrs. Harbinsale." Jane felt rather than saw her friends' eyebrows rise. She'd kept Jake's secret from everyone but Mrs. Harbinsale. Until now. She hoped they'd understand. "If I do hear anything, though, I'll be sure to let you know. I promise."

Mrs. Harbinsale nodded and lifted her teacup to her lips, using the action to mask her dismay. There was nothing more to say and a full plate of shortbread still to get through.

"I hope you'll forgive my asking," Flory interjected quietly, "but why all the late-night secrecy, Mrs. Harbinsale? And how did you know where to find Jane?"

"Jake told me about the Shack once," Mrs. Harbinsale explained. "'The perfect place to hide,' he called it. My husband, you see . . . If he knew the boys had . . . if he thought that I'd . . ." She trailed to a stop. Jane saw Flory gazing intently at Mrs. Harbinsale, as though listening to all the words their guest wasn't saying. Jane could practically hear the gears turning in her friend's brain as she connected disparate bits of information to piece together a puzzle. Jane was in the dark, however, and glanced over at Amy to see if she'd clued in.

"You know, I'd almost forgotten," Amy blustered, trying to help the woman out of her embarrassment. "I bumped into him in the mall a few weeks ago. Wasn't able to stop and chat, though. How *is* Councillor . . . er, Mr. Harbinsale, anyway?" Amy blushed over her gaffe and shoved a square of shortbread into her mouth.

"Oh, you know Rand!" Mrs. Harbinsale laughed, a little too brightly. "Always some new scheme on the go! This time it's elephants. Because of the elephant in the movie, you see." Her face flushed and she spoke rapidly, as though she'd been bottling all this up and was giddy to talk about her husband's latest business venture. "He's been importing items from Asia. You'd just love some of the things, girls—jewelry and darling little knick-knacks and oh, what else, writing paper made out of elephant dung, can you believe it?" She laughed again. Jane saw an odd look pass across Amy's face. "What will they think of next?"

"And yourself, Mrs. Harbinsale?" Flory inquired politely.

"What's that, dear?" Mrs. Harbinsale was breaking a shortbread cookie into tiny pieces on her plate.

"How are you managing these days?" Flory persisted gently. Jane marveled at her friend's diplomacy. Coming from anyone else, those questions would have sounded tactless. But all Jane heard was kindness. *Flory sounds like a grown-up!* she thought in surprise.

"Me? Oh, well!" She seemed to consider something for a moment and then change her mind. "Well, you know, I have my hands full with Rand!" She reached for the napkin in her lap and twisted it between her hands. A cloud passed over the moon, blanketing the room in shadows. She spoke again:

"I read a story about an elephant once," she said, her gaze on her hands. "She was captured when she was young and they chained her to a log so she couldn't escape. When she got bigger, they were afraid she'd just run away one day and drag the log with her. But she never did. In fact, they took the log away and just left the chain around her foot, and you know what? She stayed right where she was." Mrs. Harbinsale smiled. Jane thought she'd never seen an expression so sad.

"I have an elephant story, too," Flory said quietly, "from the New Year's Day tsunami in Asia." Jane glanced over to see her friend gazing at Mrs. Harbinsale with that same look of intense concentration she'd worn earlier. "A group of mahouts and their working elephants were taking a break at the bottom of a hill near their village. The mahouts had chained their elephants to a series of stakes to keep them from wandering off while they rested. Like all the animals that day, the elephants felt the earthquake under the ocean and knew the tsunami would come. They trumpeted and stamped their feet and strained at the stakes, wanting to climb to the top of the hill. But their mahouts, not understanding what was happening, refused to release them. In a fit of terror and strength, the elephants pulled up the stakes and ran, dragging the chains and stakes along with them. They reached the safety of the top of the hill just as the giant wave crashed over the village, destroying the buildings and dragging all the people out to sea."

"Whoa!" Amy uttered a low whistle. "That's amazing, Flor."

Flory shook her head. "There's more. As the wave receded from the land, the elephants charged back down the hill, again dragging their chains and stakes with them. They rushed into the water that was roiling with debris and uprooted trees and bodies and they began to pluck survivors out of the sea. They saved the children first, returning to the water again and again until every living child had been taken up in their trunks and carried to the top of the hill. And then they went back for the adults. They worked until they had rescued every survivor."

The little room fell silent once again. Jane groped blindly in her bag for a tissue. Finally, Mrs. Harbinsale stood, holding a warm and steady hand out to each of the girls in turn. "Thank you," she said simply. "You've done more for me tonight than you can know." Declining to go back the way she'd come, she slipped through the door and stepped out into the night just as the moon reappeared to light her path.

22
STAYIN' ALIVE

THE FOLLOWING THURSDAY, Jane arrived at the Urban Wildlife Rescue Center to find Evie, Daniel, Anthony, and Katrina in a huddle in the exam room. Through the small window in the swinging door, she saw Anthony wave her in. Checking her watch hurriedly as the door swung closed behind her, she said, "Sorry, am I late? I didn't realize there was a meeting!"

"Hey, Jane," Evie gave her a warm smile. "Don't apologize, this isn't anything official. Pretty impromptu, actually. The three of us staffers each received big news over the past week and we're just letting all the volunteers know first chance we get. Anthony, you want to go first this time? We'll make it quick—I know you've got lots to do with Avis still away."

Big news? Jane thought. *What now*? She was beginning to feel as though she'd stepped onto a roller-coaster back in September and forgotten to get off. One good thing was that Katrina was back. At least she wouldn't have to feed and clean all the animals on her own this week. *She's still looking a little green*, Jane thought. *I hope she keeps her germs to herself.* Jane suddenly realized she'd missed half of what Anthony had said and tuned back into the conversation.

"So this label loves our albums, totally dug us at Saturday's gig, and they're taking us on!" Anthony was jumping up and down and clapping his hands, his shock of long black hair swinging across his grinning face. "They're sponsoring us on a cross-country tour next summer, and if we rock from coast to coast—which we will!—they'll produce and market our next two albums! *Aaaahhhh!* Black Turtle on tour, can you believe it?!" His excitement was infectious, and Jane found herself jumping up and down and laughing with him. In the back of her mind, though, she tried to picture the UWRC without him and couldn't.

"My turn," Daniel laughed, clapping Anthony on the shoulder. "I wish my news was half as exciting, but it does involve some cross-country travel." Jane's smile stayed put, but she felt her stomach drop at his words. "As you both already know, I finish vet school in the spring." Jane and Katrina nodded. "Well, I've been offered a position at a teaching hospital. I'll be practicing in the clinic, teaching other vet students, and helping run their youth internship program in the summers."

"Daniel, that sounds amazing!" Katrina enthused. "Your dream job!"

Daniel nodded, his grin matching Anthony's. "I know. I had to say yes."

"Where?" Jane managed in a small voice. "When?"

"Prince Edward Island," Daniel answered, turning his cornflower-blue eyes directly on her. "Next fall." Prince Edward Island. The other end of the country. Three thousand miles away.

Holding her smile in place, Jane said, "Congratulations, Daniel! It really does sound like the perfect job for you!" She barely recognized the sound of her own voice. "And Evie?" She turned to the senior staffer, preferring to face the worst head-on rather than wait. "Where are you going? Will you be leaving next year as well?"

Slowly, Evie nodded. "It's a lot, isn't it? This is why we felt we had to tell you in person." The secret smile Evie had worn throughout the meeting burst into full bloom as she announced, "I'm pregnant!" She laughed as though still overcome by the surprise of it herself. "Can you believe it? I . . . we're going to have a baby! I'm due at the end of June!" She laughed again.

Before Jane had a chance to digest the news, Katrina blurted out, "But Evie, you're not even married!"

Jane heard the exam room clock tick twice before Evie spoke. "Well, Katrina, that's true," she answered evenly, "although as you probably noticed last summer, every other animal on the planet manages to procreate and raise their offspring without the help of the multimillion-dollar wedding industry." She laughed, easing the tension in the room a little. "That said, Jack—my boyfriend—and I are thinking we might tie the knot soon after the baby's born. And you're all invited!"

"Ooo!" Anthony cooed. "Need an extra bridesmaid?" Everybody laughed. Everybody but Katrina, Jane noticed.

"No satin and no seafoam green," Evie teased him. "I promise!" She turned serious again. "As for what this means for the UWRC, other than the obvious maternity leave come summer, I will be working very little or not at all in the care center after today. There are zoonotic diseases that can harm a developing fetus, and I'm not taking any chances. I'll be spending most of my time in the other building doing administrative work. Revised diet manual, here we come! So starting tomorrow, Daniel is officially Head of Animal Care at UWRC. No more Mr. Nice Guy!" She laughed, giving her colleague a playful punch on the shoulder.

"And after the summer?" Jane asked. "When Daniel goes to Prince Edward Island, and Anthony's on tour, and you're on maternity? Who'll run this place?"

"Who indeed, Miss Ray?" Daniel responded, waggling his eyebrows at her. "And what are *you* doing after graduation, hmm?"

"All right everybody, enough joking around!" Evie broke in. "There are animals to feed and meds to administer. Let's get to work!"

"Yes, boss!" Daniel teased.

"For one more day," Evie laughed, "and don't you forget it!"

Jane did the outside rounds in a daze, overwhelmed by the news she'd heard and all the changes that would mean for the UWRC. She missed having Avis there to talk it over with, missed her elderly friend's way of making sense of things and seeing the silver linings. All Jane could see right now was a UWRC empty of all the people she cared about. She'd always thought she was here for the animals, but she wondered now if her commitment to them would be enough to keep her coming once all her friends were gone.

Dumping her last load of dirty dishes next to the sink, she did a quick tour of the care room only to discover that Katrina wasn't even half finished. She was surprised; there were hardly any animals in care right now. "Um, hey, Katrina . . . you want a hand in here?" she asked, not wanting to insult the more senior volunteer.

"That would be great, actually, Jane, thanks," Katrina answered, nervously running a hand through her hair. "I . . . I can't seem to concentrate this morning."

"Still not feeling well?" Jane ventured as she took stock of the work still to be done. Two crow diets to make, three floor pens to clean out, and the cedar waxwings' aviary looked as though it could use some fresh greenery.

"Oh . . . no, it's not that," Katrina said. "It was just . . . something Evie said that's got me worried."

"Yeah, it was a lot to take in," Jane agreed. "I'm still kind of in shock myself."

"Shock . . . yeah," Katrina mumbled. "I'm . . . I think . . . Jane, would you mind taking over in here? I think I need to go home!" With that, Katrina grabbed her bag and hurried out of the care room.

So once again, Jane handled the full caseload on her own. Finishing just after noon, it hit her that she still had a full afternoon of classes and then her shift on the *Shapeshifter* set to face. Suddenly, she felt exhausted. Slinging her pack across her back, she waved at Anthony, who was on the phone, and headed out the door.

She was at the trail head with her bike when she heard him calling, and turned to find him running after her. "Message for you!" he huffed. "That was George Morton on the phone, Avis's husband. He's worried about her. Sounds like her hip is healing just fine but she's all down in the dumps and won't leave the house. He thought she might perk up if you called her." He handed Jane a scrap of paper with a number on it.

"Me?" she asked, incredulous. Avis was a grown-up, and an old one at that; she was just a kid. What could she possibly say that would help? She thought back to Flory's gentle diplomacy with Mrs. Harbinsale. Yeah, but that was Flory. Flory was one in a million.

"She'll be over the moon just hearing your voice,

Jane girl," Anthony was saying as if he could read her thoughts. "Won't matter what you say. Hey . . . are you okay?"

"It's just . . ." Jane struggled to keep her voice steady. Any more sympathy from Anthony and she'd be in tears. "So many changes all at once, you know? Graduation coming, missing Avis, and now you guys all leaving. I can't keep up!" She attempted a laugh but it came out sounding choked.

"Adapt or die, Jane Ray!" Anthony responded. *Wow. Harsh. So much for sympathy.* Jane's self-pitying tears dried up in an instant. "You're an animal, too, Jane, so do what an animal would do," he carried on. "Don't get all stuck in your ways like some fuddy-duddy old biddy. You're just seventeen! Go with the flow! Life's a wild dance, girl, and the whole world will be your partner if you'll let her!" Leaning her bike against a tree, he grabbed her hand and started spinning her down the trail. She couldn't help but laugh. "All these changes will be wonderful if you'll let them—not just for me and Dan and Eves, but wonderful for you, too!" He stepped back from her, struck an iconic disco pose, and started to sing:

Well, you can tell by the way we move and spin
it's a wild world we're livin' in.
From dinosaurs to modern man,
we keep turnin' to a cosmic plan.

And now it's all right Ms. Jane Ray,
and don't you try to run away.
If you look, you will see
that these things can set you free.

Whether skin or feathers, we all can live together.
We're stayin' alive, stayin' alive.
Feel the earth movin' and every creature groovin'
and we're stayin' alive, stayin' alive.
Ah, ha, ha, ha, stayin' alive, stayin' alive.
Ah, ha, ha, ha stayin' aliiiiiiiiiiiiiiiiive!"

Laughing till the tears finally came, Jane boogied with him through the woods until she realized she'd missed lunch and was about to be late for classes. She also realized she wasn't tired any more. Throwing her arms around him, she said, "Thanks, Anthony. And yes," she added, holding up the scrap of paper, "I'll call her." She hopped on her bike and raced along the trail, pumping hard in time to a disco beat and feeling better than she had in days.

23
AVIS'S WARNING

ARRIVING ON SET a few minutes late that afternoon, Jane slipped in through the back door of the barn and was changing into her rubber boots when she heard Denny Arcola berating Digger Hutchinson in the far corner by Gaia's stall. "Not that one, *this* one!" he shouted, fury in his voice. "How stupid can you be? No, not tomorrow, *now*! I said, *NOW!*" Making her way down the corridor toward the northeast corner, Jane cleared her throat to announce her arrival. Immediately, the shouting stopped. Rounding the last corner, she came upon Denny crouched at Gaia's feet in her stall.

She peered into the dim light, trying to make out Digger. "You're early today!" Denny greeted her, his face still contorted with anger. She watched him reassemble his features into the usual slick smile. She was about to point out that she was actually late when he said, "You know what, kid? You're a good worker. Why don't you take the afternoon off today? With pay, of course. Early Christmas present from me, whaddaya say? Gaia and I have a little work to do on our own today. Isn't that right, Gaia? Big scene coming up on Saturday, lots of rehearsing over the next two days, eh girl?" He slapped the elephant's left front leg. Jane winced. She was about to offer to stay and help when she caught his eye; the look there made it clear that his offer was non-negotiable.

With an unsettled feeling in her stomach, Jane changed back into her shoes, grabbed her bag, and left the barn. Something was wrong. She mounted her bike and headed for the trails, quickly putting the film set behind her. That slap on Gaia's leg—it hadn't been nearly hard enough to hurt an elephant, so why was it bothering her? And why hadn't Digger said anything to her? *Because he wasn't there.* The truth slammed into her like a freight train and she almost lost her balance. Denny hadn't been yelling at Digger. Digger wasn't there. He'd been yelling at Gaia. And that slap to her leg had been delivered in anger. Jane was pedaling hard for home, beads of sweat running down the sides of her face despite the cold. *Don't think about it,* she told herself, pushing back the realization that was creeping in at the edges of her awareness. *You're probably wrong. You must be wrong. Call Avis. Just call Avis. Forget about it.*

Anthony had been right—Avis was thrilled to hear her voice. Jane soon forgot to worry about what to say and just told her friend stories about the animals in care at the UWRC, about her classes at school, and about Anthony's, Daniel's, and Evie's news. Avis in turn related the tales of her surgery and recovery, her ongoing physio treatments, and her growing boredom at home. "I swear, Missy, I've read every mystery book my local library has on its shelves!" she sighed.

"Well, can you come back to the center soon?" Jane asked hopefully.

"Sounds to me as though you're getting along just fine without me!" came the reply.

"Are you crazy?" Jane almost shouted, forgetting to be polite. "That place is a disaster without you! Haven't you been listening? We have no work experience students, Katrina's never there, and now the entire staff is taking off to follow their stupid dreams! And you're at home feeling sorry for yourself? Man, Avis, do you think you could put down the Agatha Christies and maybe come in for your shift one of these days?"

There was silence on the line, during which it occurred to Jane that that may not have been the pep talk either George or Anthony had in mind. She was horrified. She heard a muffled sound on the other end of the line. Oh no, please no, was Avis crying? "I'm so sorry, Avis," she started. "I didn't mean . . ." Suddenly the sound turned to snorts and guffaws. Avis wasn't crying. She was cracking up.

"Well done!" Avis cried breathlessly through her laughter. "You certainly know how to give a girl a kick in the pants when it's needed!" She wheezed some more. "And I haven't laughed this hard in months! So you miss me, do you? Well, I must say, that feels mighty good. Oh, George'll be so pleased to have me out of the house. But I make no promises about helping you with the animals just yet, Missy. I may just come and give Evie a hand in administration for a while until I'm a little steadier on my feet."

"Anything you want, Avis," Jane said, hugely relieved. "Just as long as I'm still welcome at coffee time."

"Of course! I've missed you too, Jane Ray," Avis said simply. "And although I've been fortunate to have been well taken care of in all this, I've missed being needed myself, missed taking care of the animals, even taking care of you when you'll let me!"

At those words, Jane couldn't hold back her fears any longer. In a rush, she told Avis about her job on the *Shapeshifter* set; her work with Gaia, and the elephant's health problems; the changes in the animals' behavior since October; their discovery of the mysterious stranger in the hay; and the sharp increase in the animals' unease since he'd been flushed out and chased from the scene. Lastly, she told her what had happened that afternoon, about her realization that Denny Arcola had been yelling at Gaia, had been angry enough to hit her. Spent, and relieved finally to have told the whole story, Jane fell silent and waited for Avis's reassurance.

But it didn't come. Instead, Avis said in a grave voice, "Jane, from all that you've told me, I can only say that something is terribly wrong." Jane felt that sick feeling begin to build in her stomach again. Avis continued: "I'm not going to guess what it might be, since I may be wrong—I pray desperately that I am—and I don't want to prejudice your observations. But you and Amy and Flory must face this, whatever it is. If I'm right, those animals' lives are hanging in the balance. You must go back to the set, Jane, and discover the truth."

24
THE BOSS

JANE, AMY, AND Flory were crouched in the darkness behind the boat rentals cabin at Elfin Lake, half a mile south of the *Shapeshifter* set. It was Friday night, a few minutes after six o'clock and their after-school shift had just ended. They'd clocked out, left the set by different exits and rendezvoused here, as agreed. Quickly, they changed into the crew gear Amy had "borrowed" from the supply tent—long-sleeved shirts and pants, gloves and shoes, vests and ball caps, all black—listening as Flory reviewed their strategy. They'd spent the night in the Shack, forgoing sleep and the warmth of their homes as they laid plans for circling back to the set, getting back into the barn, and getting to the bottom of Jane's mystery. There was no time left to second-guess their decisions. Avis's words to Jane had made that clear. Time had run out.

Flory flipped open a rudimentary handheld device and pointed to several small shapes as they came into focus on the screen. "That's the producers' tent and that's

Craft Services," she explained. "Over here, this one's the barn." Jane and Amy watched over her shoulder as they adjusted their caps.

"And personnel?" Amy asked. "Did we get that function working?"

Flory nodded and pressed a button on the device. Instantly, the screen came to life with fifty or sixty dots all moving in and between the static shapes. "That's everybody," she said, "from David and Lynn right down to the lowliest gopher. Everyone, that is, except us." Amy and Flory had spent part of the night rebuilding a modified global positioning system to replace the one they'd lost the night of their first break-in. During her shift today, Flory had managed to link it in to the personnel tracking and identification system she had devised for the *Shapeshifter* producers. With the gadget she held in her hand, she could see not only every building on set but also every individual worker's whereabouts at any given moment. And by touching the stylus to any dot, she could tell exactly who that dot was.

"Best of all," Flory continued, "I tagged the ID badges on our targets, so with a flip of this toggle switch . . ." Here, she flipped the switch, and suddenly there were just four dots on the screen. Two moved inside the shape she'd said was the barn, and two moved around its perimeter.

Amy uttered a low whistle. "Nice work, Morales," she said. "So that's Dumb and Dumber inside the barn and, what, two guards outside now?"

"Front entrance and back," Flory confirmed. She pointed to each of the interior dots in turn: "This one's Arcola and this one's Hutchinson. Jane, according to what you overheard today, they're taking the horses out to the far west trails at 18:30 hours, is that correct?"

Jane glanced quickly at her watch. "Any minute now," she nodded. The three of them watched the screen as the two dots Flory had indicated moved toward the front entrance of the barn, stopped just outside it and then proceeded to the southwest. Moments later, they heard the clip-clop of the horses' hooves as the company headed past their hiding place and into the woods.

"And . . . mobilize Trojan Horse!" Flory commanded, nodding at Jane.

"Flory, it's just a cart, for crying out loud!" Jane said, surprised by her own vehemence. "Cut the cloak and dagger stuff, okay? This isn't a joke."

Amy raised her eyebrows. Flory busied herself retying her shoes, but not before Jane saw her wipe a hand across her eyes. Now what had she done? Her best friends had stayed up all night with her. Given up their Friday evening for her. Were risking their jobs—and maybe more—for her. What was her problem, anyway?

She felt a small, soft hand on her shoulder. "I understand." It was Flory. "You're scared, right?" Jane nodded, ashamed. She should have been the one comforting Flory, not the other way around. "Me, too," Flory said.

Jane turned and wrapped her arms around her friend. Flory hugged her back, hard.

Amy snorted. "All right, you two, enough mush," she said. "Let's move!"

Jane spun the dolly around. On it were three large grain sacks, one filled with oats and the other two empty. "Amy, you're alfalfa," she teased, pulling lightly at her friend's unruly hair. "Flory, you're Superior Grain Mix!" She held the cart still as her friends climbed into the empty sacks, then she tied them closed at the top. "Hang on," she muttered, and then steered the cart onto the paved pathways of the *Shapeshifter* set.

Reaching the barn without incident, she nodded to the front-door guard who recognized her and let her in. Once inside, she quickly ran the dolly into the feed room and let Amy and Flory out of their sacks. Taking the positioning device from Flory, she left the barn again by the front entrance, saying good night to the guard. Pretending she was checking her cell phone, she noted the position of the second guard: north side. She turned south and ducked into the Craft Services tent. Perry, her favorite line cook, was just covering up the dinner buffet. "You're working late, Jane!" he waved when he saw her. "Can I put together a nice supper for you? Or are you here on behalf of your friend?" He grinned and held up a watermelon.

"Um, hey, Perry!" she responded nervously. "I was just, uh . . ." She glanced down at her "cell phone" and saw that the rear guard had completed his perimeter check and was heading back toward the north side of the barn. "Er, can't stay. Bit of a situation at home," she stuttered, pointing to the device in her hand. "Hang onto that watermelon, okay? I'll come by Monday. Have a great weekend!"

She ran back into the cover of darkness and made her way to the barn's rear door. All clear. She tapped twice and heard the bolt slide away. Then Flory was there, taking the positioning device from her and pulling her inside. They were in!

"Okay, everybody," Flory gathered them close. "Last walkie-talkie check. I've jammed all the other channels so we've just got each other and nobody else can listen in." They ran through the three-way test she'd shown them. No glitches. "Perfect! All right, positions, everybody! Amy, you're here at the rear door, Position One. Jane, you're back in the empty stall next to Gaia's, Position Two. I'm on front door until D and D return, Position Three-A, and then I move south to the exotics wing, Three-B." She paused. "Now, are we clear? We are here as observers. No heroics. This is an information-gathering mission *only*. Once we have our information, we will rendezvous at the Shack to decide on next steps. Agreed?"

"Agreed," Jane and Amy murmured together. After a quick clasp of hands, Flory and Jane moved out.

Jane lost track of time as she lay in the hay next to

Gaia's stall, telling the elephant in quiet whispers why she was there, that her friends Amy and Flory cared about animals too and wanted to figure out why Gaia and the others were so upset all the time, that she was sure after today everything would be okay. Whenever she paused to take a breath or gather her thoughts, she listened, believing that she could hear in the elephant's chirps and grunts some genuine understanding of all that she was telling her. She started violently when the radio receiver buzzed against her hip.

"D and D on the move," came Flory's voice through the static. Jane checked her watch: 7:30 p.m. They'd be back in the barn within fifteen minutes. She felt a shot of adrenaline burst into her bloodstream and send her heart racing. Her vision intensified, setting the beams of the walls and roof and stall gates into vivid relief. Her hearing sharpened and she caught the first stirrings of restlessness in the animals around her. *They knew*! D and D were on their way back to the barn, and they knew it! She fought back a wave of nausea as the awareness that had been taking shape at the corners of her mind came a little more clearly into view. Never in her life had she wanted so badly to be wrong.

"D and D moving in," her receiver hissed. "Hold your positions. I'm moving to Three-B."

Never in her life.

Flory ducked into a dead-end corridor between the horse stalls and the exotics wing just as the wide front door of the barn swung open. Starlight cast a pale glow over the barn's entranceway and she could see the breath of the men and the horses hanging in the cold night air. The horses were panting with exertion. She listened as the men returned the horses to their stalls using rough language and loud slaps to the rump. A chorus of whinnied protests met with the crack of a whip against the cement floor of the barn corridors. Flory jumped. She felt something in the cage at her back begin to pace, and the hairs on her neck rose.

Suddenly she smelled smoke. The horses smelled it, too, and began to whinny and stamp in fear. Denny Arcola came into view, dragging on a cigarette. "Forget the horses, Dig," he was saying. "It's Friday night. Nobody's gonna know if we clean them tonight or tomorrow. Just go deal with that damned elephant, would you? She's been defying me for the past two days, won't do a thing I say, and they need her for the battle scene tomorrow. Maybe she'll listen to you."

Flory heard Digger shuffle off toward the far side of the barn and then pressed herself flat against the wall as Denny passed by her post. "D-two headed for Position Two," she whispered into her walkie-talkie.

"I'm too old for this garbage," Denny was saying to himself. "Stupid little peons bossing me around out there—'Restrain your horses, Mr. Arcola, show us what they can do, Mr. Arcola, is that all you've got, Mr. Arcola?' I'll show you what I've got, you small-time, self-righteous bastards! I'll show you what they can do, all right. I'll show you who's boss!"

Flory saw Denny push open the gate two units down and reach for something in the corner of the cage. There was a dull thud followed by a deep moan. Peering up over the wooden guards that surrounded the chain link caging, her eyes widened as she saw Denny wind up and swing a baseball bat into the shoulder of a large black bear. There was a sharp crack and the bear roared in pain. "Up, damn you! I said, up! Mr. Arcola's the boss around here, and everybody does what Mr. Arcola says. Got that? Now, get up!" He brought the bat down across the bear's back. The bear groaned and retreated to the far corner of its stall.

Flory crouched in the corridor, shaking. She didn't know what she had expected to see tonight, but nothing could have prepared her for this. Nor for what happened next. The bear howled, an almost human cry, and Flory looked up in time to see Denny pressing the lit end of his cigarette to the bear's front left paw. The bear reared up on its hind legs, seeming to do the dance she'd seen so many bears do at circuses and roadside zoos. Was this how all those bears had learned to dance?

Without thinking, Flory pulled her cell phone from her vest pocket as her own words echoed in her head: *We are here as observers. No heroics. This is an information-gathering mission only.* Right. And Denny Arcola was the patron saint of animals. Setting her phone on video, she waited for Denny's next move. She didn't have long to wait. Slamming the gate behind him as he exited the bear's stall, Denny grabbed a rope from the wall and barreled his way into the cage closest to her, cigarette once again dangling from his lips. "How 'bout you, tiger? You next? You ready for one of Mr. Arcola's special training sessions? Maybe *you* know who's boss, huh?"

Flory heard a low growl start alarmingly near her feet. There really was a tiger in there. The growl turned to a roar when a whip cracked against the wall that separated Flory from the tiger. "Or maybe you *don't*!" Denny's seething tone sent a chill of fear down Flory's spine. Edging her phone up over the wood and through the chain link, she peered over the wall and saw Denny tossing a circle of thick rope over the tiger's massive head. Yanking on the slipknot he'd created, Denny tightened the rope around the tiger's neck and then threw his weight against the rope, choking the animal. Flory held the phone as steady as she could as she watched the tiger flail against the cage floor, trying desperately to extract itself from the chokehold. When still it refused to submit, Denny leaned over, pulled the cigarette from his mouth and burned the tiger's nose. The tiger emitted a strangled cry and then went limp. At last, Denny released the rope and exited the cage. Flory saw the tiger's body rise and fall slightly with ragged breaths before she slumped to the floor.

The sound of Digger returning from the far side of the barn roused her to alertness once again. "Hey Den, she won't do it," he called from the far end of the horses' stalls. "Den, you hear me? Gaia, she won't do what I want."

"Damn well figures," Denny muttered. "You want something done right, you gotta do it yourself." And then louder, "Hang on, Den. Just cleaning up in the exotics. Sharpen the bullhook while you're waiting, test the reflexes in her knees a coupla times, see how she likes that. Just watch out for her trunk!"

So Gaia was next. Flory felt sick. She didn't know how much time they had, but she knew she couldn't come up with a plan on her own. Folding her phone shut, she reached for her walkie-talkie and buzzed the Position One code—meet at the rear door. Then she radioed Jane, letting her know that Digger was returning to Gaia's stall and to wait until he'd passed her before making her way back. She went to stand and her legs folded beneath her. Holy Mother, she couldn't collapse now. She prayed for strength, listened for Denny's whistling in the distance, then crawled back to the rear door on her hands and knees.

25
TXT MSG

AMY LEANED AGAINST the back wall, her face a grim white. Jane held a hand to her mouth, afraid she was going to be sick. Flory stood between them, replaying the footage of Denny Arcola choking and burning the tiger Jane had been caring for since September. The images were blurry—comprehensible with Flory's moment-by-moment explanation but otherwise difficult to make out—and the sound was a wash of ambient noise punctuated by louder vibrations the girls knew to be the tiger's cries. Despite the poor quality of the video, though, the animal's suffering came through loud and clear to the three girls in the barn.

"I'm going to throw up," Jane mumbled, pushing Amy aside and reaching for the door handle.

Amy grabbed her by the shoulders and turned her around. "Not now, Jane," she whispered fiercely, shaking her. "Look at me . . . *look at me*! Now breathe. Take a deep breath. Good girl. You can throw up, cry, do whatever you need to do later, okay? Right now you need to hold it together for Gaia and help Flory and me think. We need to do something, and we've probably only got a few minutes to come up with a plan. Okay, okay, I know, breathe. Listen, I know we agreed 'observation only' but I couldn't live with myself if we just stood by and let this happen now that we know what's going on." Jane and Flory both nodded. "Okay, good. So . . . I'll throw out ideas, you two can shoot them down, and we'll see what sticks, okay?" Jane and Flory nodded again.

"Okay, so . . . we call in the guards," Amy began.

"And get apprehended for trespassing while D and D cover their tracks," Flory shook her head.

"We use your phone and call the police," Amy tried again.

"They'll get here too late," Jane said, stumbling over her words in her rush to get them out, "and besides, just the sound of someone arriving in the lot will be enough to warn D and D to stop whatever they're doing to the animals. No, we need to catch them in the act!"

"Didn't Flory already do that?" Amy questioned, pointing at the cell phone.

But Flory looked quickly at Jane, understanding. "When we look at this video, we see what happened in graphic detail," she said. "But I think our prior knowledge of the barn and the animals is filling in that detail. Here, look again, imagine this blown up to the size of your TV screen and you're Joe Average watching the news." She replayed a short clip and Jane and Amy saw blurry forms moving through darkness, heard static punctuated by unintelligible shouts. Flory's video was useless to them.

"Well, okay then, so what we need is a better camera," Amy pressed. "I'm closest, so I run home, grab our video camera and run back?"

Flory paused, considering the idea, then shook her head. "Too much time, too many chances to get caught, and then . . . hey, wait . . . a camera!" She slapped her forehead. "We're on a film set, for gosh sake! Amy, couldn't you get us a camera?"

"Yeah, sure," Amy answered ruefully, "a *film* camera. I just don't know how to operate one!"

Jane had been silent throughout this last exchange. The talk of videos and televisions and news and cameras had jogged puzzle pieces loose in her brain. In a flash, the pieces coalesced into a clear memory: she felt his hand on her arm, heard his calm, earnest voice say, *Here's my card . . . I'd like to hear from you, Jane.* She knew his phone number and email address by heart.

"Flory, quick, give me your phone!" she said, practically grabbing the mobile from her friend's hands. As she composed a text message to Noah Stevenson and attached Flory's video, she quickly reminded her friends about the reporter she'd met at the wildlife center.

"Wait, we're pinning this mission on a guy you met

once, three months ago?" Amy asked, incredulous.

Jane looked over at Flory, her confidence momentarily shaken. Flory nodded and said, "Yes, I think we are." Jane hit Send.

Two minutes later, the phone vibrated in Jane's hand. She opened it to find a message on the screen:

```
6 blks awy
w camra
where r u
```

He was there. He'd answered. He was coming. He'd understood. Flooded with a feeling she couldn't name, she hit Reply and typed:

```
barn
cm on foot
guards
will txt wn coast clr
tap 2x back dr
```

As she hit Send, there was a sudden commotion on the far side of the barn and then Gaia's alarm call reverberated through the building. The three girls froze. "It's starting," Jane whispered.

"Go!" Flory commanded, kicking into action. "Both of you, Position Two. I'll wait here for Noah." She held her cell phone in one hand and the positioning device in the other, watching the two outside dots move across the screen. "We'll join you before you know it. Now, go!"

26
RAMPAGE

"So you think you're a star, hey, big girl?" Denny Arcola's voice rang in the rafters. "'The darling of Cedar's Ridge,' is that what they're saying? Well, here's a little lesson for ya: You can never believe what you read in the news!" His bullwhip cracked. The tip opened a gash across Gaia's left back leg. She trumpeted in pain and pressed herself against the far wall of her stall. Denny laughed.

Amy squeezed Jane's hand as she felt her friend begin to shake. Creeping down the corridor, they could make out Denny at the front of Gaia's stall, with Digger just to his left. The wound in Gaia's leg was oozing blood and she was backed into the far corner, facing the animal wranglers. She raised her head, sensing a new presence, but the men were too intent on their task to notice. The girls slipped into the empty stall next to Gaia's just as Denny raised his voice again.

"Just who the hell do you think you are, you dumb beast?" he yelled, taunting her by swinging the whip in his hands. "Think you can do what you want, when you want, don't have to listen to Digger here? Don't have to listen to *me*?" The whip cracked again as it tore a strip of flesh from her left front knee. "From now on, dammit, you'll do as you're told!" The reverberations of her trumpet calls seemed to shake the barn's very foundation.

"She knows we're here," Jane whispered desperately. "She's calling for help . . . for us! Oh, Amy, she must wonder why we don't come! We've got to do something!"

"Who takes care of you?" Denny carried on, oblivious to everything around him. "Who feeds you? Who put this roof over your stupid head?" He lunged at Gaia's head. Terrified, she emptied her bowels in the corner of the stall. "Ahh, geez, look at that . . ." He raised his arms in disgust. "And who has to clean up your stinking mess every damn day? I do! *I do*! And for what? So you can ignore whatever Dig and I tell you to do? I don't think so. You've got a job to do and you're damn well going to do it!"

Jane heard an electric buzzing sound that she recognized from the night she'd first seen Ilsa riding Gaia. Suddenly it hit her—whatever Denny was about to do to Gaia, he'd been doing then. This had been going on for months. Feeling sick again, she raised a hand to her mouth. Amy wrapped an arm around her shoulders and held on tight. Where were Flory and Noah? What was taking them so long?

"Steady, girl," Amy whispered, squeezing her hand. "Your cameraman will be here any minute. Gaia's hanging in there. We can, too."

"We're here," came a small whisper at Jane's ear. She turned to find Flory crouched behind her, mobile devices in hand. And there in the dark, just next to Amy, was Noah Stevenson, a palm-sized digital video camera held steadily at shoulder height, capturing everything. He must have sensed her gaze; without moving the camera, he turned and looked directly into her eyes. He nodded slightly and then turned back to the scene before them.

"Left, up!" Denny shouted, then reached forward and touched the rod he was holding to Gaia's left front foot. The buzzing intensified to a sharp crackling as the rod administered an electric shock. Jane raised her hands to her mouth in horror. Amy looked away. Denny moved counterclockwise, preparing to use the same tactic on each of her feet.

"He's shocking her with a cattle prod," Flory gasped. "Jane, I thought you said Gaia had infections in her feet!"

"She does," Jane choked out through her hands. "She's in pain all the time. This . . . this . . . it's unbearable." Suddenly she rose up from her crouch and lunged toward the stall gate. "I can't watch this! I have to stop him. It's too much for her. It's too much!"

Amy tackled her and pinned her face down in the hay. She wrestled violently, frantic to help her suffering friend. Then strong, gentle hands lifted her from the barn floor and placed her softly down on her knees. Noah leaned in close, taking her hands in his, and said in an intense whisper, "Jane, we'll stop him. Forever. This is the last time Gaia will ever have to go through this. And our footage will put this guy away. Just a few more seconds and we'll have everything we need." He reached past her and took his camera back from Flory, who'd had it trained on Denny and Gaia.

Noah kept the camera rolling as Denny used electric shock to force Gaia to lift each of her feet in turn. Then, red-faced and sweating, the wrangler handed the cattle prod to Digger and said, "Your turn, Dig. Crank it up another notch or two, see if she'll dance for you!" Digger moved forward slowly, obviously not as keen on the task as Denny was. "Whatsa matter there, Dig, you got cold feet?" Denny laughed. "I bet I know how to warm 'em up for ya!" He grabbed the prod out of Digger's hands and began to chase him around Gaia's stall.

Then Noah's cell phone rang.

For a moment, the barn went still and silent as nobody moved. "What the hell . . . ?" Denny panted, holding the cattle prod aloft. It rang again. "Geezalmighty . . . there's someone in here!" Lifting the prod overhead like a war club, Denny let fly with a wordless holler and charged through the stall toward the corridor.

Noah was up and running before the girls had even reacted. "Every station in town will have this footage within half an hour," he called back over his shoulder, "and I'm calling the police as soon as I get to my car! Now get out of here!"

Not realizing the man running through the barn was just one of four witnesses, Denny and Digger tore after him, screaming obscenities. "Flory, the guards!" Amy cried. "They'll catch Noah on the way out!"

"I'll handle them," Flory responded. "But I think Noah's going to need more help than that. Look, D and D are gaining on him!"

"I'm on it!" Amy exclaimed. "Basic diversionary tactics one-oh-one." Crouching, she popped the wheels into her shoes and sped off down the corridor.

"Jane?" Flory called back, glancing down at the positioning device as she ran toward the front door of the barn.

"I'm staying here with Gaia," Jane answered simply. Flory raised a hand in salute and was gone.

Slipping through the front door and closing it behind her, Flory dashed through the frosty night toward the lake, all the while telling herself it wouldn't be so bad, she wouldn't be in the water for long. She dove in head first and let out a long underwater scream. It was bad. Surfacing, she gasped with the cold for several precious seconds before she found her voice and began to call for help. Almost immediately, she saw both guards round the sides of the barn and race toward the lake, their flashlights sweeping icy arcs across the shoreline. "Here!" she cried, waving her arms. "I'm over here!" She heard splashing; they were on their way. Diversion one complete. She hoped Amy was doing as well.

Noah slammed himself through the back door of the barn, hoping to knock down any guards that might be lurking outside. The door swung wide and he stumbled into the darkness. Now to find his way back to the car before those two goons caught up with him. Hearing them shouting and swearing in the corridor behind him, he realized they were closer than he'd thought and picked up his pace. He made it through the back lot and up to the road, all the while hearing the men gaining on him. Now where was his car? He was sure he'd parked it just up to the left. Or was it over to the right? Without warning, someone shoved him hard from behind and he crumpled to the ground, wrapping his body around the camera to protect it as he fell and bracing himself for the next blow. But it never came.

"Hey, you stooges, I'm over here!" His attacker's voice floated close by, but it was moving away from him. "Yoohoo! What's the matter? You scared? Come get me! I'm right over here!" The voice had moved again. A decoy!

It sounded like the redhead. She was stronger than she looked, Noah thought, rubbing his knees ruefully. How on earth had she caught up to them? No matter—she'd bought him time to escape with the incriminating footage and he wasn't going to waste it. Up and running again, he almost barreled into his car in the dark. Fumbling for his keys, he nearly dropped the camera onto the pavement. *Slow down, Stevenson. Take your time. You're okay. Now find your keys and get out of here*!

Amy could hear D and D panting about fifteen feet behind her. They'd given up swearing and were saving their breath for the chase. She grinned into the dark. Thanks to her Wheelys, she hadn't even broken a sweat. She planned to keep them running, further and further from the set, until they were worn out. Then she'd circle back to the barn and wait with Jane and Flory for the police to arrive. Her decoy act had worked like a charm.

A car started about half a mile back. *Good*, she thought, *the cameraman found his wheels.* She turned quickly and saw taillights vanish into the night. Pressing on, it was several minutes before she realized she hadn't heard a peep from either of her pursuers for some time. *I'd better slow down and let them catch up a little.* She waited, scanning the darkness for short and round, tall and thin. *Geez, I was going faster than I thought.* She waited a little longer. And then it dawned on her: they weren't going to catch up. They weren't coming at all. At some point, without her even noticing, they'd turned back.

Letting forth a primal howl that contained in it all her revulsion for what she'd seen that night and all her fear for the friends she'd left behind at the barn, she dug her wheels into the pavement and raced back toward the set.

Jane pressed the warmth of her body to Gaia's side, careful not to touch her feet or any of the open wounds on her legs. Slowly, as she ran a soft hand over her shoulder and whispered quiet words of comfort into her ear, she felt the massive body stop trembling and start to come to calm. Looking up, she saw the scars of old puncture marks on her face and trunk and wondered how she could possibly have missed them before. "I'm so sorry, girl," she whispered sadly. "For everything."

The back door of the barn slammed. Lifting her trunk in alarm, Gaia tried to back up even further, but there was nowhere left to go. Jane spun, looking for something she could use as a weapon, but the men had taken all the weapons with them. She looked up into the elephant's ancient eye, took a deep breath, and let it out slowly. "Not without a fight," she said, and then she moved out in front of Gaia's head. Planting her feet on the floor, she let her arms hang by her sides. And then she waited.

Denny Arcola came sauntering up the corridor, Digger Hutchinson tagging behind him. "You!" he said when he saw her, but there was no surprise in his voice. "So ol' Digger here was right after all. 'We don't need a kid,' he said. 'She'll only get in the way,' he said. Well, fancy that, Digger. You were right about something after all. I shoulda listened to you." He stared at Jane as he spoke, his customary slick grin gone, the harsh lines of his face exposed.

"You curious about what we do here, little girl?" he asked, his dark eyes boring into hers. "Keep showing up after hours when you're not supposed to be here. You must be awful curious! Well, why don't I give you a little lesson. Would you like that? A private lesson. I'll show you all my tricks. I got lotsa tricks. Only problem is, they're secret, so you can't tell anybody. Although I think by the time we're through with your lesson, you won't be spillin' any secrets."

He laughed then, and Jane shuddered involuntarily. "Whatsa matter, not so brave without your friend?" Jane realized he thought there'd only been two of them. The thought gave her some comfort, but it was short lived. Moving with astonishing speed, he reached behind him and spun something into the air. The bullwhip cracked at her feet. She screamed. Gaia trumpeted in response, stamping her front feet on the dirt floor.

Passing the whip to his left hand, Denny reached behind him again and grabbed the cattle prod from Digger's hands. Lunging forward, he clipped Jane's left leg before she could move away. It felt as though her leg had been torn from her body. She doubled over, gasping.

"Denny, no! That setting's too high! It's set for the elephant. Turn it down!" Dimly, Jane could hear Digger's voice but she couldn't make out what he was saying. Get up. She knew she had to get up. Protect Gaia.

"Oh yeah, softie?" Denny sneered. "Let's see how she likes this setting!" He swung his arm over in a high arc and Jane ducked, only to have the prod catch her flat across her low back. She fell to the ground at Gaia's feet. Barely conscious, immobilized by the pain, she watched helplessly through half-closed eyes as Denny reached behind her and laid the prod to Gaia's diseased front feet. She expected to hear the elephant's trumpet, but it didn't come. Then she realized she wasn't hearing anything. Nothing but the sounds of her heart and blood pumping in her ears.

He was trying to get Gaia to trample her, she realized, make it look like an accident. Sure enough, Jane felt the ground tremble beneath her. Gaia was stamping her feet in pain and fury. *Any minute now*, Jane thought, feeling herself on the verge of blacking out. *I forgive you, girl. Please forgive me, too.*

She felt something touch her head and braced herself for the crushing blow. But the touch moved down her neck and over her shoulders, down the length of her torso and legs to her feet, infinitely gentle, a feather. She felt herself roll forward, pushed by some unseen force. And then the force moved under and around her, and she was lifted into the air.

Weightless, she felt herself flying, floating, free from pain. In her mind, Gaia was with her, both of them free, Gaia wild again, roaming the jungles of her home, winking at Jane from behind a succulent green bush. *So we both died*, Jane thought. Denny had finished them both off. Suspended, she gazed up at azure blue sky and down at a jungle jeweled with flowers of every hue and thought to herself that maybe death wasn't so bad.

She landed with a thud on something solid and warm and bristly. A familiar smell filled her nostrils and she struggled to place it. Then the trumpets of angels filled her ears, rousing her from the afterlife and she found herself on Gaia's back looking down at Denny Arcola and Digger Hutchinson. Disoriented and dizzy, she grabbed the tops of Gaia's ears and hung on.

His face contorted with anger, Denny advanced on Gaia with the bullhook in his hand. The sharpened tip gleamed in the threads of moonlight that wove their way through the slats in the barn's roof. Still coming to, Jane thought, *I was supposed to rescue Gaia. But she rescued me. Now it's my turn*! She bent forward, placed her lips to the elephant's ear and whispered, "Okay, girl, this is it. Work with me. I can't do it like your singsong man, but I'll try my best!" Ignoring the pain, she sat up straight and in a clear, sure voice, said, "Gaia, move up!"

With a trumpet call that sounded like no other Jane had ever heard, Gaia charged. Rocketing out of the corner of the stall, she swung her trunk, knocking Denny to the ground, unconscious. Jane felt the sickening crunch of bone beneath her as Gaia stepped on the man's leg, crushing it. Gathering momentum, the elephant broke down the stall gate and rumbled into the corridor, knocking Digger against the wall. He fell to the concrete floor, holding his head and screaming in terror before passing out at the sight of his own blood.

Down the corridor she moved, her bellows echoed by a chorus of cries from the other animals in the barn. As she reached the front doors, they swung wide revealing Flory and Amy and two very frightened guards on the other side. The four jumped clear as the elephant rushed through bearing Jane on her back.

Jane brought her to a halt at the edge of the lake with a single word. She stayed, but she would not be silent. As white moonlight melted across the black lake, every resident of Cedar's Ridge was roused by the sound of an elephant trumpeting the story of her fear and pain, her rescue, her freedom. The sound would echo through the city for weeks to come.

27
PJ'S

PJ's 24-HOUR CAFÉ stood half a block down High Street from Cedars, Jane's dad's restaurant, between the civic square and Shopping City Mall at the top of the Ridge. One of the oldest establishments in the city, PJ's was known for its comfort food—everything on the menu came with a side of mashed potatoes—and like the blinking neon sign promised, it was open all night.

It was just after midnight, and Jane, Amy, and Flory were seated at a booth in the back corner, Flory on her cell phone and the other two tucking into their meals. "This is the best food I've ever eaten," Amy gushed through mouthfuls of veggie shepherd's pie. "I don't mean at PJ's, I mean in my *entire life*." Jane laughed, accidentally spitting some macaroni and cheese across the table, which made her laugh even harder. Amy was right: everything tasted brilliant, everything was funny, her friends were beautiful, PJ's was beautiful, this booth was beautiful. Life was beautiful. And by some miracle, she was still alive.

Police, ambulance, and fire trucks had all arrived within minutes of Gaia's exit through the barn doors. Denny and Digger were taken to hospital under guard and would be placed under arrest as soon as they were conscious and could be read their rights. The police took statements from the girls and Jane was told she'd be called to testify just as soon as the men were fit to stand trial. Medics tended to Jane's injuries and treated Flory for hypothermia as well as provided her with clean, dry clothes. Gaia was rushed back to the zoo for treatment, veterinarians with the SPCA and the Humane Society were brought in to tend to the animals remaining on set, and the film's producers were called to come down and make a statement.

The police were still waiting for the producers when Noah returned to the scene, close to 11:00 p.m. The girls quickly filled him in on all that had happened after he'd gotten away with the footage. Shaking his head and looking directly at Jane, he said, "I can't believe I left you here with those two lunatics. I should have stayed. I could have helped!"

"Did you get the video footage to the TV stations?" Jane asked in response.

He nodded. "Yes, but . . ."

"Then that's all that matters," she answered.

"You're wrong there," he said quietly, but he let the subject drop. "Say, anybody else hungry?" The girls couldn't remember the last time they'd even thought about food. So after numerous calls home and reassurances to parents, Noah had driven them all up to PJ's for a late-night snack. Soon after they placed their orders, Noah received a call saying that David and Lynn Sayers had arrived on set to make their statements. With hasty apologies, he'd rushed away, promising to return as soon as he could.

Now Flory flipped her phone closed and scooped up a spoonful of toasted butternut squash soup. "That was my uncle," she slurped. Her family ran Morales & Monroy, Barristers and Solicitors. "We're being sued."

"What the . . . ?" Amy sputtered.

"Are you serious?" Jane dropped her fork.

"Well, Jane is," Flory answered. "Denny Arcola and Digger Hutchinson are suing the Raincity Zoo and SayWhat? Productions for reckless endangerment, and they're suing Jane for assault with a deadly weapon."

"Gaia?" Jane asked, incredulous.

Flory held up a hand. "Wait, stay calm, there's more. My uncle says Mr. Arcola has a history of doing this and, unfortunately, of winning his cases. But that's because nobody's ever been able to prove that he was actually abusing the animals in the first place. He says that if our evidence is as damning as we say it is, there's no way these lawsuits will hold up in court."

"Amen and pass the bread," Amy said, reaching for the basket. "Jane, quit looking at your watch. He said he'd be back, he'll be back. Eat!"

"I wasn't . . . ," she started. But she realized she was. She looked across the table at Amy and Flory, her eyes shining, and said, "He's cute, isn't he?"

Amy and Flory squealed in unison. "Cute?" Flory breathed. "He's gorgeous! Those blue eyes with that dark hair, the way he smiles at you . . . and very nice jeans, too!"

Amy collapsed in a fit of laughter at that. "I think you mean, 'nice butt,' don't you, Flor? Gosh, what would Mark think, hearing you talk like that about another man? Although I have to agree with her, Jane, his jeans *are* very nice."

"And what would Sanjay . . . or Stuart or Eli or whoever you're dating this week think, hearing you talk like that?" Flory shot back, blushing.

"Hey, easy!" Amy responded, grinning. "We're all allowed to look."

"Well, now would be a good time to look," Jane said, her eyes wide. Amy and Flory turned their heads. PJ's front door swung open and Noah strode in, waving to them from across the restaurant. His coat was caked with mud from his fall in the road, and his jeans were torn at the knee. His face was shadowed with stubble, and there were shadows under his eyes from too many late-night deadlines. But he walked like he knew exactly where he was going, and why, and his eyes were lit with joy as he held aloft a small black rectangle for the girls to see.

Sliding into the booth next to Jane, he said, "We did it." He grinned around at the others. "This segment made the eleven o'clock news locally, *and* it got picked up by CNN. It'll be all anybody's talking about by morning. *We did it!*"

Their server arrived with Noah's pizza and the four of them talked and laughed excitedly as they ate. "So, David and Lynn Sayers clearly didn't have a clue that this was going on," Noah reported, digging into his third slice. "They were horrified. You should have seen their faces. They said Animal Actors Inc. came highly recommended by a colleague in the business, their references all checked out, no red flags when they ran the company name by the industry watchdog group. But apparently that's what this guy does, right? Sets up companies and then dissolves them when he's finished a gig. Covers his tracks, moves on, and then just does it again. But not this time!"

"So what happens to *Shapeshifter*?" Jane asked.

Noah nodded. "They're going to shut the production down temporarily while they figure out what to do. All the animals on set are going into rehabilitative care to be treated for injury and trauma, and David and Lynn are understandably wary about working with live animals again. When I left just now, they were talking about looking into animatronics for the animal scenes. It'll cost them, but I think it's dawning on them that making their money on the backs of animals—under any circumstances—might not be the way to go."

Their server came by and he ordered desserts and coffees all around. "Tonight's on the *Cedar's Ridge City Herald*," he laughed. "Our front-page story tomorrow is going to scoop every other paper in the country!"

"Hey, that's right," Jane broke in, "you still have to write all this up for the paper! When's your deadline?"

"Not till 3:00 a.m.," he said, glancing at his watch. "I've still got two and a half hours!" They all laughed. As they finished their coffees, though, they could feel the adrenaline wearing off and fatigue kicking in.

"Man, am I glad it's the weekend," Amy said wearily.

"Not till Sunday for me." Noah drained his coffee. "But I wouldn't have it any other way. C'mon, let's get you girls home and get me to my computer!"

Flory lived closest so he dropped her off first. Jane and Amy got out of the car to bid her good night. "Thank you, Flor," Jane whispered in her ear as she hugged her. "I . . . I . . ." She stuttered to a stop.

"I know," Flory whispered back.

In the car, Jane turned to Noah. "My house is just past . . . *oww*!" Amy kneed her through the car seat.

"You probably want to drop me off next," Amy interrupted. "I'm just down the hill on the north side of Elfin. As Noah's car pulled into the MacGillivrays' driveway, Amy ruffled the top of Jane's head and hopped out before she could say anything. Waving them away, she waited till Noah turned his head and then she gave Jane the thumbs up and a wink. Jane smothered a laugh and waved back.

Noah and Jane drove back up the hill in silence, both of them tired, both lost in thought about the events of the night. Jane started when he spoke. "Hey ... I was wondering ..." Her heart leapt and suddenly she was wide awake. "... Since it's so late already, what would you think about staying up a little later and"—her heart was pounding now and she noticed she was having trouble breathing—"... co-writing this piece with me?"

28

THERE ALL ALONG

"WHAT?" JANE SPUTTERED, taken completely by surprise.

"Hey, sorry, if you don't want to, that's cool. I just thought . . ." The car sped up. Jane felt herself blushing and was glad for the darkness. "It's just that you've been part of every big story I've ever done, Jane, and you've been on the inside with this thing all along, and I had this idea that maybe . . ."

"Sure!" *What was she saying?* "I'd love to!" *What did he mean, part of every big story he'd ever done?* "What did you mean, part of every big story you've ever done?"

He laughed softly. "That's right, I forgot. I know who you are, but you don't know who I am!"

Jane tensed: "You're not Noah Stevenson?"

"Oh, sorry Jane, that's not what I meant." He reached toward her then quickly pulled his hand back and ran it over his close-cropped hair instead. "Let me start again. Remember when you rescued that oiled bird a year or so ago and blew the whistle about the oil company to a news crew? That was me with the microphone." Jane felt her breath catch. So she *had* seen him before! She strained to remember speaking to him back then, but her memories of that day were of oil and animals and a dam breaking inside of her that released her voice. So it was *his* story that had carried news of the spill across the country!

"And then down at the Plaza of Nations last December, with you three in your bird costumes?" Noah continued. "I was the one who caught the oil executive's confession on tape." Jane remembered: the story had gone national and instigated changes in the country's oil spill response policies.

"There's something else." He sounded hesitant. "This past summer, someone made an anonymous drop-off to the *Herald* late one night. The package contained evidence of a fraud scam run by four of our city councillors. I was working late that night and I found the package, so I stayed all night and wrote the piece that appeared in the paper the next day. I . . . I've always kind of thought maybe you were my secret source. Silly, hey?"

He glanced over at her, a shy smile lighting his face. Her eyes wide, she met his smile with one of her own and shook her head. "I was." He nodded in acknowledgment and then turned his eyes back to the road. Jane's mind reeled. Tonight, having Noah respond to her call, put his job and maybe his life on the line, send Gaia's story out to the world, she'd felt a trust and a sense of partnership she'd only ever experienced before with

Amy and Flory. And here he was telling her he'd been right there all along. Looking back now, she realized she'd felt it. She'd just never known where the feeling came from. Until now.

They were stopped at a light at the southeast end of the Ridge; to the left lay the road home and to the right lay the road to the offices of the *Herald*. The light turned green but Noah stayed where he was. The roads were empty. He was waiting for the green light from her. "Let's write a story together," she said, smiling over at him. Grinning, he swung the car to the right and they headed down the hill.

At 3:00 a.m., their story filed, and high on caffeine and adrenaline, Noah and Jane climbed into his car and headed back up the hill. At the top of the Rays' steep driveway, he stopped the car and turned off his headlights. Soft white flakes dusted the windshield, the start of the season's first snowfall. Noah sat for the longest time, just looking at his hands on the steering wheel, until Jane wondered if he wanted her to walk the rest of the way. She was reaching for the door handle when she felt his hand on her arm. Gentle as his touch was, it burned the way it had back at the wildlife center that day. "I've got a million things I want to say, Jane," he started, "and I can't find the right words for any of them! Some writer, hey?" He laughed.

"That sounds like the story of my life!" Jane responded. *Especially right now,* she thought.

"Maybe if I . . ." He turned toward her, his eyes like stars. "I was . . . would it be all right if I . . ."

She turned to face him then, her eyes meeting his in a silent yes. He reached out and cupped her face with his hands before leaning in to place his lips on hers. Like his hands, his mouth was soft, so soft, but it burned, and she wondered if her touch felt like fire to him, too. She reached up and placed a tentative hand to the back of his neck and he let out a soft gasp. Smiling against his mouth, she welcomed his kiss and he responded, asking, exploring, inviting her to respond to him, too. She felt his arms encircle her, pressing her close, and she leaned against him, tasting his kiss, breathing in his scent, and feeling his body wrap itself around her like a song.

In some quiet corner of her mind, she realized the way she felt in his embrace matched the way she'd felt when he responded to her message last night. When he'd appeared by her side in the barn. When they'd worked together, side by side, on tonight's story. Loving, warm, true.

Love—where had *that* word come from? She pulled away quickly and uttered a nervous laugh. "I'd better get inside."

"Yeah, right, of course," he answered gruffly. "Before your dad comes out here with a flashlight." They both laughed nervously.

"Thank . . ."

"I'll call . . ."

They both started to speak at the same time, and laughed again. "Good night, Jane," he said quietly. His hand like a breath against her neck, he brushed her lips with his. And then she was out of the car, half-running, half-sliding down the snow-slick drive, and he was starting the engine, backing up, driving away, gone.

Inside the house, she leaned against the door, breathing hard and felt Sweet Pea and Minnie wend their way between her legs. "Hey, little ones," she whispered, reaching down to pet them. "I'm home. And I'm going to sleep for the next twenty-four hours straight! Won't you love that? Someone to nap with all . . ."

"Jane, that you?" Her dad's groggy voice called from her parents' bedroom. He was already up to go to the food markets before heading to the restaurant.

"It's just me, Dad," she whispered as she passed their doorway. "Everything's okay. Bit of a . . . situation on the set yesterday."

"Am I going to be reading about my daughter in the news again?" he growled in mock exasperation, poking his head out of the bedroom.

She grinned and nodded. "With my own byline this time!" She kissed him on the cheek and continued down the hall.

She washed up in the bathroom then made her way to her bedroom, kicking off her shoes and sliding into her pajamas. Shutting the light, she threw back the bedcovers and heard something flutter to the floor.

Curiosity overcoming her fatigue, she switched on her bedside lamp and searched until she found the small white rectangle beneath her dresser. A note from her dad? No, it was an envelope. Sitting on the bed now, her heart racing for the hundredth time that night, she turned it over to find her name and address written out in that familiar block hand. It was a letter from Mike MacGillivray.

29

BUTTERFLIES IN THE SNOW

S NOW FELL ON Elfin Lake, covering the thin layer of ice at its surface and painting the woods around it in shades of white and gray. The flakes fell thick and fast, and the few souls who ventured onto the trails soon found they could not rely on familiar landmarks to guide them home. The world was changed.

Jane stepped carefully along the western trail, halting as chickadees, sparrows, and towhees darted out of the underbrush to gather up the seed some passerby had scattered over the snow. She had filled her pockets with peanuts and sunflower seeds before leaving the house, and she emptied them as she went, marking a crooked trail that disappeared almost as quickly as she made it.

Rounding a bend, she came upon an old wooden bench. A short distance off the path, it sat close to the shoreline facing the lake. It was empty. She checked her watch: two minutes to three. Inhaling a deep breath of cold air and snowflakes, she brushed the thick cushion of snow from the seat and sat down to wait.

Staring across the lake to the eastern shore, it was a moment before she realized what was different. It wasn't only the snow that had transformed the landscape that day. The *Shapeshifter* set was gone. Overnight or perhaps that morning—the barn and the animals, the tents, the trailers, the cars—everything, everyone. Gone. She felt a dull ache take hold of her heart, knowing that what the animals had endured that fall would take much longer to erase.

Thoughts of the animals fuelled a sense of discomfort and confusion she couldn't shake. Noah's kiss, Mike's letter, and Gaia's rescue had permeated her dreams and addled her sleep. She'd stayed in bed till noon, Sweet Pea and Minnie her constant companions. But every time she closed her eyes she dreamed, face to face with another fork in the road, the shock and pain of Denny Arcola's cattle prod, piles of white envelopes to open, stacks of newspapers to read. She'd heard the phone ring in her sleep, but when she finally rose to see the number on the display, she found she couldn't bring herself to call back. He'd called twice more before she left the house, and both times, she'd stood still, heart pounding, and let it ring.

She checked her watch again now: almost ten minutes after three. Mike's letter had said three o'clock at the bench on the western shore. Had he missed the ferry because of the snow? Or maybe changed his mind?

Something struck her hard in the back of the head and she screamed out in terror. "*Whoa, whoa, whoa . . . Ray girl! It's me!*" Mike MacGillivray darted around to the front of the bench and crouched in front of her, brushing the snow from her hat and parka. He was dressed in an old blue ski suit and Jane recognized Amy's orange toque and mitts. Tendrils of sandy hair poked out from beneath the toque, and familiar eyes gazed up at her with concern. "That's some set of lungs you've got there, Jane Ray! Hey . . . what's with the tears? What's going on?"

He sat down beside her on the bench and wrapped a strong arm around her shoulders. Hesitating only briefly, Jane leaned into him and poured out the story of the past four months. She hadn't realized how badly she'd needed to talk about it all until this moment.

When she finished, she lay her head on his shoulder and rested, and for a few minutes, there was just the snow falling, their breath in the air, the hush of winter. Then he said, "Flory got those decorations up at the Shack?" She laughed softly, her head bouncing slightly on his shoulder.

"December first, right on schedule," she answered.

"Twinkly lights?" he asked. She nodded against his arm.

"That calendar with the little pop-out doors?" he asked. She nodded again.

"Mistletoe?" She paused before nodding again. "Well, the Shack's only about a half a mile from here. I'm thinking if that mistletoe's close enough for you, it's close enough for me."

Jane felt the now-familiar butterflies take wing inside her as Mike reached his free hand around and tilted her face toward his. Keeping his arm draped across her shoulders, he leaned in and kissed her, his lips soft and warm and sweet. He pulled away too soon, grinning down at her with a look she remembered from childhood, a look that always meant mischief. "I just kissed little Janey Ray!" he exulted, laughing.

She blushed. The last thing she wanted right now was for him to think of her as a kid. She leaned in again, meaning to return his kiss with all the pent up longing of the past year, but he was talking again, looking in the other direction, waving a hand toward the far side of the lake. "I'm staying with Ben tonight," he was saying, "Amy's . . . boyfriend or ex or whatever he is. Man, that girl. Such a flirt. I don't know where she gets it from! Anyway, great guy, he's pulled together a group of my buddies from high school for a poker game tonight, and then I'm back on the early ferry tomorrow. I'm really glad you had time to meet up today, Jane."

Jane felt a sense of panic rising in her as she realized this was it, this was all she was going to get of Mike MacGillivray until who knows when. A week ago, kissing him in the snow on the shore of Elfin Lake would have seemed like a dream come true. But now she wanted more—she wanted him home, back in Cedar's Ridge, she wanted to go out with him. She wanted him to ask her to be his girlfriend.

"Will . . . are you coming back?" she stuttered. "When will I see you again?"

He shrugged, looking down at his hands. "My parents don't want me in their house as long as I'm farming and not going to engineering school," he said, "and I get free room and board at Cortes as long as I'm farming. So . . ." He let her finish the thought on her own. "We're laying pretty low over the next couple of months, of course, but we'll start planting in late February and then I'll be there for the spring and summer. I . . . I can't ask you to wait around for me, Jane." He looked at her then. "Or can I?"

"I graduate in June," she responded, her heart leaping with possibilities as she contemplated the freedom that would mean. Freedom from routine, freedom from the past, freedom to travel, freedom to leave Cedar's Ridge, to go anywhere she wanted.

"You got a date for grad yet?" he asked, grasping both her mittened hands in his. Eyes shining, she shook her head. "Well, then, Miss Ray, would you do me the honor of allowing me to escort you to your high school graduation?" She cried out in delight and threw her arms around him. He laughed, saying, "I take it that's a yes?" and held her tight.

After a couple of minutes, she started to shiver. "Not the best day for sitting around watching the world go by, hey?" he said, standing and holding a hand out to her. She rose slowly, wanting to savor every moment.

"Listen, you'll be busy, I'll be busy. It won't seem so long," he said, leading her back to the trail. He glanced up toward her house, then back across the lake, and then he leaned down and planted a warm kiss on each of her cheeks. "Merry Christmas, Butterfly. I'll see you in June," he promised, lifting his hand in a little wave.

She waved back. "June!" She watched him walk down the trail until he disappeared behind a curtain of snow.

30

AMY CHOOSES A GRAD-DATE

COME JANUARY, JANE, Amy, and Flory returned to their routine of spending their after-school hours at the Shack. "The glamour was nice while it lasted," Amy mused as she stood at her lab table sifting a dark, murky substance through a mesh screen. "I loved telling everybody at school that I was working on a film. 'Call my agent, baby!' Man, I'm going to miss saying that!"

"I'm going to miss the extra money," Flory admitted, looking up from the computer where she'd been typing madly. "Or rather, going shopping with the extra money!" She giggled.

"I miss Gaia," Jane said, glancing out the window to where snow fell from a sky the exact color of the elephant's skin. "But other than that, I'm glad it's over." She looked back to her notepad, wrote another few words, and then glanced up toward the lab, sniffing. "Speaking of Gaia, Ame, the smell in here right now reminds me of her stall . : . *before* I would clean it. What are you, uh, cooking up over there?"

"New project," Amy replied, her voice clipped. "Top secret. No way I'm going to tell you two what I'm up to, not after the way you busted my last two ideas. You'll just have to wait for the unveiling along with the rest of my public."

Jane caught Flory's eye and had to swallow a laugh. "Sure thing, Ame," she responded. "What about you, Flor? You sound like a centipede with tap shoes on that keyboard over there. Or is it top secret, too?"

"Not at all," Flory replied matter-of-factly. "I'm working on my valedictory address, actually. I prefer to get a bit of a head start rather than leave it till the last minute."

Amy stared at her through narrowed eyes. "Flor, the grade twelves don't vote for class valedictorian until May," she said finally, tempering her voice so that she sounded like she was speaking to a two-year-old. "Don't you think you're being a bit . . . presumptuous?" She looked to Jane for support.

But Jane raised her eyebrows and said, "I don't know about you, Ame, but *I'll* be voting for her . . . and I'm on the nomination list myself!"

Amy thought about it for a moment and then shrugged. "Good point," she conceded. "Congratulations, Flory!"

"Thanks, Amy!" Flory smiled and turned back to the computer. "Hey, Jane," she said suddenly, turning around again. "What are *you* working on? You've been crossing out everything you write for the past hour!"

Jane blushed and then smiled. "It's a letter to my grad date!" Flory squealed, Amy mock-groaned, and Jane laughed in delight. Over the holidays, she'd told her two best friends about her encounter with Mike and his request to accompany her to grad. The idea of it still sent her heart racing so she brought it up every chance she got.

"I still can't believe that lame brother of mine didn't come and see *me* while he was here," Amy grumbled. "First Christmas ever that our whole family wasn't all together. My mom and dad just pretended like everything was completely normal, no presents from Mike, one big empty place at the dinner table, 'please pass the tofurkey, dear.' It was nuts."

"Couldn't you have gone to see him?" Flory interjected quietly. "You knew where he was staying." At that, Amy looked even grumpier and pushed the trays and bowls around on her lab table for several awkward seconds.

Finally, she asked, "Did he . . . say anything about Ben when you saw him, Jane?" She kept her gaze trained on her work.

"Sorry, Ame," Jane said softly. "We weren't . . . Ben didn't come up."

Amy nodded, then returned her focus to the crusty brown tray in front of her. The three of them went back to their respective tasks, but Amy soon broke the silence again. "I'm considering asking that Noah Stevenson if he'd be my grad date," she said as she transferred a bowl of lumpy, viscous brown matter onto a waiting screen. "I know he's busy with work and stuff, but he's so cute, and he seemed like a really nice guy. What do you think?"

"Uh, enlighten me, Amy—what's wrong with the hundred and fifty guys in our graduating class?" Jane asked sharply. Flory looked over at her and she felt herself blush. "It's just that all one hundred and fifty of them would die to take Amy Airlie MacGillivray to grad," she hurried to explain. "Why deprive them?"

Amy's eyes went wide. Jane felt her pulse quicken, as though she'd revealed a secret to her friends that she was still keeping from herself. She breathed a sigh of relief when Amy said, "Jane Ray, I like the way you think!" She crossed the Shack floor quickly and stood behind Flory at the computer desk. "Flor, where's my Facebook page? Cool. Now, click on my friends and select all the guys from Cedar's Ridge Senior Secondary. Perfect."

Jane was beginning to worry that Amy must have misunderstood what she'd said. "Ame, what exactly are you doing?"

"Yes, Amy," Flory added, "what are you doing?"

"Keep up, people," Amy barked. "Stay with me here. Now Flory, compose a message."

"To all of them?" Flory squealed.

"All of them," Amy nodded. "You got it? Jane, you with me? Any guy who doesn't have a date by grad night is getting an invitation to go with yours truly!"

Jane's eyes went wide and Flory uttered an appreciative whistle. "So every guy has a date for grad!" she said. "Nobody's left out!"

"And I dance every dance!" Amy exulted. She leaned forward, grabbed the mouse from Flory's hand, and clicked on an icon at the bottom of the screen. Instantly, the Shack filled with the sounds of a top-forty dance tune, blaring at full volume, and she began to bounce through the room. "One at a time, gentlemen, one at a time. There's more than enough of me to go around!"

"You should submit this to the Guinness Book of World Records!" Flory shouted over the music. "The most grad dates ever!"

Jane snorted. "More like Ripley's Believe It or Not!"

Howling with laughter, the three girls danced around the little room until the sky grew dark.

31
WHAT MAKES YOU WILD

ON THE FIRST Thursday of the New Year, Jane arrived at the Urban Wildlife Rescue Center to find Avis waiting for her at the door.

"You're back!" she shrieked and threw herself at her long-absent friend.

"Careful, my hip!" Avis cried, holding her at arm's length, but her face was flushed with the pleasure of Jane's welcome. "And I'm only partially back. I won't be able to work with the animals until this leg's a lot better." She frowned. "George'll be driving me back and forth for a while, and I'll just be stuffing envelopes and licking stamps and such while I'm here. But enough . . . come inside, Jane . . ." She crooked a finger and pulled open the door. "There's a little someone Daniel introduced me to this morning that I'd like you to meet!"

Leading the way into the exam room where Daniel was prepping meds, Avis reached both hands into a kennel and pulled out a small bundle wrapped in a yellow towel. Peering over her shoulder, Jane saw a quivering brown nose poke its way free, accompanied by a prodigious set of black whiskers. And then two brownish-black eyes and two large brown and white ears emerged and she laughed, recognizing the patient from previous weeks. "Bunny!" she cried softly and reached for the bundle.

"*Sylvilagus floridanus alacer*," Daniel corrected with a grin, "the Eastern Cottontail. Native to the central southern United States, introduced into western Washington State around 1930, been expanding its range into BC's Lower Mainland ever since. Loves grasses and clover in summer and bark, buds, and twigs in winter. Rarely seen in care, but phenomenally popular with staff and volunteers alike at UWRC!"

"How's she doing this week, Daniel?" Jane asked, re-sisting the urge to cuddle her like a pet.

Daniel made a noncommittal noise. "'Bout the same," he replied, "which is to say, not great. We should be seeing more improvement by now. We'll give her another session of physiotherapy this morning and see how it goes."

"Goodness, she looks just fine!" Avis interjected. "Whatever happened?"

"We're not sure," Daniel replied. "She was found in the mall parking lot, sitting almost underneath a car. She didn't even try to evade capture. Her hind end seems to be completely paralyzed, so we're thinking impact from being hit by a car or maybe a predator attack or being struck by something. It's interesting—she's very alert and she's eating tons. Her forelimbs are working fine and she'll hold the syringe when you feed her. She doesn't seem to be in any pain. But she can't hop! Her hind limbs aren't working at all."

"*Eugghh*," Jane said as she unwrapped the towel. "Bit of a mess here, bunny!"

Daniel made a sympathetic face. "She had diarrhea in the night—whether from her meds or all the physio or something she ate, I don't know—and of course she couldn't move or feel it so she's soiled herself. I was actually hoping you two would bathe her hind end for me. Just fill the sink with warm water and one of you can hold her while the other washes her gently with a cloth. Once you've got her clean and dry, you can feed her breakfast and then pop her back in her kennel. Evie and I will take care of her physio later this morning. Thanks, ladies. Oh, and Avis, good to have you back!"

He left the exam room and then stuck his head back in: "Almost forgot—Katrina's been taken off the schedule. Evie didn't mention why, but it sounds as though she may not be back. Jane, I know it's a big load on your own, so I've got a couple new work experience students coming next week. If you can just get through today I'll be eternally grateful!" He ducked out of the doorframe and was gone.

Jane and Avis worked side by side, Avis supporting the rabbit so that just the hind end was submerged in the warm water, and Jane working patiently beneath the surface to remove the matting and clumps. The rabbit's long, narrow back feet hung in the water, swaying as Jane worked but otherwise motionless. It was a long process—Jane emptied and refilled the sink three times—and as she worked she realized that with Gaia and now with this rabbit, she was having an experience with a wild animal that few other human beings ever get to have. To be close to it for such a length of time; to hold it and feel its heart beating; to tend to its injuries and even to its most basic bodily needs; to be a link to its survival. She felt a tenderness rise up in her for this animal she held in her hands, a feeling much like what she felt for Sweet Pea and Minnie but also subtly different. There was an awe in it, awe for the animal's willingness to be helped despite its instincts to the contrary. And there was a gratitude in it, for being the one allowed to help. She glanced up, catching sight of an expression on Avis's face that reflected the way she felt, and she smiled at her friend.

With the rabbit cleaned and fed and tucked safely away in her kennel, Avis went to the house to help out in administration and Jane worked quickly through her rounds in the care room and outside. She wondered briefly what had caused Katrina to quit her shift, but at the same time she realized a little guiltily that the care center was a lot less tense with her gone. At a tap on her shoulder, she looked around to find Anthony standing there, hands on hips. "Coffee time, girlfriend—or did you forget? *Some*body's been buzzing me on the admin line!"

Jane laughed. "I wonder who that could be! I totally forgot, Anthony, it's been so long! Woohoo—coffee and cookies with Avis!" She scrubbed down in the exam room and headed out through the garden, anxious to fill her friend in on all that had happened since they'd last spoken.

Fifteen minutes later, still gossiping as they washed up the dishes, Jane heard a light tap at the basement door. Peeking through the window, she was surprised to see Amy standing outside. "What are you doing here?" she asked as she ushered her friend in from out of the cold. "Shouldn't you be in chemistry?"

"A fine welcome," Amy snorted as she pushed past Jane and grabbed the last gingersnap from the plate. "Hey there, Mrs. Morton! Good to see you up and about! That hip of yours going to let you boogie with us on grad night? Did Jane tell you about my grad date?"

"Indeed she did," Avis chuckled. "A stroke of brilliance, I must say. It's lovely to see you, Amy. Please remember me to Flory, would you? Jane, I'll meet you back at the care center. I can't resist paying another visit to that little rabbit!" Jane watched her step gingerly over the doorsill and hobble away up the path.

Closing the door and glancing around, Amy turned to Jane and said, "I need your help, animal lady."

"Of course!" Jane replied, mystified. "What's up?"

Amy lowered her voice to a whisper: "I need feces. As much as you can get away with. Any kind. Actually, the . . . thicker and lumpier the better. If you could just gather up whatever you can get your hands on each Thursday and bring it to the Shack after school, I'd really appreciate it. Thanks, Jane, you're awesome!"

"Wait a minute, *what*?" Jane was shaking her head. "What on earth do you need feces for? And what am I supposed to do with a containerful between noon and three o'clock—just store it in my locker? Amy, listen, first of all, I don't even think it's legal. And besides, these animals are sick! The threat of zoonotic diseases is bad enough, but with these guys, their poop is practically a lethal weapon!"

Amy frowned and folded her arms. "So is that your final answer?" she asked. "You won't help me?"

"Help you *what*?" Jane cried, exasperated.

"With my entrepreneurial venture," Amy whined, thoroughly frustrated now. "My secret project. I need a free supply of raw materials, and, well, things with Buster aren't working out so well. I don't know if it's something he's eating, but . . ."

"You mean that experiment the other day was your dog's . . . ? *Waaait* a minute," Jane said, a memory floating to the surface. "This wouldn't have anything to do with Mrs. Harbinsale's 'elephant dung stationery,' would it?"

"Maybe," Amy pouted.

Jane groaned. "Amy, elephants are herbivores, you goofball!"

"Yeah, and I'm a vegetarian," Amy shot back. "What's your point?"

"My point is, it's the grasses and leaves they eat that give the paper its texture. Not to mention its neutral smell! Ame, for the kind of stationery you're talking about, you need elephant dung. Lots of it. And for that you need elephants. Lots of them. Which means you need to go far, far away!"

Amy grimaced at her. "Okay, okay, I can take a hint." She sighed. "Back to the drawing board, I guess."

Jane gave her a sympathetic smile. "Come on, I'll walk you to the trail head."

Jane had her hand on the care center door handle when she heard shouts inside. Was that Avis's voice? It couldn't be. She pulled open the door to find Anthony standing behind the reception desk facing into the exam room, his hands on his heart. The exam room door was propped open and Jane heard, "You can't do this, Daniel. She's perfectly fine!" It *was* Avis! The elderly woman was standing with her back to the door, pointing an accusing finger at the senior rehabilitator.

"She's a wild rabbit, Avis," came Daniel's patient

reply, "and she can't hop. She can't move, she can't forage for food, she can't escape from predators. I know deep down you must understand."

"She eats, Daniel!" Avis cried, her voice trembling. "She's bright and alert and her appetite is tremendous. She's full of life!"

Daniel nodded. "That may be so, but she's been here for almost three weeks and hasn't regained any mobility in her hind end. There's no positive prognosis at this point. She's paralyzed, Avis. She isn't going to get better. I've talked it over with Evie and we've decided she isn't fit to be released to the wild."

"I'll take her home!" Avis cried. "I'll look after her. She deserves to have a life!"

"Avis," Daniel responded calmly, although Jane could see he was struggling with the decision himself. "She's a *wild* animal. She deserves to have the life she was born to! She'd be living a shadow of a life, kept in a cage in your home, in *anyone's* home. She was born for the wild, born to run free in the woods and be with her own kind, to mate and procreate and to live out her life by her instincts and by the calls of the Earth." Here, he took a deep breath and brought his hands together. "She can't do that any more, and rather than let her die as prey because she's paralyzed, I'm making the decision to end her life painlessly and humanely. Without suffering. I'm sorry, Avis. You don't have to agree, but I have to ask you to respect my decision." He caught sight of Jane standing behind Anthony. "Jane would you . . . take Avis for some fresh air in the garden?"

Stepping into the exam room, Jane reached her arms around Avis's shaking shoulders and led her friend out of the care center. Walking her slowly to the bench beneath the old apple tree in the garden, she cleared a place for her in the snow and then sat down beside her. Avis buried her face in her hands and sobbed.

Jane waited, her hand resting softly on Avis's back, wishing she knew what to say or do. "Just because she can't walk properly is no reason she should have to die!" Avis whispered through her hands.

Jane wrapped her arms around her friend and held her. She could feel her thin bones through her winter jacket, the shuddering of her breath as she tried to rein in her sobs. She expected this to feel strange, a teenager trying to comfort an old woman, but instead it felt natural, even familiar. And she realized she recognized the feeling as the same one she'd felt holding the rabbit in her hands. Placing herself between Gaia and the wranglers. Feeling Flory take her hand. Knowing Amy had her back.

"What makes her wild aren't the same things that make you wild, Avis," she said, searching for the right words. "She needs her legs and her natural habitat to be free to be who she is. But young or old, injured or well, you're always you. And you're always wild. And free."

Avis leaned into Jane's embrace and allowed herself to be held. "I love you, Avis," Jane whispered.

"I love you, too, Missy. I love you, too."

32

THE SUITS

TIMO LAUSANNE WATCHED from the doorway of the enclosure as the SPCA's veterinarian made a thorough re-examination of Gaia and reported his findings to Sen Chanta. The vet had come in December immediately upon Gaia's return from the *Shapeshifter* set and assessed all of the acute injuries that had been added to her chronic conditions—from flesh wounds to burns to untreated infections. "Osteomyelitis," he'd pronounced. Advanced deterioration of the bones in her front feet due to long-term untreated infections. Arthritis in the joints of all four feet. Outside nails on all feet damaged and ulcerated. Those on her left front foot bruised, splitting open, and separating from the foot. Bruised, abscessed, and rotting foot pads. Poor circulation due to lack of movement and exercise, and kidney dysfunction due to her body's struggle to rid itself of the infections. Within days of returning to the zoo, her stereotypical head bobbing and weaving had begun again, the stress and inertia of being back in this environment already taking its toll.

"Her condition is critical," the vet had warned Timo as he'd cleaned and treated her wounds, trimmed her nails and foot pads, and administered antibiotics. She had stood patiently throughout, Sen Chanta at her side, as if she understood that the pain of the treatments was different from the pain she'd experienced just days before. "I've left strict instructions with Sen here for her care over the next while and I'll return in four-week intervals to check on her. Of course, if you're not seeing improvements, don't hesitate to call."

Timo had paid the vet's bills, ordered the medications he'd prescribed, bought the recommended foods for the changes to Gaia's diet. And he would pay the bill again today. But he was done paying bills for this elephant. She was a mess, too old for the business, too decrepit to be of use to anyone. She'd been a liability to him for some time, and he'd been more generous than most zoo operators would have been, keeping her on this long. But this morning's phone call had made up his mind for him: it was time to cut his losses and let her go.

He'd known he was in for it when his secretary had announced, "Pimentel & Pomeroy for you, Mr. Lausanne. Shall I put them through?" He nodded wearily. Pim-Pom, he called them behind their backs. His lawyers. No matter how many times they'd saved his hide, he was never glad to hear from them. It was never good news.

"Mr. Pimentel, Mr. Pomeroy! To what do I owe the pleasure today?" It was his standard greeting. The two of them laughed their standard response over their speakerphone, mincing giggles that were indistinguishable from one another. In fact, Timo thought, Pim and Pom were indistinguishable from one another. Small, neat, fussy men in matching hand-tailored Hong Kong suits. Expensive ties, manicured nails, gleaming teeth, cufflinks.

"You're being sued," they answered in unison. He detected a hint of glee in their response. Understandably. His misfortune was their livelihood.

"Ah," he replied, unconsciously gripping the edge of his desk. "I see. And who is it this time, pray tell?" In his mind, he listed off the usual animal rights activists, scouring his memory for something he might have done to tick one of them off.

Pim-Pom cleared its throat, a sign to Timo that the joking was over, that what was to follow might just be worthy of his concern. "A Mr. Dennis Arcola," the lawyers answered. "For reckless endangerment and assault resulting in grave bodily injury."

"Are you talking about that lunatic that roughed up my elephant?" Timo exclaimed, astonished. "The list of charges against him is longer than her trunk! What is *he* doing suing *me*?"

"Indeed," came the reply. "It seems Mr. Arcola has engaged one of the better personal injury lawyers in the country, and it seems as well that they may have a case."

"What *case*?" Timo spat, angry now.

"Is it true"—Pim-Pom answered his question with one of their own, a habit that infuriated him—"that you did not disclose the full extent of Gaia's medical conditions before negotiating the rental and proposed sale of said elephant to Mr. Arcola's company?"

"Wait a minute, just who's on trial here?" Timo cried. "You're *my* lawyers, dammit! Why, you almost sound as though you're taking his side! My god, you saw the footage just like I did. The man was vicious. Prior conditions or no, any animal would have behaved as she did. She was acting in self defense . . . or does that not apply to animals?"

"It may not, Timo," Pim-Pom conceded. "Firstly, the charges against Mr. Arcola are for what he did to his employee, not what he did to your elephant. The animal cruelty laws in this country have no teeth and everybody knows it. And secondly, Mr. Arcola and his lawyer have approached the federal wildlife ministry claiming Gaia is violent and poses a threat to the population at large. They are petitioning to have her destroyed."

By the time Timo hung up the phone, he had a headache and his ulcer was back. Have her destroyed, they'd said. After all these years, after all he'd invested. To lose the film revenue *and* the sale to Animal Actors Inc. and wind up with nothing . . . and now a costly lawsuit on top of it all. He grabbed his cell phone from his belt and speed-dialed Marcozi's number. Maybe his broker's rich client still wanted something for his study. If they could make it look like it was all arranged before this lawsuit business, then at least he could put a few dollars in the coffers to show for all this. *Come on, Marcozi, pick up. Dammit.* He left a voicemail, asked his secretary to hold his calls for the afternoon, and retreated into town for a long lunch.

Now, as he watched Sen Chanta talk to Gaia, her trunk wrapped around him and his hands under her chin, he felt an ache that he didn't think was his ulcer and wondered how in hell it had all come down to this. Why him? Why now? But there was no point asking such questions, no time for them. The conversation he'd been avoiding couldn't wait any longer.

"Sen," he called quietly from the doorway, feeling as though he was intruding. The caretaker waved a hand to show he'd heard him. "When you have a moment this afternoon, could I see you in my office? There's something I need to tell you."

33
JANE RECEIVES A VISITOR

"Your attention please . . . ," the PA system blared, interrupting the last few minutes of Mr. Zachary's creative writing class. "Would Jane Ray please report to the office after the three o'clock bell? Jane Ray to the office, please. Thank you."

Blushing, Jane closed her notebook and packed up her pencil case, knowing she wouldn't be able to concentrate any longer. With a nod from Mr. Zachary, she shouldered her bag and left the room. Hurrying down the long hallway, she wondered what on earth had happened to get her in trouble with the principal. Some half-baked scheme of Amy's, no doubt. She shook her head, laughing to herself.

But when she arrived at the office, there was Mrs. Dixon, the secretary, perched behind the counter, a suspicious look on her face as she eyed a stranger standing in the waiting area. At the sound of Jane's footsteps, he turned, and Jane felt a flicker of recognition stir in her, though she did not know the man. Small, dark, and wiry, he had a kind face that was lined with worry and darkened by sleepless nights. Dressed simply in a black woolen coat and a brown twill shirt and pants, he had a quiet, calm presence that Jane found immediately comforting, and strangely familiar.

"Jane," Mrs. Dixon took her aside and spoke in a hushed tone, "this Mr. Chanta says he's a friend of yours. His story seemed rather unlikely, but I agreed to check with you before I sent him away. Do you know him?"

Jane turned back to face the stranger and was about to shake her head when he said, "Hello, Jane! It is a great pleasure to see you again!" Though he smiled, his eyes held a look of desperate pleading. But it was his voice that Jane took notice of, a singsong cadence that sparked another flash of recognition.

As if responding to a call, shards of memories within her began to rise to the surface: A sheaf of papers covered in a small, round cursive, the words "Sen Chanta" at the bottom of each page. This man's name. The voice on the tapes, the voice in the barn, the one Gaia had responded to, this man's voice. The dark head in the hay, the man running away through the woods, this man. The man in the picture in her old family photo album—this same man. This was Gaia's caretaker!

"I know him," she said definitively to Mrs. Dixon. Then she stepped forward and offered Sen Chanta her hand. "I'm so glad to see you again!" The look of relief on his face was so acute Jane thought he might cry.

"Is there somewhere we might speak?" he asked her. "I would not ask, I would not have come, except that it is urgent, and I do not know what to do."

Jane felt an anxiety rising in her that she thought she'd left behind in December. "Is it Gaia?" she asked. He nodded. "Come with me," she said, and strode out of the school.

Detouring past the Shack, she scribbled a note for Amy and Flory to let them know where she was going and that she'd see them later. Then she led Sen Chanta through the trails to the bench on the western shore of Elfin Lake. It was early March and already the trees and salmonberry bushes were budding. Bright yellow skunk cabbages dotted the little creeks running into the lake, and the trails, so recently treacherous with snow and ice, were now slippery with mud. Along with the *caahs* of crows in the trees and the insistent tapping of a woodpecker somewhere nearby, Jane spotted a killdeer as it darted out from the underbrush and across the trail and caught the brilliant flash of a violet-green swallow as it swooped through the air and into one of the lakeside nest boxes. From the southern horizon came the telltale V-formation of a flock of Canada geese winging their way toward the lake. Cedar's Ridge still shivered under winter's spell, but spring was on its way.

Sen wasted no time. "If something is not done, Gaia will be dead by summer."

Stunned, Jane stared at him, waiting for an explanation. Haltingly, he told her what he understood of the situation at the Raincity Zoo, of the lawsuit against his boss and the investigation that was underway by the wildlife ministry of the federal government. If they agreed with the charges, he explained, Gaia would be destroyed. It could happen as early as June.

Jane began to protest but quickly realized she was arguing with the wrong person. Sen obviously found the situation as outrageous as she did. "Wait," he said darkly. "There is more. My boss is angry that he has lost so much money on Gaia. She is expensive now, with all her health problems, but she does not bring many visitors to the zoo any more, and the money he hoped to make from the film has slipped from his grasp. He cannot sell her—no other zoo would take an old elephant who is sick and cannot breed—and now the government may destroy her. He is desperate." Here Sen paused and Jane felt a dread at what was to come.

"There are places," he began, "private places for people who wish to hunt big game and hang trophies on their walls. People who are too lazy or cowardly or who don't have enough money to travel to Africa or Asia for their sport. Animals like Gaia . . . ," Sen paused again, gathering strength for what he had to say, "animals who are old or sick or injured and who no longer provide their zoos with a profit are sometimes sold to these places. Big wooded areas with fences all around. The 'hunters' are outfitted in safari gear and driven through these 'parks' with their rifles in hand until they get a 'kill.'" His voice dropped to a hoarse whisper. "People pay a great deal of money to play this sport. My boss would like to get his hands on some of that money."

Aghast, Jane stared across the lake to the former site of the *Shapeshifter* set. What had she done? In rescuing Gaia from months of abuse, she had sentenced her to death. Probably a violent one. And now this man who loved Gaia had come to her looking for a solution, another rescue. What could she do? What could anyone do now?

His voice broke in on her thoughts: "Her life began in violence, and I have thought all these years that as long as I stayed close, I could prevent it from ending the same way. All I have ever wanted for her is peace. But it seems there is no peace for elephants in this world."

Because she had no answers, because she had nothing else to offer this man who had sought her out as his last resort, Jane leaned forward and said, "Tell me about Gaia."

34

A LAND LIKE THIS ONE

I WAS BORN TO *the Phnong people of Cambodia forty-two years ago this July. My family were mahouts—elephant trainers—and I grew up in a small village north of Kâmpóng Chhnāng where the Mekong River meets our great lake, the Tonlé Sap. It is a land much like this one, still lush and green and wild, with monsoons from May to November that make your greatest rains here look like spring showers. My father and my uncles were mahouts, employed with their elephants to haul teak wood logs out of the forest, and I knew that I, too, would one day join them in their work. This pleased me because from my first memory, I loved elephants.*

The first sounds I recall are their trumpet calls, the first smell the sweet grassy musk of their skin. As a child, I loved to go to the camp with my father in the early mornings, when all of them were lined up, waiting to be harnessed and led into the forest. That's when I would talk to them. I did not realize at first that what I was doing was anything special. In my mind, I told stories about my days at home and the games I played by myself or with my friends, and I could sense them listening. When I was done, they would tell me of their long days in the forest, of their feats of strength and of their aches and fatigue. They also told me of remembered ones, ones left behind, but I did not understand these stories, for I had not yet experienced such loss. My uncles soon noticed that the elephants followed me and listened to me, did the things I asked of them. They began to speak of my "gift," and at first, I was proud, believing that indeed I had an extraordinary talent. I know now that the gift was not mine, but the elephants' gift to me.

When I turned twelve, my father deemed that I was ready to begin work, and that I should have an elephant of my own. After much discussion and planning with the other mahouts, it was decided that I would join them on their next catch. Like a child, I asked why they did not simply let one of the female elephants produce a baby for me. They laughed and said being pregnant would keep her off the job for too long.

The morning of the catch, my mother gave me the garb of a mahout to wear—a smaller version of my father's clothes—and a sack of food, and said a prayer for my safety. At the camp, we were met by my father's two eldest brothers, a guide, and a foreigner whom my uncle explained had promised to pay them handsomely to find him an elephant to take home with him. My uncles rode the massive bull, Boon Tam, the guide and the foreigner rode the guide's elephant, named Sitheng, and my father and I rode together on one of my favorites in the camp, little Sema. As we wound our way into the forest, my father leaned forward and said to me, "Today, Sen, you will become a man."

Though at one time there were thousands of elephants in Cambodia, now there are just a few hundred, and even then, at the time of the catch, elephant families were sparse in the forests and always on the move. It took our guide until midday to pick up a recent trail, and then it was several hours more before we saw them, resting in the shade half a mile or so down the riverbank. My uncles directed us to wait, and then set off toward the family on Boon Tam.

There were seven of them: five adult females and two young ones. The smallest, a baby of about four years, was nursing from its mother while the other youngster, a sibling stood protectively close. I was overjoyed to see a whole family together like this, and though I did not realize it at the time, part of my joy lay in the sight of these creatures wild, unbounded by ropes and unanswerable to human commands. My father leaned forward again, pointing at the baby, and said, "That one is yours, Sen!"

I did not understand what he meant. My mind still did not connect what I saw in front of me with the animals back at the camp. It never occurred to me that the elephants I knew and talked to every day had once been free like this.

My eldest uncle shouted a command and Boon Tam began to charge. I saw the little group of females tense, then heard the matriarch utter a low rumble. The sound spurred all seven of them to action, and soon they were running into the thick of the woods. Boon Tam charged past the spot where they had entered the forest, then doubled back, heading them off. They turned, leaving the confusion of the woods for the openness of the river-bank. Feeling the ground beneath me tremble and still too innocent to be afraid, I watched in awe as eight elephants thundered toward me, Boon Tam gaining on the little family.

I saw something fly from my uncle's hand, out over Boon Tam's head, and suddenly the baby, my baby, lay bawling in the mud. The other six females turned at the sound and trumpeted in answer. Cautiously, they edged back toward Boon Tam and the baby, seeking a way to free the little one from her tether. But my uncles directed Boon Tam to hold them off. Soon, Boon Tam was in the middle, us and the baby on one side and the rest of the wild females on his other side. As the females crowded him, seeking a way past, my uncles let fly another lasso and captured the second young one. The foreigner's elephant. Slowly, they edged Boon Tam toward us, bringing the two small elephants with them. The females remained where they were, thwarted, trumpeting their anguish. I felt their cries in my body as though they were my own.

Suddenly my father shouted, and then the guide and the foreigner were shouting, their cries of fear mingling with those of the elephants, and I looked up to see one of the females skirting around Boon Tam and charging our group. It was my baby's mother, the one I had seen nursing her. It happened so fast. My uncles could do nothing; they were holding on to the ropes with all their might. My father tried to turn Sema around to make her run, but she, and Sitheng, too, had joined their voices to those of the wild females. In moments we would all be smashed to pieces.

A loud crack split the air. The charging mother faltered but then kept coming. I looked around to see what had caused the noise when it came again. Again, the mother stumbled and slowed, but she did not stop. She was almost upon us. Again the sound came, and again. My eyes were on the mother elephant as she stumbled for the last time and fell still, less than twenty feet away. All of us watched her die, the elephants, too. The baby cried itself hoarse. And then I saw the foreigner wipe his gun and put it away. "We'll come back later for her head," he said.

No one spoke as we corralled the two small captives into the middle of our group and led them back to camp. I was learning what it meant to be a man—silent, strong, deadly—and I wished with all my heart that I might remain a child. I knew that this baby elephant would be mine to train and to work with from this day forward, and that thought was my one hope, but it, too, turned to ash.

That night, after the foreigner left with his baby and his trophy, my uncles put my baby into a crush, a pen hardly bigger than she was. The next morning, when I arrived at camp to begin my training, the men were beating her with sticks and ropes. She was thrashing frantically against the rails of the crush. I cried out and ran to her but my uncles held me back. This is the custom, they said. She must be made to submit, to obey commands, to take riders on her back. I learned that she had been kept awake all night without food or drink, and would be for days. I was required to listen as they commanded her to lift her feet, and to watch as they stabbed her feet with nail-tipped spears when she did not respond as they wanted.

For a month, I stood by as she endured this, sometimes even taking part in the "training." And then I stole her. The night before, I packed a bag of food for myself and a bag of supplies—the tools of my trade and some herbs and salves—and then we took to the woods. In the beginning we simply ran, with no thought of where we would go or what would become of us. I was sad to leave my family at first, but at twelve, I saw what I was doing as a great adventure. I did not realize that I would never see them again.

The baby and I developed a routine in which we bathed in the river and then I tended to her cuts and wounds. We traveled mostly in the early mornings and late evenings and rested during the heat of the day. I did my best to care for her feet, but I know now that those early injuries set the stage for the problems that have plagued her all of her life.

Then one day I heard her voice. On the day of the catch, and for the month afterward, it seemed my "gift" had disappeared. But perhaps she had begun to heal and recover, had learned to trust me a little. Perhaps I had begun to forgive myself. And so I heard her ask me who I was, what had become of her family, where we had been and where we were going. I did my best to answer her honestly, but for her last question, I had no answer. I told her simply that wherever we went, whatever may happen, I would always be with her and I would keep her safe.

For the next two years, we worked—anywhere we could find a job that would let us be together and provide enough for food and safe shelter. Using only my gift and a few gentle touches, I taught her to respond to commands and to learn skills that would put us in demand wherever we happened to be. She was playful and curious, and learned quickly. We hauled teak wood from the forest at a logging camp. We transported goods between remote villages. We plowed fields and carried the harvests to the trains. When I learned the other mahouts drugged their elephants to make them work longer and wanted me to do the same, we left and worked at a resort for a time, providing rides to wealthy tourists.

Eventually, we came to a city, where we lived on the streets, again offering rides to anyone with a few coins to spare. It was a rough life, and the little one was becoming ill from breathing exhaust from the cars, drinking dirty water, eating garbage out of ditches. To make matters worse, the government was demanding that all street elephants have licenses—expensive licenses. I was torn about what to do next, when one day, a young tourist from America said to me, "You could make a fortune doing this back where I come from!"

I asked him if it was safe where he came from and he answered yes. Was it as beautiful as my country? More so, he said. It was the greatest country in the world. Why, there were even places where elephants like mine had their own homes and got fed every day and people came to visit, especially children. The zoo, he said. It sounded to me like a magical place.

So we went back to the tourist resort for another year and I saved my money. With the help of the resort's owner, I sent letters to several zoos in America, and also in this country. I received only one reply, from the Raincity Zoo here in Vancouver. They had been looking for a baby elephant, would be pleased to arrange the necessary permits and to pay for her passage. I did not tell them I was coming as well, for fear they would say no. But I had promised my girl I would not leave her.

The crossing by ship was terrifying, for me, yes, but even more for her. She was kept below in the hold, alone with the cargo, and we encountered several storms on our way. She became ill and would not eat, and she fell, injuring her left front foot. With no veterinarian on board, I was left on my own to tend to her as best I could.

We were greeted in port by the zoo's owner, then a Mr. Liam Luffin. I had thought to sneak a ride back to the zoo in his automobile, but he spotted me and asked just what did I think I was doing. He was a kindly man, though, and when I told him my story, he offered me a job, said he needed someone who could teach a baby elephant how to give rides to the kiddies.

He named her Gaia. At first, the zoo seemed like the magical place I had imagined it would be. Safe, with fresh food and clean water, and shelter at night. But soon I learned that Gaia could not leave her small enclosure, could not forage for her own food, had nothing around her to engage her bright mind, and would rarely have company of her own kind. That when she was not giving rides to children, she would be standing still on concrete for hours and days and weeks. For years.

Then one day I overheard the name of the foreigner who had come with us on the catch and returned to America with Gaia's sister. He owned a circus—another new word for me—somewhere in the United States. I thought perhaps life at a circus would be a better fate for an elephant than the one I had chosen for Gaia. Hiding my actions from Mr. Luffin, I wrote a letter to the circus, explaining who I was and asking if there was room for another elephant and trainer.

A few weeks later, Mr. Luffin appeared in Gaia's enclosure, a reply letter in his hand. Thoughtlessly, I had used the zoo's return address on my letter. "This is how you repay my kindness, Chanta?" he asked me sadly. I felt ashamed. We opened the letter together and read the ringmaster's reply. Gaia's sister had indeed been part of his act for several years, but just the month before, her rider had run away from the circus, taking the elephant with her. No trace of either the young woman or the elephant had been found. So there was in fact an opening if I was interested in coming to Illinois.

"What do you know about circuses, Sen?" Mr. Luffin asked me. "Nothing," I answered him. And so he told me. About the training methods and the confinement and the traveling and the tricks. "It's up to you," he said to me, walking away. "I just thought you should know what you were getting into."

The circus sounded worse than anything I had seen so far. I couldn't take Gaia there. But returning to Asia was not an option either. Even if she could have survived another ocean crossing, where would we have gone that was safe from mining and hunting and poaching? And so, in the end, we stayed.

I believe my bright and curious baby girl is still in there somewhere, but with her constant head-bobbing and her ceaseless boredom, it is difficult to be sure. We still have our gift, but she no longer has much she cares to tell me, and my own life changes so little from year *to year that I haven't many stories for her, either. I have kept my promise to stay with her and, up until recently, I have kept her safe. I have always thought that we would live out our lives together, Gaia and I. We are both just middle-aged. But now . . . now death seems to face her at every turn. And she has hardly lived.*

35

THE RUNAWAY

*S*HE HAS HARDLY *lived.* Sen Chanta's words echoed in Jane's head as she made her way back along the lake trails to the Shack. What did it mean to save an animal's life? Was it enough that it simply continued to exist? Or was there more to life than that? If an animal couldn't live out her life by her instincts, moving where she wished, mating as she chose, facing the risks of the wild but reveling in its freedoms as well, was she truly alive? Had she saved Gaia's life that December night, or had she merely prolonged a miserable existence? And if she hadn't saved her, not truly . . . could she still?

Pausing with her hand on the doorknob, Jane heard peals of laughter emanating from inside the Shack. Peering through the window, she saw Flory spinning around the little room, a pale periwinkle-blue dress held up to her petite frame. Sleeveless, with a low V-neck, it had an empire waist and a flowing, knee-length skirt. In one hand dangled a pair of silver shoes and a tiny silver bag to match. Her graduation dress. It was perfect.

And there was Amy, up on her lab-table-turned-catwalk, sheathed in a gleaming teal-green sari dress, the scoop-neck, cap-sleeve cropped top baring her slim waist and accentuating her curves, the floor-length wrap skirt shimmering like a mermaid's tail over jeweled gold sandals. Jane had completely forgotten that today was the day they'd agreed to show each other their grad outfits and plan all the finishing touches—makeup, hair styles, nail polish, accessories. Her dress—a vintage "Marilyn Monroe over the subway grate" that she'd found at Legends in Vancouver—was at home hanging in her closet. She was considering running home to get it when Flory spotted her through the window. The Shack door swung wide and her friends' laughter burst out into the cool afternoon air, rolling over Jane like a balm. Anything was possible with friends like these, she thought. Even the impossible.

"Close that door, I'm cold!" Amy ordered from atop her runway.

"That's because you're practically naked!" Jane laughed. "Wooooo, baby! The boys of Cedar's Ridge Senior Secondary won't know what hit them! And you look stunning, Flor. Like a princess or a little pixie!" Her friends beamed.

"You've got it going on yourself with the corduroy and the rubber boots there, Ms. Ray," Amy replied as she clambered down from the lab table and changed back into her jeans. "Totally unique. I didn't see that look in any of the magazines this year." Jane giggled and struck a provocative pose.

"What happened, Jane?" Flory asked as she placed her outfit in a garment bag and hung it over the door. "We found your note but it didn't make a lot of sense. Who's Sen Chanta?"

Slowly, then gathering speed as her tale took shape, Jane told her friends about meeting Gaia's caretaker and relayed all that he had told her of the elephant's history. She ended by sharing with them the thoughts that had circled through her mind as she'd walked back to the Shack.

Several moments passed in silence. Then Amy said, "Well, so it sounds like we're only half done, right?"

Flory nodded. "We still have an elephant to rescue," she said soberly. She sat down at the computer. "What are we waiting for? Let's get to work!" Mutely, Jane hugged both her friends hard, then had to rummage in her bag for a ratty tissue to blow her nose.

"So here's what I think," Amy started, setting a chair next to Flory at the computer station. "We take up a collection at school, steal Gaia from the zoo, and ship her back to Cambodia to be released into the wild. Hey? Right? Sometimes the first ideas are the best ones, ladies. Don't be too hard on yourselves if you can't top it."

But Jane was shaking her head as she dragged another chair over to the computer. "Aside from the jail time the theft would probably earn us, Ame, sending

Gaia back to Cambodia is a no-go for a whole bunch of reasons. Mahouts in Cambodia are still wild-catching elephants, farmers are still hunting them, tuskers are still poaching them. Honestly, I don't know if there are any wild places left that are safe for elephants!"

Flory was typing madly as Jane spoke. "Okay, so no wild Cambodia. But look, here's a website for the Phnom Tamao Rescue Center in Phnom Penh. A sanctuary in her home country, Jane!"

A sanctuary for rescued elephants. It had never occurred to Jane that such a place might exist. But would it be that different from a zoo? "Are there photos?" she asked eagerly. "What's it like?" Flory scrolled and clicked as Jane and Amy looked on in amazement. The sanctuary was set in the jungle with shelters for the elephants and acres of lush space for them to roam and forage. They could enjoy the company of the other elephants or wander off on their own, and specially trained mahouts kept them company, fed them and gave them their baths, and tended to any old injuries they might have. "Painting lessons?" Jane squealed, laughing. "These elephants paint?"

"Only if they want to," Flory said, reading the photo caption.

Jane sighed. "It looks like heaven." She hesitated, hating to put a damper on the discovery. "But from what Sen said, Gaia would never survive another trip overseas. What we need . . ." She tried to laugh. "I don't suppose there's a Phnom Tamao somewhere near Vancouver?"

Flory went to work, narrowing her search and then broadening it back out again. After a few moments, she shook her head. "I'm sorry, Jane. There are sanctuaries throughout Asia and Africa, but they might as well be light years away."

"Wow," Amy whistled. "But that's a lot of people doing a lot of stuff for elephants! Makes you think that despite everything we've seen and heard, there might be some hope." She clapped her hands suddenly. "Okay, *focus people!*" she shouted, leaping up from her chair and bobbing and weaving around the room like a boxer. "C'mon, *think*! Think, Jane!" She clapped her hard on the shoulders. "There must have been something in what this Sen Chanta said today that gave you some ideas! There must be some reason he thought talking to you would help! What was it? *Think!*"

Jane shook her head miserably, running Sen's story over and over in her mind. "I can't!" she cried, panic in her voice. "I can't do it!" She grabbed her old running shoes from under the gardening table and yanked them onto her feet. "I've got to get out of here. I need some air. I'm sorry!" With that, she dashed out the door and disappeared up the trail.

"Geez, what, is she running away to join the circus?" Amy huffed. "Doesn't she know running away from your problems never solves anything? What? Flory, what's that look on your face? I suppose you think this is *my* fault, is that it? Well, so I was a little hard on her. But I just think he must have said *some*thing . . ."

"He did!" Flory breathed.

"Huh?"

"Amy, you're a genius!" Flory laughed.

"Yeah, a regular Einstein, sending my best friend off the deep end like that," she frowned, feeling badly now.

"Don't you remember that part in Sen Chanta's story where he told Jane about writing a letter to the American who owned a circus and who had Gaia's sister?" Flory said in a rush.

"Yeah, so . . . ?"

"Well, the letter the American wrote back said that the woman who rode that elephant had *run away from the circus, taking the elephant with her*!" Flory crowed, hands in the air.

"Right, Flor," Amy responded with exaggerated patience. "*Never to be seen again.* Or did you forget about that part?"

"Don't you see?" Flory exclaimed, ignoring the fact that Amy clearly did not see. "It's the one piece of the puzzle we don't have: Who was she? Where did she take that elephant? I have a hunch that if we can track down that circus rider and find out where she and that elephant went, we'll have a lead that just might help Gaia!"

"Well, now," Amy said, reaching under the computer

desk for a dog-eared phone book. "Let me just look her up right now! Oh, right. We don't know her name or anything about her. Oops! Sorry, Flor, *dead end.*" She let the heavy book fall to the floor.

"There's got to be a way to find out," Flory persisted, tapping her fingers idly on the keyboard.

"Why do you have to be so stubborn?" Amy retorted, frustrated now. "We don't have time to be chasing red herrings, Flory. If this circus rider thing was important, don't you think we'd have figured out . . ." Her voice trailed off, causing Flory to look around sharply. "Ohhh . . . hang on, *I* know how to find her!"

"Are you mocking me, Amy?" Flory asked suspiciously.

"No. Dead serious," Amy answered. "Flory, can you still hack . . . er, get access to the *Shapeshifter* cast and crew database?"

"Of course!" Flory responded, her hands already flying over the keyboard. "Why? Who are we looking for?"

"Ilsa," Amy stated. "Lundgaarten. The woman who rode Gaia on set. She used to tell me stories of her days in circuses, vaulting on the show ponies and doing tricks on the elephants' backs, traveling all over the country. She told me it was like a sorority, like any industry, I guess, where the girls all knew each other, all kind of looked out for one another. If anyone will know anything about a rider who stole an elephant, Ilsa will!"

"Got her!" Flory exclaimed as she clicked on a name in the list. "Ilsa Lundgaarten."

"She's local?" Amy asked peering over Flory's shoulder. "Brilliant." She grabbed the red phone. "Flor, read me out that number. I think we just found our missing puzzle piece."

36
ON THE BACKS OF ELEPHANTS

JANE STOOD IN the middle of the Shack floor, red-faced and huffing from her run, staring at *Shapeshifter*'s Jungle Queen. "What are *you* doing here?" she blurted.

"You tell me," responded Ilsa Lundgaarten in a bored voice. Dressed head to toe in black, legs crossed, hair piled high, the glamorous performer looked distinctly out of place at the rickety gardening table. She glanced at her watch and then reached into her purse, pulling out a cigarette. "Light?" She looked around at the three of them. "Will this take long?"

"Forgive me if I wasn't entirely forthcoming on the phone," Amy fawned, walking toward her with a flaming Bunsen burner in her hand. Ilsa hastily returned the cigarette to her purse. "Now that Jane's here, we can fill you in. We'll be quick."

As succinctly as they could, Jane, Amy, and Flory explained that they were looking for clues to the identity and whereabouts of a circus rider who ran away with her elephant about thirty years ago. Any information she might be able to provide would be greatly appreciated.

Ilsa narrowed her eyes and looked directly at Jane. "Why do you want to know?" she asked.

In a torrent of words, Jane retold Gaia's history as she had heard it from Sen Chanta earlier that day, and then recounted their own gruesome discoveries on the *Shapeshifter* set. "Gaia's life is in danger once again," Jane said, seating herself across from the film star and leaning in close. "If this circus rider found a safe haven for her elephant, then we want to know. We're willing to do anything it takes to rescue Gaia!"

To Jane's astonishment, Ilsa burst out laughing. "Wowee, kiddo, you're just like her. You'd get along like a house on fire!" She fluttered her hands and fussed with her hair. "Such high drama over an *elephant*," she smiled, but there was an edge to her voice now. "What about Denny? In a wheelchair for the rest of his life, career ruined. Ever think of him? Huh? And for what? Trying to keep that massive beast in line just so those rich Hollywood types could get their movie made!" Her eyes were as hard as her voice now. "Denny was no different from anyone else I've ever worked with. A little heavier handed, maybe, but no damn different. That's what it's *like*. What you just described, all doe-eyed and trembly-voiced? That's an elephant's *life*. That's *life*." She looked pointedly at each one of them in turn. "I may be the only rider here, girls, but we *all* made our money on that elephant's back, didn't we?" She stood and started toward the door.

Jane sat still, her back rigid, her face hot. Out of the corner of her eye, she saw Flory cover her face with her hands. Amy stood beside her, tight-lipped, unmoving.

At the door, Ilsa stopped, the cigarette back in her hands. "For what it's worth," she said quietly, "her name was Aurora." Jane turned toward her but was unable to look her in the eye. "That was her stage name. I don't know her real name—none of us used our real names. She was a dreamer—like you. She tried to get them to change things, to treat the elephants nicer. They wouldn't listen. So she ran, and she took the elephant she loved with her." Ilsa cleared her throat and stared at the floor. "She did what we all want to do, Jane. Except that there's nowhere to run to, is there, so what's the point? I just wish I could figure out how she managed to disappear with a ten-thousand-pound elephant." She laughed softly as she pulled open the door and stepped into the early evening darkness. "If I didn't know better, I'd have said it was magic." She closed the door quietly behind her.

37
GAIA'S GIFT

EMPTY PIZZA BOXES and pop cans littered the old gardening table. Amy sat sprawled against her lab bench, eyes closed, nodding in time to the music playing through her headphones. Flory was updating her Facebook page. Jane lay spread-eagled on the floor, an arm over her eyes, dozing.

They had tried punching every combination of "Aurora," "elephant," and "sanctuary" they could think of into various search engines, and had actually turned up thirty-year-old news archives about the circus rider's dramatic disappearance. But they had learned nothing about where she was now, nor found anything that would be of any help to Gaia.

Exhausted, Jane let her mind play over the events of the past nine months—all that she'd seen and learned, all the stories she'd been told. In her memory, she heard Sen Chanta's singsong voice and Gaia's greeting calls, smelled the elephant's scent, recalled the rough, bristled texture of her skin both as a child visiting the zoo and again recently, when Gaia had saved her life. Turning inward to the images in her mind's eye, she saw Gaia traveling down a wide concrete road in the heart of a bustling city, a baby elephant at her side. They walked in step; their movements were identical. The baby was Gaia's own young self. At every intersection, something rose up to block their way. But every time, whether through wisdom or sheer strength, they overcame the obstacle and carried on. Far ahead of them in the distance, silhouetted against the rising sun and surrounded by lush, green jungle, was a third elephant, a matriarch, a grandmother. She was waiting patiently for her younger selves to arrive, had been waiting a long, long time. But they were in sight now and she knew they would come. As the sun crested over the horizon, she stepped forward and raised her trunk in greeting. They were almost there.

Jane rose up from the floor with a gasp and shouted, "Dawn!"

Flory jumped and squealed, startled. Amy yanked her headphones off and said, "Wrong again, girl. It's just after 7:00 p.m."

"*Dawn!*" Jane shouted, leaping up and down like a lunatic. "Aurora's real name is Dawn!"

"*Aaaaahhhhh!*" Amy hollered, jumping up and throwing her arms around Jane. "Of course!" Together, they bounced around the room like a two-headed kangaroo, laughing and shouting.

Flory's hands flew across the keyboard and then she broke in with a triumphant screech. "I found it, I found it!" she cried. She was bouncing in her chair and waving her arms. "Come and see! Oh, Jane, Amy . . . you'll never believe it!"

The three friends crowded around the computer screen and gazed at the website for the New Dawn Elephant Sanctuary. Located just outside of Nashville, Tennessee and covering almost three thousand acres, New Dawn was a wild expanse of rolling hills and pasture, grasses and sedges, washes, creeks, dense woods, and over a hundred varieties of trees, and the elephants were free to roam where and when they liked and to take cover in the open-door shelter whenever they chose. Home to seven Asian females, all of them rescued from circuses and zoos, New Dawn forbade visits from the public; the elephants' sole companions were the sanctuary dogs and cats, the wild birds and butterflies, and each other.

"What's that moving in the corner?" Amy asked, eagerly tapping the screen. "Elecam—does that mean we can see the . . . *Aaiiee!*" she screeched, ecstatic, as Flory clicked on the link. "Look at them! Have you ever seen so many happy elephants in one place?"

There were two elecam feeds, one from the barn and one from out on the acreage. The girls leaned in and watched two keepers, a man and a woman, feeding and bathing an elephant in the barn. The elephant tousled the man's hair with the tip of her trunk and he laughed. In the woods, two elephants waded through a creek bed and then turned to wait for their friend, a smaller female who carried a car tire in her trunk. In the distance they could hear a fourth elephant calling to her companions.

"'Contact Us,'" Jane urged. "Click on 'Contact Us,' Flory!" She let out her breath in a rush. "There's her name: Dawn Shields . . . the woman who ran away from the circus!"

Amy was holding out the red phone. Swallowing hard, Jane dialed the number as Flory read it out. Staring at the screen, she saw the woman in the barn reach for her belt. "She's got a cell phone!" Flory exclaimed. "This is live! Jane, you're about to talk to . . ."

"Dawn Shields," a weary voice answered.

"Ms. Shields, my name is Jane Ray. I'm calling from Cedar's Ridge, British Columbia, in Canada, and I hope I'm not . . . well, actually I can see I'm disturbing you. Sorry about that." Amy rolled her eyes and looped her hand in small circles as if to say, get on with it!

"Did you say Cedar's Ridge?" Dawn was looking directly at the camera now. "Isn't that where that girl almost got herself killed last year trying to save an abused elephant? It was all over the news down here."

Jane's heart rose. "That girl was me," she said. "The elephant's name is Gaia. Ms. Shields, her life is still in danger, and I—my friends and I—we're looking for somewhere safe and wild and beautiful where she can live out the rest of her life in peace. Somewhere like your sanctuary." And with Dawn Shields murmuring words of encouragement and understanding on the other end of the line, Jane told Gaia's story for the third time that day.

When she was done, Dawn was silent for a moment. Jane peered at the screen, wondering if they'd lost the connection, but Dawn was pacing up and down the length of the barn. "Jane, there was something you said about Gaia's early history that rang a bell for me. I don't know whether you know anything about my own story, but I started this sanctuary because of an elephant named Terra. And if I'm hearing you right, she and Gaia . . ."

Jane nodded vigorously, suddenly overcome with excitement and wishing Dawn could see her, too. "I almost forgot!" she broke in. "That's what convinced us to start looking for you in the first . . . Wait a minute . . . what did you say her name was?" Jane was shaking now.

"Terra," Dawn answered. "It's the Roman name for the Goddess of the Earth." She waited for Jane to continue but heard only dead air. Looking up at the camera again, she called, "Hello? Jane, you still there, honey?"

Flory turned and administered a series of light slaps to Jane's face, bringing her back to earth. "They have the same name!" Jane breathed into the phone. "'Gaia' is Greek for Goddess of the Earth! Dawn, you guessed right, Gaia and Terra are sisters. And they have the same name!"

Dawn was laughing and crying all at the same time. The girls watched the screen as she brought a hand to her heart. Several moments went by before she could speak again. "So how soon can you get her down here?" she asked, grinning at the camera through her tears.

Jane exclaimed and threw her arms around Amy and Flory. "She'll take Gaia!" she cried raggedly through her own tears. "Gaia's going home!"

Suddenly, she realized there was a tinny little voice emanating from the phone receiver and she brought it back to her ear. "Listen, Jane," Dawn was saying, "I don't want to pull any punches, darlin'. It costs six hundred thousand dollars a year to care for one of these girls. Best medical care there is." Jane gasped. "Now, I got loyal donors all over the world who'll cover that once Gaia arrives. But what *you're* going to have to do is get her down here. And by my best guess, from where you are, food, trailers, hay, gas, that's going to be about twenty-five thousand dollars. Think you can pull it off?"

Jane covered the receiver with her hand and whispered to Amy and Flory, "I need to check with you guys about something Dawn's asking for. She says she needs us to . . ."

"Are you nuts?" Amy asked, incredulous. "Just say yes!"

Flory was nodding her agreement. "Whatever it is, Jane, we'll make it happen."

Wide-eyed, Jane held the receiver to her mouth and squeaked, "Yes!" Dawn grinned and gave them the thumbs-up from the screen. Jane laughed as the enormity of what they'd all just accomplished sank in. There would be time later to think about all that would still need to be done. "Hey, everybody," she shouted, "Gaia's going to Tennessee!"

38

THE CAMPAIGN

THE CAMPAIGN TO send Gaia "home" to Tennessee was launched the following week. The girls plastered Cedar's Ridge with posters, Gaia's sweet face front and center, and convinced almost every store and restaurant owner in the city to let them place a donation box at the cash counter. Children at the elementary schools organized bake sales, plant sales, and even manure sales. As well as taking up a collection among themselves, Cedar's Ridge Senior Secondary students ran car washes every weekend at the local gas station—Cedar's Ridge drivers had the shiniest cars in town that spring—and the grad class held a twenty-four-hour dance-a-thon.

As word began to spread, many of the business owners and community leaders who remembered visiting Gaia at the zoo as children called to make corporate donations, and those who had profited most from the *Shapeshifter* boom gave extra. David and Lynn Sayers called from Los Angeles to offer the girls their support, and pledged five thousand dollars.

One afternoon, Amy picked up the red phone to find Ralph Mailer on the line. She promptly burst into tears. "Well, if it ain't my guardian angel!" he boomed into the receiver. The summer before, the larger-than-life bush pilot had had a heart attack while flying the girls from Crowsnest Pass back to Vancouver with an emergency shipment of West Nile Virus vaccine. Amy's quick response had saved his life. "You girls're up t'yer tricks again, I see! So *I* thought, since I used to drive long-haul 'fore I flew planes, I could lend you a hand gettin' that elephant of yours down to Tennessee! Friends of mine got a truck and trailer all lined up specially. All you got to do is say yes!" Amy said yes.

By early June, the campaign had raised just over twenty thousand dollars. Between classes, homework, volunteering, and exam prep, Jane, Amy, and Flory were swamped. But rather than overloading them, running the campaign—and feeling the support of their friends and neighbors—energized them. Amy managed the postering and community donation boxes. Jane oversaw special events and kept the financial records. But it was because of Flory's behind-the-scenes work that all of it was possible.

The day after their encounters with Sen Chanta, Ilsa Lundgaarten, and Dawn Shields, Flory had contacted her uncles at Morales & Monroy, Barristers and Solicitors, briefing them on Denny Arcola's lawsuit against Timo Lausanne and the government's investigation of Gaia. They immediately contacted the government lawyers on the investigation to explain that an option had come up that would allow Gaia to live while eliminating any possibility of her being a threat to the public. By the end of March, the investigation was put on hold, pending the outcome of efforts to send Gaia to the New Dawn Elephant Sanctuary.

Next, she went to work on Timo Lausanne. Indicating to her uncles that the zoo owner was highly financially motivated at the moment, she suggested he be allowed to plead to lesser charges in the assault case in exchange for letting Gaia go without financial compensation. But when Morales & Monroy tried this ploy, they hit a roadblock. Denny Arcola's lawyer said he'd consider lowering the charges, but Pimentel & Pomeroy were so sure they could win the case as it stood that they advised their client not to negotiate. Flory could see she'd lost her bargaining chip.

At that point, she played her trump card. With a quick scan of her cell phone's message history, she found the number she was looking for and hit the Call button. "Hello, Mr. . . . oh, you recognized my number! I'm very well, thank you, and you? Excellent! Yes, they're both well, too. I'm, uh, calling to request a favor. I'm sure you're aware of our fundraising campaign? Yes, well, we've hit a little snag." She laid out the situation in detail, explaining that their goal was for Timo Lausanne to release Gaia to the New Dawn Elephant

Sanctuary without charge. "You certainly don't owe any of us anything," she concluded, "but since you were so involved before, I wondered if maybe you would . . ."

"In a heartbeat," came his quick answer. "I'm glad you asked. Flory, I'll need you to get me every detail you've got on Gaia's life—her birth, her history, her life at the zoo, her situation now, this New Dawn place. The Shapeshifter stuff I know already."

"Of course!" Flory replied, ecstatic. "When do you need it?"

"Tonight if you can," he said. "I'll run something tomorrow." There was a pause. "Flory?" he said.

"Yes?"

Another pause. Then, "Nothing. Listen, thanks again for contacting me with this—and keep in touch!"

And so Gaia's media campaign was launched. At first, the stories were designed simply to build public sympathy and support:

SHAPESHIFTER STAR HAD HUMBLE START

By Noah Stevenson

It was 1977 in Cambodia when the group of mahouts came across a small family of wild elephants . . .

IS YOUR 12-YEAR-OLD SMARTER THAN AN ELEPHANT?

By Noah Stevenson

Asian elephants are said to possess the cognitive capacity of the average 12-year-old human child, and have been taught to respond to upwards of 45 commands, paint pictures, and even play in an orchestra! . . .

NEW DAWN SANCTUARY NEW BEGINNING FOR GAIA

By Noah Stevenson

She watched her mother die in the jungles of Cambodia. She was beaten and left with chronic injuries by the time she was six. Grossly mistreated on a film set, she has spent the majority of her years alone in an enclosure little bigger than a tennis court. But thanks to Cedar's Ridge resident Jane Ray and her friends, she may soon . . .

Noah ran something on Gaia any time the *Cedar's Ridge City Herald* had space to fill, but before long, his stories were so popular with readers and selling so many extra papers that they were moved to the front page, and his editor told him to keep them coming. That was his cue. With Flory feeding him backroom information about the legal and financial machinations, he stepped up the campaign, and began to let the local and national TV news syndicates in on the scoop.

Jane stopped at Hilltop Grocery each day after school to buy a paper, and clipped every one of Noah's articles. "It's . . . for the UWRC," Jane mumbled when Flory pointed out that she was already keeping an archives file.

"Ah," Flory nodded, understanding.

"He's really starting to play hard-ball, isn't he?" Jane said, scanning the latest headline.

"He is," Flory agreed, smiling to herself.

ZOO OR PRISON?

By Noah Stevenson

Gaia the elephant is ready for retirement, and a place is waiting for her at the New Dawn Elephant Sanctuary in Tennessee. But Raincity Zoo owner Timo Lausanne won't let her go . . .

GAIA'S HEALTH TAKES TURN FOR WORSE

By Noah Stevenson

Old injuries, chronic infections, and recent mistreatment have put Gaia the elephant's health at serious risk. But an interview with Cedar's Ridge veterinarian Dr. Reid confirms that conditions at the Raincity Zoo are only making things worse . . .

And finally, the one that brought storms of letters to the editor, phone calls to City Council, and protestors to the gates of the Raincity Zoo:

WILL ZOO SELL CITY'S SWEETHEART FOR SPARE PARTS?

By Noah Stevenson

Rather than release Gaia to the New Dawn Sanctuary in Tennessee, Raincity Zoo owner Timo Lausanne is in negotiations with the African Experience Safari Range in Florida to sell the ailing elephant to be hunted for sport . . .

In the second week of June, Timo Lausanne raised the white flag. In a press release submitted to every media outlet in the country, he stated that he had always had Gaia's best interests at heart; that he had been unaware of the nature of the business African Experience Safari Range was running; and that due to her deteriorating health and the fact that the Tennessee facility offered resources Raincity Zoo was not in a position to provide, he was releasing Gaia to the care of the New Dawn Elephant Sanctuary.

They had won. Gaia was now just five thousand dollars away from going home.

39

WHITE ELEPHANT SALE

JANE AND FLORY arrived at the White Elephant Sale to find Amy already in intense negotiations with Donna Lise Harbinsale for her entire supply of elephant dung stationery. "Deal!" Amy shouted, laying a crumpled wad of cash on the card table.

Donna Lise fluttered her hands and bobbed with excitement behind the table. "Oh, my goodness," she exclaimed. "My first big sale of the day!"

It was sunny and warm and she was dressed in a pink t-shirt, rolled up denims, and flip-flops. Jane couldn't recall having ever seen her in anything but a suit. She'd had her hair cropped close to her head in a flattering pixie-cut and let her natural silvery gray grow in. She looked like a different person. Jane guessed she probably was.

The big picture ad in the *Cedar's Ridge City Herald* had read:

HELP ME MOVE—HELP GAIA MOVE!

Donna Lise Harbinsale moving to smaller home,

selling family treasures and elephant souvenirs to raise last $5,000 for Gaia! Come early!

Then it listed the time and her new address.

A long-time socialite and wife of one-time businessman and City Councillor Rand Harbinsale, her name alone was enough to draw a crowd. Some people came for the gossip factor and some to get steals on her family heirlooms. But many more came to support her cause.

"I've been on my own for just over a month now," she was telling the girls excitedly. "The manager's good about pets, so I've adopted a little cat for company, and I found full-time work as a bookkeeper just up the street." She grinned happily. "I love it!" She had a suite in a heritage low-rise not far from her old neighborhood, and she'd set up her sale items in the grassy courtyard out back. Several tables held displays of porcelain figurines, crystal glassware, fine china, and silver tea services. The rest were piled high with elephants. Elephant photos, jewelry, trinkets, toys, statues, carvings, garden decorations, and planters. Stuffed animals she'd knitted and children's clothing with elephant appliqués that she'd sewn. Hundreds, maybe thousands, of elephants.

"Rand was thinking of setting up some sort of import-export business," she explained as she toured the awe-struck girls through the milling crowds. "But he missed his window of opportunity," she said, referring to the shutting down of *Shapeshifter*. "All of these things were just sitting gathering dust, so when I left, I just brought them along!"

"That is one motherlode of merchandise," Amy whistled. "I hope he gave you a hand with the lifting!"

"Oh, I didn't tell him I was leaving," she said, her cheery tone faltering slightly. "I couldn't, you see, so I left him a note. When he got home that night, all these things were gone—and so was I."

"And what's that over there?" Amy asked to break the awkward silence that followed Donna Lise's revelation. She was pointing to a table whose wares were covered with a tarp.

"Come see!" she whispered, suddenly furtive. Glancing around to make sure no one else was looking, she lifted the tarp from the left side of the table. "Rand did these," she said. "They're . . ."

"Fake elephant paintings!" Amy cried, recognizing the style from those she'd seen online, and then she doubled over laughing. Jane and Flory struggled to keep their faces straight, but Mrs. Harbinsale was laughing, too.

"They're awful, aren't they?" she giggled. "I knew I couldn't sell them, but I just can't seem to throw them out!"

Suddenly Amy stopped laughing, her eyes wide. "Ladies," she whispered conspiratorially, "are you thinking what I'm thinking?"

"No!" Jane and Flory whispered back. "We haven't got a clue where your mind has gone, Ame," Flory added in a normal voice. This brought on fresh gales of laughter.

"C'mon people," Amy finally sputtered out, wiping her eyes. "These are limited-edition Rand Harbinsale originals! Don't you think there might be a few people in Cedar's Ridge who'd pay a hefty sum to hang one of these in their living room?" With that, she whipped the tarp off the paintings and began to assemble a display that showed them off to their best advantage.

"AUCTION!" she hollered, grabbing the attention of every sale-goer instantly. "Ten minutes, ladies and gentlemen. Have your checkbooks ready. We will be auctioning off twenty-three paintings, original artworks, by none other than Randall Harbinsale, former City Councillor and General Manager of Cedar's Ridge Golf & Country Club!" Her announcement was greeted by wild applause, and people rushed to Amy's display, jostling one another for front-row positions. She held up her hands for silence. "For those of you who are captivated, as I am, by the simple, childlike images created by sanctuary elephants in Southeast Asia, the Harbinsale Collection is the next best thing! Now, what do I hear for this lovely, um . . . this one here?" Bidding on the first painting started at a hundred dollars.

Shaking their heads in wonder, Jane and Flory turned back to the covered table. "And what's this pile?" Jane asked, indicating a pyramid-like stack under the tarp. Donna Lise turned back the cloth and the girls gasped.

"Elephant meat," Donna Lise said unnecessarily. "Two hundred and fifty cans. I'm sure you can understand why I'm keeping it under wraps."

Flory put a hand on Jane's arm. "This should go to some use," she said quietly. "It should serve Gaia somehow." She thought for a moment. "Mrs. Harbinsale, Jane, how many cans can you carry?" As Amy's auction continued, the three of them walked through the crowds, Jane and Donna Lise fetching and carrying the brightly labeled cans and Flory pausing to talk with each of the sale-goers in turn. She spoke to them not of slaughter but of the importance of keeping a reminder close by that they had done something to make a lasting difference in one elephant's life. Every one of them was happy to pay the ten dollars she asked.

By four o'clock that afternoon, Donna Lise had entered every sale in a spreadsheet and tallied the results: "Seven thousand three hundred and eighty-two dollars and twenty-five cents," she announced, laughing through tears as the girls screamed and turned cartwheels on the grass. "We did it! Oh girls, she'll be free. *Free!*"

"Congratulations, mom." A tall young man emerged out of the late-afternoon shadows. "I'm so proud of you. *For everything.*" Lying on the grass behind Donna Lise, Jane looked up at the sound of the familiar deep voice and caught her breath. Thin, with long, wavy dark hair, browned by the sun and hardened by a year of life on the run, he looked like a different person, too. But her heart knew him. It was Jake Harbinsale. "C'mon over here, Bobster," he called, "and give your mom a hug!"

A young boy stepped shyly away from the wall and edged toward Donna Lise. Gone was the spoiled little prankster Jane remembered. This boy had had to grow up fast. Donna Lise was sobbing soundlessly, overcome at the sight of her sons, missing for so long. "Where have you . . . ? When did you . . . ? How did you find me?" she gasped as she held her arms out to Bobby.

"We saw your ad," Jake grinned. "Wondered if you might like a couple of roommates."

"I sold the bunk beds!" she laughed, blowing her nose and wiping her eyes.

"We're pretty good with sleeping bags," Jake answered, "aren't we, Bob?"

"Oh, my boys!" Donna Lise cried. "You're home!" Jake leaned across the table to hug her and Jane saw her wince. Jake must have felt it, too.

"Still?" he asked, his face darkening.

She shook her head. "It's over, Son," she said. "I have a new home, a new job . . . a new life. And my boys are home safe. It's all over."

Jane was about to get up and go over to Jake to say hello when she heard another familiar voice echo through the courtyard. Facing his mom and with his back to the courtyard, Jake stiffened. He looked over and caught Jane's eye; so he *had* seen her! Almost imperceptibly, he shook his head. *Whatever happens*, he seemed to be saying, *don't react. Don't give me away.* She nodded slightly and then watched as he whispered something to his mom.

"Just what in hell do you think you're doing, Donna Lise Harbinsale?" Rand Harbinsale shouted across the courtyard at his wife. The last of the day's browsers fell silent and turned to watch as the dark, heavyset man strode toward the cash table.

"You're my wife!" he spat. He made the word sound dirty. "You made some vows, lady! Or have you forgotten?" He became aware that he had an audience, but rather than bringing him to his senses it seemed to fuel his tirade. "You think you can just leave whenever you like? Go where you like? Do what you like? Hunh, Donna Lise? Just up and leave without a word to your husband of twenty-five years?"

His face was flushed a deep scarlet now and the veins in his neck and forehead bulged. Donna Lise stood perfectly still, not saying a word. Her silence infuriated him further. "What kind of a wife does that?" he yelled, his voice cracking with the strain. "What kind of wife steals from her husband? Airs her family's dirty laundry in front of the whole neighborhood like this? Runs around in dungarees with her hair chopped off like a bloody boy's? You want a new look, Donna Lise?" He pushed up his sleeves, unconsciously opening and closing his hands. "I'll give you a new look!"

Donna Lise never moved as he came at her. Never moved as Jake spun at the last second and knocked his father to the ground with a single blow. Never moved as Jane ran up and put her arms around her shoulders. Cradling his fist, Jake stared at his father lying unconscious on the grass. "Flory," he said without looking around, "do you happen to have one of your family's business cards with you?" She tucked it into his hand and he glanced at it briefly before slipping it into his pocket. Then he turned, nodding at Jane before he met his mother's eyes. "Now," he said. "*Now* it's over."

40
FLORY GIVES A SPEECH

"PROGRAMS! GITCHER PROGRAMS HEEEEEERE, ladies and gentlemen! FREEEEE PROGRAMS!" Amy Airlie MacGillivray stood at the entrance to the high school gymnasium hawking Graduation Ceremony Programs as hundreds of grads, parents, siblings, and friends poured into the gym. Winking as she shuffled past her, Jane grabbed a program and then laughed when she felt the cover's rough, nubbly texture.

"Is this what I think it is?" she called over the din.

"One hundred percent pure!" she heard Amy shout before the crowd carried her into the fray.

The atmosphere in the gym was electric. Two hundred and fifty grads were there to receive their diplomas, and with only one day left in the school year, the excitement had reached a fever pitch. Jane looked around at the crowds of people, everyone searching for seats or shouting and waving to friends across the room, everyone dressed in their formal best. Chairs scraped across the wooden floor, a thousand voices rose, programs rustled, and the microphone screeched as Principal Hirji tested the levels. The noise was deafening.

Spotting her parents, Avis and George Morton, the MacGillivrays, and the Moraleses all laughing and talking together in the middle of a row in the bleachers, Jane waved. After making her way up to say hi and receiving congratulatory handshakes and hugs from all of them, she squeezed her way back to the floor, found a seat with her grad class near the end of a row, and left a couple of seats free for Amy and Flory. Flipping open the program, she scanned for Flory's name: "Miss Florencia Morales, Class Valedictorian" was all it said. She'd left an agitated Flory backstage rehearsing and making last minute changes to her speech, highly unusual for the meticulous planner. Jane and Amy had had no success prying any information out of her about it. "I want it to be a surprise," was all she'd said.

Suddenly the lights went down and a hush fell over the room as Principal Hirji approached the microphone. Jane felt someone slide into the seat next to her and turned, expecting to see Amy. It was Jake Harbinsale. "Hey," he said, greeting her with a warm smile. "My last chance to see all my friends before they take off into the big wide world," he said, his expression turning wistful. His year on the run had put him behind; he'd start grade twelve in the fall. He took her hand and squeezed it and then sat back with her to watch the ceremony unfold. Amy slid into the seat next to him as the lights came up on the stage.

After her welcoming remarks, Principal Hirji called the graduating class to the stage. The concert band played as, one by one, all two hundred and fifty of them filed past their beaming teachers and accepted their diplomas from the principal. Next came the awards. Among them, Amy was called forward to receive the Top Student Combined Sciences prize and a scholarship of five hundred dollars. Flory appeared from the wings when her name was called; she'd won the British Columbia University Entrance Scholarship, full tuition for four years. Jane was surprised to find herself called to the stage twice: once to receive the Creative Writing prize for best published piece, for the article she and Noah wrote about Gaia; and a second time for a Community Service Award.

Arriving at the top of the stairs, she gasped in surprise when she saw Evie, Daniel, and Anthony there to present the award. She ran forward and hugged them. As Jane accepted the certificate, Evie said into the microphone, "This award comes with the offer of a full-time job at the Urban Wildlife Rescue Center—for the summer, or for as long as Jane would like to stay. Given all that she has done for us, and for animals in this community, we can't think of anyone we'd rather have on our animal care team than Jane Ray." Jane was dumbfounded when the audience rose to give her a standing ovation.

Back on the floor, Amy and Jake guided her to her seat as the room went black and a spotlight came up on a microphone in the center of the stage. A hush fell over the room. Jane felt her heart racing as the seconds ticked by and Flory did not appear. People in the audience began to cough and fidget with their programs, and a flurry of urgent whispers ran through the grad class as everyone made a guess as to what was going on.

And then she was there. Shiny black hair and eyes like polished stones glinting in the spotlight, neat black dress suit and pumps—every inch the lawyer. She smiled shyly into the darkness and the room broke into encouraging applause. Clearing her throat, she looked down at her note cards, back out at the audience, and then down at her notes once more. Then, with a fierce sweep of her arm, she tossed the cards into the air and grabbed the microphone from the stand.

"*SEX, DRUGS, AND ROCK 'N' ROLL!*" Flory screamed into the mic like a strung-out rock star and raised her right hand, flashing the devil's horns to the assembly. For a moment, a thousand people sat silent in the darkness, stunned. Then the crowd went wild.

The grads rose, screaming and cheering, stamping their feet, and banging their chairs against the floor. Parents rose, shocked, their outraged shouts from the bleachers mingling with the din below. Teachers scurried through the aisles trying to restore order and Principal Hirji was staring at her school's star pupil in disbelief, clearly debating whether she should march up the stairs and wrest the microphone away.

"Ee . . . an . . . why . . . ger!" Flory was speaking again, and at the sound of her voice, the room began to quieten and people took their seats again as they strove to hear what she might say next.

"Sex, drugs, and rock 'n' roll," Flory repeated in a normal voice now. There were a few more wolf whistles and shouts, and Flory waited until the gym was silent. "That's the anthem of the wild teenager, isn't it? We've got this energy inside just bursting to be used, to be expressed, let out to shine. I can feel it right now in myself! I can see it right now in all of you! Can you feel it? CAN YOU FEEL IT?" The gym erupted again.

"Nuclear fusion's got nothing on us right now! The power that fuels the stars in the universe has got nothing on us right now! And where has our culture of pop stars and celebrity idols shown us we can channel all this wild energy? Sex, drugs, and rock 'n' roll!" A ripple ran through the audience as people began to realize she wasn't headed in the direction they'd expected.

"And do you know what's worse? What's worse is that it's not even an option for *all* teenagers. Oh, no! It's only for the wild child. Do you know what I'm talking about? Yeah? I think you do. I think you've spent the last two or three or four years just like me—weighed down by your label: the brainy nerd—that's me; the dumb jock; the artsy flake; the geeky misfit; the wild child. And just like that anthem, we start to believe that this is who we are, that *this is all there is*. That all this energy inside of us is some kind of cosmic joke, a mistake, just something we're supposed to shove to one side or stuff back down as we struggle to cram all that we are into these little labeled compartments. Something we can only let out in manageable bits through the holes we make in our skin—and in our lives—to relieve the pressure.

"But I want to tell you something tonight that nobody ever tells us, because they're too scared. I want to tell you that those labels are meaningless. That that anthem is a mirage meant to keep us looking in the wrong direction. I want to tell you that WE ARE ALL WILD!" The grads cheered. "That energy you feel inside of you is *yours*, and you're *meant* to feel it, and meant to *use* it and to live your life by it!

"All around me, all year long, I've been hearing people say, 'I can't wait to graduate. I can't wait to be free!' Well, I want to say something else tonight that nobody ever tells us: *We're already free!*" She waited as another round of whispers ran through the crowd. "We've been free all along! And if you can get your mind around that, then you'll always be free, whether you work in a factory or run your own business, raise a family or live alone, roam the planet or stay right here in Cedar's Ridge for the rest of your days.

"You have *always* been free to choose—the attitude you bring to class . . . or whether you even show up at all! How you treat your friends, and whether you respect yourself—and I mean respect yourself enough to be your best self, no matter what's going on around you. And you're free to choose now—whether you'll listen to everybody else as they tell you which college to go to and which job to go for, or whether you'll listen to that quiet, persistent whisper inside that's guiding you in the pursuit of your *own* dreams.

"You've always been free to accept the idea of teen culture that's been laid on us by society—you know, the lazy, selfish, rude, violent, aimless, apathetic teenager—and use it as your excuse for being less than you know you could be. But don't you see? *That's what they want*! They want us to channel that energy of ours into useless pursuits because they're afraid of how powerful we are! You *really* want to rebel? Try showing up—with all of that power right on the surface where they can see it— ready to learn, ready to share it, ready to give, ready to do what you've been told is impossible.

"We are all wild. We're made of the dirt of the Earth and the dust of ancient stars. We have the instincts of wild animals, and if we listen and if we let them, the rhythms inside us will align themselves again with the turning of this Earth.

"And as for sex?" There were gasps and titters from around the room. "Well, we may be the only animals on the planet with the choice to do it purely for pleasure. But unless you're ready to bring another being into this world, wait a while! Channel that energy into some of your other passions. And if you *really* can't wait? Then for the love of all things holy, use a condom!" The girls squealed and the guys roared. Flory crossed herself and grinned.

"As for drugs, sure, you can choose an artificial high that makes you feel better and keeps the world at bay for a while. It's tempting sometimes. *Or* you can choose the highs that come with remembering you're not separate from the world at all, but as special and necessary as the sun on your face, or the rain, or the sight of the North Shore mountains covered in snow, or an eagle in flight, or a work of art, or making your own art, or holding a friend's hand.

"And as for rock 'n' roll, all I have to say is choose carefully what you let in." She pointed to her ears, her eyes, and her mouth. "Not only are you what you eat, you are also what you consume—TV, movies, games, the Internet, too. And there are rappers and YouTube critics and bloggers and newscasters who will try to tell you that the world is broken. But let me tell you that if you let that in, it will break you, too.

"The world is not broken. Yes, there are some of us in this world who are hungry. Who are sick. Who are homeless. Who are at war. I say 'us' because those of us who sit, safe and comfortable, in this gym tonight are actually part of one big, wild family, connected by blood and memory, by ancient history and the myths and mysteries of our origins. We're connected by animal instinct and the will to survive. And beyond that, the will to thrive, to be all that this energy inside of us tells us we can be. Not at one another's expense, but together, because of one another, for one another.

"And as members of this wild family—as the *wild teenagers* that we are—we get to choose what we will do about the hungry and the sick, the homeless and the war-torn. What we will do about a world that has had so many of its wild places razed and its wild creatures caged and hunted into extinction." Flory paused to catch her breath and then looked out again at her friends.

"Tomorrow night, we party." She smiled. "After all, we have a lot to celebrate. But for tonight, I'm asking you—teenagers and adults—to remember your wild selves, and to remember that it is not our small, labeled, diminished selves but our wild selves that the world needs right now: passionate and compassionate; peace-loving and wise; energized and ready to act.

"To the Graduating Class of Cedar's Ridge Senior Secondary School—this wild world needs you, all of you. And you're ready. In a way, you always have been. Because you were born to be wild.

"Thank you." Flory bowed.

Before she could straighten, a thousand people rose as one and thundered their response back to her for over ten minutes. Jane felt a tap on her shoulder. Amy leaned across Jake and said, "That girl is going to kick ass in court!"

41

I HOPE YOU DANCE

JANE HEARD THE MacGillivray station wagon rattle into the driveway and took one last look in the mirror: white, 1950s-style, halter-neck dress with full skirt; red sequined belt, clutch bag, and strappy sandals; screen-siren-red lips and nails; hair pinned up at the sides with loose curls cascading down her back; ridiculous grin. Yep, she was ready.

"Honey, is that Mike?" her dad called from the living room. "Can we get some pictures before you go?"

"Oh!" her mom gasped as she entered Jane's bedroom. "Jane, you look just . . ." She fluttered a hand to her mouth.

"Thanks, mom," Jane hugged her. Listening for the doorbell, she ran to the back window and saw that Mike was stopped halfway down the driveway with the engine still running. "Dad, I don't think he's coming in," she shouted on her way down the hall. "No fodder for the paparazzi!" she laughed as she twirled and posed for the camera. She kissed them goodbye at the door, crossing her fingers as she promised to come straight home after the dance.

"Hi, Mac!" she cried breathlessly as she clambered into the old brown behemoth. "How did you get your parents' car? Things must be better at home, hey?"

"You look beautiful, Butterfly," he answered as he navigated the wagon back up the steep driveway and onto the road.

"Thanks!" She laughed delightedly. "Oh, Mike, so much has happened since I last wrote—go slow!" In the few blocks between home and school, Jane crammed in as much as she could about Flory's valedictory address, her job offer from the UWRC, and the results of the campaign to send Gaia to Tennessee. "We leave first thing tomorrow," she grinned, breathless with excitement. "I still can't believe I get to go with her!"

They pulled into the school parking lot, which already looked like a bumper car ride at an amusement park, and sat idling, waiting for limos to move and a parking spot to appear. "There's Amy!" she squealed, bouncing in her seat and waving through the window. Amy was improvising a Bollywood dance on the flagpole plaza surrounded by about seventy-five grade twelve guys—all those who didn't have girlfriends or special dates for grad—every one of them looking like the luckiest guy of the night. "Hey, wait a minute . . . isn't that Ben?" She peered at a stocky, handsomely tuxedoed young man ensconced happily in the midst of a colorful mass of grade twelve girls.

Mike nodded beside her. "He got wind of Amy's grad date scheme and decided to make the same offer to all the girls who didn't have dates by tonight," he explained. "Can't imagine what he's trying to prove."

Before she could comment, she noticed Amy waving like a drowning woman and pointing toward the school entrance. Glancing over, Jane spotted Flory standing with Mark, both of them waving, too. When she looked back, she saw Ben raise a hand to Mike in terse salute and then move determinedly toward Amy. But one of his entourage waylaid him en route with a boutonniere and a kiss.

"Jane, there's something I need to tell you."

She was so preoccupied with the scene on the plaza that she almost missed the urgent note in Mike's voice. Turning to face him, she realized she hadn't really looked at him until now. He wore a dark suit and white shirt, but no tie. The shirt hung open at the collar, his hair was unkempt, and he obviously hadn't shaved for a couple of days. There were dark circles under his eyes and the lids were red as though he'd been crying. Jane felt the oxygen in the car disappear and the doors and windows close in around her.

"I've been meaning to tell you . . . I tried to write . . . I shouldn't have waited till tonight . . . ," he stammered. "But I wanted to see you, tell you in person. I thought I could hold out till after the dance, but I can't . . . You're my Jane Ray, my Butterfly. I . . . care so much about you, but . . ." Mike's voice faltered.

Jane held her breath and waited: *But . . .*

". . . Katrina's pregnant," he said finally. He focused his gaze on a spot just behind her head. "Due in July. She'll . . . we'll have a baby by next month. I've quit the farm. Re-applied to the engineering program. Got myself a warehouse job in town, night shift. We'll get married. It's done. It's all done." He stopped, and his eyes shifted, seeking hers. "I'm sorry." Her head was shaking an insistent *No, no, no* and she struggled to breathe. "I'm sorry," he said again, waiting for her response. "God, Jane, please say something!"

"You said . . . ," she tried to answer him. "Last year . . . ," she tried again. "While you were writing to me, you and she . . . All this time, I believed . . . I hoped . . . we were going to . . ." A ragged cry escaped and she clapped a hand over her mouth.

"I did, too," he answered, his eyes pleading with her to understand.

But she would not. "*Then why?*" she wailed, giving rein to the tearing feeling inside. "Just because . . . What about all *your* dreams? You don't *have* to do this—you have a choice!"

"This *is* my choice," he said fiercely, his voice cracking and his eyes brimming with tears. "There were only bad choices, Jane. I made the best one I could."

Footsteps sounded on the pavement behind her and Jane turned to find Amy and Flory standing outside her car door, their faces anxious. "I asked Ben to tell Amy,"

Mike said shakily, leaning over the steering wheel. "I knew you'd . . ."

The door opened and Jane found herself lifted out of the car and to her feet. Her legs buckled under her but Amy and Flory had her weight. "I'll see you later," Amy said to her brother before shutting the door.

"Take me home," Jane whispered to her friends as they stumbled toward the plaza.

"No," Amy said. "Absolutely not. This is our grad night—the only one we get—and we're going to dance."

42

CONGRADULATIONS

THEY DANCED.

Flory danced with Mark and with boys she'd made friends with over the years, some of them she'd known since kindergarten. Amy danced with every one of her dates, allotting them half a song each. But at eleven o'clock, with an hour still to go, she spent the rest of her grad night with Ben. Both girls took time out at the banquet tables to snap photos and visit with friends, some of whom they'd keep in touch with but many they knew they'd not see again after that night. Jane never left the dance floor.

The school gymnasium had been transformed from the assembly hall of the night before into a starlit ballroom. A black dance floor covered the wooden ball courts and swaths of shimmering cloth hid the bleachers from view. Small tables were scattered around the periphery, cabaret style, bunches of white helium balloons floating above them. Canapés and pastries were laid out on banquet tables against one wall and caterers served beverages through a window in one of the equipment rooms. Moving spotlights swept across the floor and reflected off revolving, glittering mirror balls suspended from the ceiling as the deejay spun a mix of current hits, classics, and top-tens from the past twelve years.

Jane never stopped moving. She danced to every song, sometimes with a partner but often on her own. She threw herself into the music, letting it take her over, letting it crowd out thought and feeling and memory until there was just music and rhythm and the pulsing, pounding vibrations of bodies and bass rising up through the floor. At times, the crowds faded completely away and she no longer heard the music but simply felt it hammering through her like the pounding of blood in her ears. Each time her mind threatened to reclaim her she threw herself harder against the wall of sound until the thoughts retreated again and there was nothing but movement.

People pointed and whispered, wondering what had gotten into shy Jane Ray. Some of them had seen her stagger in from the parking lot and assumed she was drunk. But most looked on in wonder at the energy and passion that kept her in perpetual motion. What they didn't see was the anguish behind it. Amy and Flory knew it was there and joined her on the floor several times, sharing it in the only way they could. "Drink something, Jane," Flory encouraged, handing her a tumbler of water. "You're soaked with sweat." Jane took it and poured the water over her head, shaking loose the pins in her hair and letting it hang free. A little while later, she kicked off her sandals and danced the rest of the night barefoot.

One of the people who watched from the sidelines was Noah Stevenson. Flory spotted him and crossed the room to say hi. "What brings you here?" she asked, although she thought she knew. "Not covering the Community beat after all those front-page stories, are you?"

"Believe it or not, I am," he answered, shrugging and glancing at his camera. "The annual 'CongraDulations' feature for the *Herald*. Our regular guy got sick at the last minute and asked if I'd fill in. Believe me, I wouldn't have volunteered."

"Oh?" Flory responded, surprised.

He nodded his head toward the center of the gym, where Jane was spinning in the arms of one of Amy's dates. "Thought there was something starting up between us back in December, that night we all rescued Gaia from those wranglers," he said, his eyes never leaving the dance floor. Flory nodded; she'd thought so, too. "But she never returned my calls. I don't know if she just changed her mind or what. It disappointed me more than I expected, though, I'll tell you that." He looked down at her then with a lopsided smile. "Hey, you shouldn't be here listening to my tales of woe,

Flory—you should be out there partying!" She hesitated for a moment, glancing out at Jane, then touched his arm lightly and headed back to Mark.

Noah moved around the room gathering shots for the CONGRADULATIONS feature. Couples dancing, guys gorging themselves at the banquet tables, groups of girls huddled together talking and laughing, Amy and Ben and their hundred and fifty dates in a Broadway-style kick line. But again and again, his eye was drawn back to the wild girl at the center of the maelstrom, and his flash blinked like a strobe light as he caught and stilled her movements a fraction of a second at a time.

When at last the evening was over and only the last dance was left to play, the deejay announced that it was time for everybody to find a partner and end grad night right. As couples sought one another out, and as Amy's and Ben's dates happily paired off, Jane swayed by herself beneath the mirror ball, her fury finally spent. Noah stood against the wall, his camera forgotten in his hand, his gaze locked on her, feeling helpless. Suddenly, he felt a soft tap on his arm and looked around to find Amy and Flory by his side, Ben and Mark hovering close behind. "You'd better warn him this could backfire," Amy was saying. Flory nodded and then stood on tiptoe to whisper something in his ear. His face reflected a succession of emotions as she filled him in on where Jane's attentions had turned last December and then what had happened earlier that night.

"So it's not that we're asking you to do anything," she finished, "but we just thought we should tell you in case you wanted . . ." She and Amy stared after him, open-mouthed, as he ditched his camera under a chair and started across the dance floor.

Jane was searching the room for Amy and Ben, Flory and Mark, a landmark, an anchor, when she felt a hand at her back. *There*, she thought. *Solid ground.* She leaned back and felt herself encircled by strong arms, supported, partnered. She swayed and he moved with her, following her movements at first and then leading her in arcs across the floor before finally turning her to face him. She looked up into Noah's eyes and fell still for the first time that night.

"Where did you come from?" she asked, reaching out a tentative hand.

"I've been here all along," he answered, meeting her eyes and taking her hand in his own.

She thought of his phone calls. More than six months had passed since then. "I was unkind," she said, her gaze wavering.

"You didn't mean to be." It was a question rather than a statement. She shook her head, her eyes searching his. As the last of the music faded away, he bent to her and grazed her lips with his, and she felt the full intensity of his feelings contained in that spare touch.

And then it was over. Her friends encircled her, leading her away and shepherding her home.

Noah stood under the lights watching her go. Retrieving his camera from beneath the chair, he stared at it for a moment and then looked back at the doorway where he'd last seen Jane Ray. He knew he wouldn't sleep that night. He had work to do.

43

AN ELEPHANT NEVER FORGOTTEN

THE CARAVAN ASSEMBLED at dawn. Ralph and Shelley Mailer were already at the Raincity Zoo when Jane's parents dropped her off, making a final inspection of the truck and customized trailer. "Maybe you better ride shotgun," Ralph teased her. "Anything happens to me, you can just grab the wheel . . . hyeh, hyeh! Say, your little pals coming along?"

Jane shook her head. "They're both still in bed sleeping off last night's grad party," she explained with a rueful smile. "Like I should be." Secretly, though, she was thankful she'd had this reason for getting up, getting dressed, eating, leaving the house this morning. She was afraid that without it, she might not have done any of those things.

There was a small crowd of well-wishers and a couple of TV news crews there to see them off. Jane scanned the group quickly but saw no familiar faces. The zoo's owner, Timo Lausanne, took the opportunity to make a speech about how pleased he was for Gaia and how grateful he was to the community for their support. Sen Chanta was standing just behind him and caught Jane's eye, smiling. Next to him was a familiar-looking stranger. After the speech, Jane approached and Sen introduced her to Peter Shields, Dawn's partner from the New Dawn Elephant Sanctuary. He had flown up and would accompany Gaia throughout the journey, Sen explained, acting as a link between her old life in Vancouver and her new life in Tennessee.

"I saw you on the elecam," Jane said as she shook his hand.

"I saw you on the news," Peter replied, acknowledging her with a warm smile. "Dawn's really looking forward to meeting you."

Jane and Peter followed Sen into the enclosure where the mahout gave Gaia a bath and fed her breakfast: hay, cereal, apples, and grapes. "Hey, girl!" Jane said happily as the elephant recognized her and reached over to embrace her with her trunk.

"Today is the day," she heard Sen say to the elephant as he pressed himself to her side and rubbed her chin.

"Time's a wastin', folks," Ralph called out from the cab of the truck as he maneuvered the trailer into loading position. "Let's get this show on the road!"

Sen led Gaia from her enclosure and the little crowd applauded. A few people cried, though whether from sadness over Gaia's departure or regret that no one had tried to secure her freedom earlier in her life, Jane wasn't sure. "This happens on Gaia's time," Sen announced as they approached the trailer. He spoke then in low tones meant just for the elephant, explaining as he had been doing for the past month what was happening, where she was going, how long it would take, what she'd encounter when she got there.

Right away, she stepped her right front foot onto the ramp, and Jane guessed they'd be pulling out within minutes. But she underestimated the discomfort Gaia felt with the unfamiliar surface; her distrust of the small, enclosed space; her memories of having traveled like this before, to the film set. It took Sen four full hours to coax her up the ramp and into the trailer. The well-wishers had straggled away by then and Timo Lausanne had retreated to his office, so the caravan party celebrated with a small hurrah. And then, with the sun high overhead, they were on their way.

Ralph drove the truck and Peter rode with him so that he could check on Gaia any time he needed. The others followed in a rental car, Shelley driving with Sen in the passenger seat and Jane in the back. Shelley kept up a steady stream of conversation, her background as a rehabilitator lending her a natural curiosity about Sen's work with Gaia. Sen answered all her questions, but he never took his eyes off the trailer in front of them, and Jane realized she hadn't given any thought as to what this journey might mean to him. She made a mental note to talk to him the next time they were alone.

The journey from Vancouver to Tennessee was roughly three thousand miles, a diagonal line from northwest to southeast that cut across nine states. Notified in advance by Peter, the customs officials were waiting for them when they arrived at the American border and, after a cursory inspection of passports and permits, they waved them past the lineups and onward on their journey. It would take them three-and-a-half days, and forty hours on the road.

The caravan stopped every two or three hours so Peter could check on Gaia, feed her, give her water, or clean the soiled hay out of her trailer and replace it with fresh. The stops also gave her time to relax without the strain of moving and bouncing. She had a constant supply of hay, which Peter and Sen supplemented with cabbages, bananas, carrots, apples, and grapes, and she ate well and played with her food all through the trip. Her trailer was fitted on both sides with wide windows, which Peter kept open during the day so she could look out at the countryside passing by. They made three overnight stops—in Butte, Montana; Mitchell, South Dakota; and Perryville, Missouri—during which both Peter and Sen slept in the hay by Gaia's side.

As they traveled together, the members of the little group grew close, sharing meals and motel rooms, discussing intensely the fate of elephants around the world, and wondering about the future of one beloved elephant in particular. It was after lunch one day at a

Kansas City truck stop that Jane came upon Peter and Sen talking together behind the trailer. Peter waved her over. "I hear you have this 'gift' Sen talks about," he said. Jane looked at Sen in surprise. The mahout nodded.

"I watched you with Gaia for many days," he explained. "I saw that you understand how to listen to an animal, that you have the ability to make yourself understood. I saw that Gaia wished you to understand her. This is the essence of the gift." Jane blushed, not sure what to say. She'd known since she started volunteering at the Urban Wildlife Rescue Center that she was able to communicate somehow with animals, and she knew that the ability was growing stronger. But the kind of gift Sen had told her about? Like he had with Gaia? Before meeting him, she'd never known such a thing was possible. And now, to think that she might possess such a thing herself . . .

"Sen's been teaching me over meals and at night," Peter was saying now. "Anything and everything he can remember about being a mahout, and about his connection with Gaia. Every bit of information will help us do a better job of caring for the elephants at the sanctuary. Of course, Dawn and I have asked him to join our staff, which would eliminate the need for this crash course! But he's refused." Peter elbowed the smaller man good-naturedly.

"*What*? Why, Sen?" Jane gasped, not comprehending. "To be able to stay with Gaia—that sounds ideal!"

The mahout shook his head, his expression a mixture of sadness and acceptance. "I have kept my promise to her," he said simply. "Now, there is a promise I made to myself that I must keep." He would say no more about it.

On the fourth day, the group rose early and packed up the caravan as Peter and Sen tended to Gaia. "Say goodbye to Perryville," Ralph shouted as he jumped into the cab of the truck. "Next stop, New Dawn Elephant Sanctuary!"

They covered almost five hundred miles that morning. Just before noon, Ralph pulled off the highway onto a rough access road that led through the woods to the sanctuary acreage. Up ahead, Jane could see a banner billowing across the entrance: *Welcome home, Gaia*!

Dawn stood by the gate waving them in and another young woman crouched beside her, videotaping the caravan's arrival. The elecam! Grinning, Jane stuck her head out the car window and waved, knowing Amy and Flory were at the Shack watching. What she didn't know until later was that thousands of people, back home and here in Tennessee, were watching, too.

With practiced precision, Ralph backed the trailer into the open-air barn, as Jane, Shelley, Sen, and Peter got out to meet Dawn and stretch their legs. "They're out in the forest," Dawn answered when Sen asked about the other elephants. "But believe me, they all know someone's coming today! I'm sure we'll see them later."

Despite the new sounds and smells, despite the strange voices, despite the fact that she could not see what lay behind her, it took Gaia just an hour to leave her trailer. She reached her toes back to test the ground, shuffling in a hesitant dance as if she wasn't sure it would be there to meet her. And then all at once, she took a full step, placing her weight on her back foot, and then another, and another. Within a minute, she was down the ramp and in the barn. She let out a happy trumpet and a cheer rose up from the caravan crew and the sanctuary staff. Gaia had arrived.

As Peter and Dawn offered her hay and treats and gave her a bath, Jane noticed that her head-bobbing, which had plagued her for years at the zoo, had completely disappeared. Curious as a newborn, she was exploring her space in the barn, paying particular attention to the open end and all that lay beyond it—warm sun, trees and grass, hills and rivers, butterflies. Elephants.

Suddenly, a distant greeting call wafted across the open air and into the barn. Falling completely still, Gaia listened, her ears directed forward toward the source of the sound. Then she lofted her trunk and returned the call. It came again, closer this time, and again she returned it. It came a third time, and now Jane could see the elephant coming toward them, trunk raised—Gaia's mirror image.

"It's Terra!" Dawn whispered excitedly. "They remember!"

"Remember?" Sen asked, confused.

Jane brought a hand to her mouth. In all the pressure of the campaign and making arrangements for the journey, she had forgotten to tell Sen how they found this sanctuary in the first place. Now, she said, "Sen, remember that letter you received from the American circus owner, about the rider who ran away with the other elephant your uncles caught that day?" He nodded, frowning.

Dawn took his hand. "That rider was me," she said, "a lifetime ago. Terra was my elephant, Sen. This is Gaia's sister."

Terra stood just outside the barn and reached her trunk into the enclosure toward Gaia. Gaia reached out in return, and the two elephants met again across the few feet and the thirty years that separated them. Trunks waving, weaving, entwining, exploring, caressing, they reunited as Terra welcomed Gaia home. Overwhelmed, Sen Chanta stood and wept.

After several minutes, Terra stepped back and started toward the forest. She looked around at Gaia, clearly inviting her to follow. Gaia took a tentative step, and then another, and then she stopped. "Too soon, maybe," Dawn whispered. "It can be days or weeks before new arrivals leave the shelter."

Gaia turned and walked back toward the group of observers at the other end of her enclosure. Towering over Jane, she reached across the wooden bars that separated them and touched her trunk lightly to the top of her head, and then to her shoulder. *I will always remember you, too,* Jane thought.

Then Gaia turned to Sen. With infinite care, she moved the tip of her trunk over his face, as if committing every curve and crevice of it to memory. Then she wound it over his shoulder and around his waist, and he lifted up his arms to return the embrace. Jane watched in wonder as tears trickled from the elephant's eyes.

Finally, Gaia raised her trunk and trumpeted a long, ragged cry. Then she turned and followed Terra out of the barn and into the sun.

44
FREE

AMY AND FLORY picked Jane up at the Vancouver airport a few hours later. With the time difference, it was still only midafternoon. Jane tried not to think about the last time she'd sat in this station wagon, and kept her mind occupied by reliving the trip for her friends and filling in all the details the elecam had left out. "What do you say we each pack a cooler and have a picnic down at the lake?" she suggested. "We could even take your boat out, Ame, and eat on the water!" She wanted to keep busy, not be alone. She'd noticed even on the plane ride back from Tennessee that her thoughts had turned brooding, and they'd only gotten worse when she landed.

"Sorry, kiddo," Amy said, glancing at her in the rear-view mirror. "We thought you weren't coming back till tomorrow. I've got a hot date with a Frenchman." So the reunion with Ben had stuck.

Flory turned around to face her. "And Mark's taking me to see Theater Under the Stars. Can we postpone it till tomorrow?"

"Sure," Jane said, keeping her voice light. *If I last that long.*

At home, Sweet Pea and Minnie greeted her at the door, ecstatic to see her after her absence. "I forget how lucky I am," she whispered to them as she bent to stroke their small, soft bodies. "I missed you, too, little ones."

The house was quiet; her mom and dad were still at work. She dragged her backpack up the stairs and down the hall to her room. *I could watch TV,* she thought, *or walk up the hill and rent a movie, or go for a run. Or all of the above. Then I'll call Avis and tell her about the trip.* There. A plan. That would take care of a good two hours. Only five more to fill before bedtime.

She saw the envelopes on her pillow as soon as she entered the bedroom. Notes from her dad, she figured, reaching for them. The first contained a news clipping:

RAINCITY ZOO BUYS BABY ELEPHANT FROM SAN DIEGO

By Noah Stevenson

"There will be elephant rides at the Raincity Zoo again," beaming zoo owner Timo Lausanne announced at his first press conference since Gaia's departure. Animal rights groups are already up in arms at what they see as . . .

So that was Sen Chanta's secret, Jane thought. He was coming back to care for the baby elephant as no one else could, as she lived out her life in captivity. Until she, too, could be freed. Until there was no more demand for elephants in zoos, or for bush meat, or for ivory. Until they were all free.

Turning the second envelope over in her hand, she found her name and address written in a scrawling, unfamiliar hand. She opened it and pulled out a cardboard case containing an unlabeled DVD. She shook the packaging looking for a note, but there was none. Curious, she walked up the hall to her mom's office, popped the DVD into the computer, and sat down to watch.

Without warning, the Beatles' "I Saw Her Standing There" blared out of the speakers at full volume.

And suddenly, she was there on the screen, her arms raised, the skirt of her white halter dress flaring out in a wide circle, her hair whipping around her head. Dancing.

It was a slide show, the images appearing, fading, overlapping and changing in time to the music. Every image was of her on grad night, each more frenetic than the last. In one frame her eyes were closed, all her senses clearly turned inward as though listening to something deep inside. Her body appeared to be moving as if driven by some invisible, irresistible force.

She felt the music again now as it pumped through the speakers, and saw that it belonged wholly to the girl in the images. But as she listened to the lyrics, she realized they told the story of the one behind the camera.

As she watched the images flash before her, she could

remember how she'd felt at each of those moments during the night, as her mind recognized by sight what she had felt only internally before. But the strangest thing was that watching herself now through this lens, she saw no fury, no pain. The look on her face was almost feral. And every movement of her body proclaimed one thing: freedom.

She knew then that she could let Mike go—as he had let her go, as Sen had let Gaia go—knowing that whatever connected them would always remain.

She was free—as Flory had said—she'd been free all along.

The last image was of her standing alone in the center of the room, spent. The moment before she'd felt that hand at her back. Noah's hand.

The music ended and the last slide flashed onto the screen, static. It wasn't an image, but words—a letter. The note she hadn't been able to find earlier:

I'll wait for fifteen minutes each day after work, next to the lake on the site of the old Shapeshifter *set. Until you're ready, or until the end of the summer, whichever comes first.*

> ~ N

Jane stared at the words on the screen but in her mind she was seeing Gaia again, following Terra into the sun. Thirty years in captivity. Unspeakable loss and pain. And yet she was ready to be free again the moment freedom arrived.

That is what it means to be wild, Jane thought. *To lay the past down in a moment and walk into the sun.*

Glancing at the time, she ran down the stairs and out onto the trails, heading for the eastern shore. With any luck, she'd get there before him. And then when he asked her when she'd gotten back, she could let him know she'd been there all along.

FLORY'S FILES

Crazy—the files I opened on Gaia have filled another filing cabinet! Jane's prodding me to go green and Amy's hassling me to join the twenty-first century, and I have to admit they both have points (although if you tell them I said so, I'll deny it). So this time, I've posted all my *Gaia Wild* files on the series site—just go to **www.wildliferescueseries.com** and click on Flory's Files under "Categories" in the right navigation bar to find all these files and more!

Is It a Zoo or a Sanctuary?

FILE NO. 0809004

More Books and Resources
About Elephants

FILE NO. 0809005

Quiz: Are You a Biophile?

FILE NO. 0809006

Tina's Story

FILE NO. 0809007

ACKNOWLEDGMENTS

I wrote this book for Tina, the elephant, who lived most of her life at the Vancouver Game Farm (now the Greater Vancouver Zoo), and who lived out the last of her days at the Elephant Sanctuary in Tennessee. This is not her story, but if it is infused with even a little of her grace and spirit then I've done what I set out to do. I also wrote this book for those who brought her some measure of freedom and peace at the end of her life, especially: Carol Buckley and Scott Blais of the Elephant Sanctuary; Peter Fricker of the Vancouver Humane Society; Julie Woodyer of Zoocheck Canada; and Nicholas Read of the *Vancouver Sun*.

In Toronto, my thanks go to Catherine Bentivoglio and her students for bringing this series to life in the classroom; Debby Degroot for her humor and support; Brad Kalbfleisch for *Elephant Rescue* and all his kindnesses; and Kelly Snow and the Lights Out Toronto crew for their warm welcome and enthusiasm.

Back home, I thank Peter Fricker again for the time he spent giving me an insider's view of Tina's liberation and journey to Tennessee; and Ernie Cooper with World Wildlife Fund for his stories and insight into the world of animal trafficking. Special thanks to Liz Thunstrom and Vanessa Lowe, professional rehabilitators with the Wildlife Rescue Association of British Columbia (WRA), for reviewing an early draft of this book. And thanks to Jackie Ward, Lani Sheldon, Deborah Austin, Mary Bruneau, Gloria Norton, and the Thursday morning crew for their ongoing inspiration and friendship.

Thanks to Naomi Broudo and Violet Finvers of Tandem Design Associates for their beautiful work on the series' promotional materials; David Fraser and Leanne McConnachie for championing the creation of my animal welfare scholarship at the University of British Columbia; authors kc dyer and James McCann and the membership of CWILL for the support and camaraderie; Lesley Fox for being Jane, only more so; Dr. Susan Mackey Jamieson, mahout in training, for her incredible generosity; Curtis G. Schmitt for celebrating and for becoming a friend; director TJ Scott for reminding me to dream big; Lori Thiessen for making the solitary work much less lonely; and Pat Tracy, my editor at the *Burnaby NOW*, for her own compassion for animals and for turning a problem into such a great opportunity.

I'm blessed to call my publisher, Robert McCullough, a friend—thank you. Huge thanks to the whole Whitecap team, and especially Taryn Boyd for getting down on the floor with me and helping me up; and my editor, Sonnet, the Force that was with me throughout (the "Stayin' Alive" lyrics are hers!).

Biggest thanks of all to my family—my mom and dad, who introduced me to Tina, and my sister, who rode with me—for giving me every opportunity to open my eyes and my heart to animals. And finally (*finally!*) to Steve, for waiting, for making the journey, and for loving me for me.

ABOUT THE AUTHOR

Diane Haynes first learned to love animals by introducing herself to the neighborhood dogs and cats and by going to zoos, circuses, and aquariums with her family. In writing *Gaia Wild*, she wrestled with the question of whether the education and inspiration captive wild animals provide to humans outweigh the animals' suffering. But though she treasures every memory of her encounters with Tina the elephant and others, she would give them all up in exchange for their freedom.

A freelance writer since 1989, Diane's articles and editorial work have garnered her numerous awards. She has steered a floatplane through the Chilcotin

Mountains, run a half marathon, sung and danced in Broadway-style musicals, and helped rescue hundreds of animals as a volunteer with the Wildlife Rescue Association of British Columbia.

In 2007, Diane founded the Haynes Scholarship for the Advancement of Animal Welfare at the University of British Columbia. She is currently the Humane Education Supervisor for the BC SPCA Kids Club and is blogging at www.wildliferescueseries.com.

OTHER BOOKS IN JANE RAY'S
WILDLIFE RESCUE SERIES

ISBN 978-1-55285-658-1
www.whitecap.ca

FLIGHT OR FIGHT

When shy Jane Ray rescues a drowning seabird from an oil spill, she finds herself face to face with national television cameras—and head to head with with the alleged culprit, SeaKing Shipping.

Impassioned by the dedication of animal rescue crews working around the clock to save hundreds of oiled birds, Jane volunteers with the Urban Wildlife Rescue Center and begins a campaign urging SeaKing to take responsibility for the spill. But the corporation won't go down without a fight, and Jane will need all the help she can get from her two best friends to keep the animals—and herself—safe.

CROW MEDICINE

It's summer's eve, and Jane Ray can hardly wait to start her new job at the Urban Wildlife Rescue Center. She doesn't know yet that her love of animals, and crows in particular, is about to be sorely tested. West Nile Virus hovers just over the Rocky Mountains, and if it hits, it will leave hundreds of animals dead in its wake.

When the Center decides to euthanize its crows to hold the virus at bay, protesters respond with vandalism and threats. Meanwhile, Jane encounters Audrey Thomas, a renegade elder who tells her she has "crow medicine," the power to take a stand and to shine her light in darkness.

It falls to Jane and her two best friends to retrieve a controversial vaccine from a station in the Rockies. But will they return in time to save the animals? Will they make it back *alive*?

ISBN 978-1-55285-806-6
www.whitecap.ca